Rosie pu... want me to... standing th... watching me?"

Andrew appeared to ponder the question. She thought she had said it plain enough.

He crossed his arms over his chest. "Aye, that is the very nut and core of it. I do. Perchance you will recall that I have paid a small fortune for that very privilege, Mistress…what did you say your name was?"

She lifted her head with as much pride as she could muster. "'Tis Rosie, my lord."

He flourished a deep bow. "I am struck near speechless by your presence, Mistress Rosie. Permit me to introduce myself. I am Sir Andrew Ford, the miracle worker."

Rosie stared at him with a mixture of bewilderment and apprehension. She was trapped alone with a charming lunatic.

Sir Andrew softened his expression. "I do but jest, Rosie. 'Tis my fashion. Now, for the love of warm water, will you please undress—or shall I do it for you?"

Dear Reader,

This month we're celebrating love "against all odds" with these four powerful romances!

Never before have two seemingly ill-suited people been so right for each other as Andrew and Rosie in Tori Phillips's triumphant new medieval novel, *Lady of the Knight*. On the heels of a starred review from *Publishers Weekly* for *Midsummer's Knight*, Ms. Phillips spins the frolicking tale of a famous knight and courtier who buys a "soiled dove" and wagers that he can pass her off as a noble lady in ten days' time. With her cooperation, he'll share the winnings. But things go awry—most notably in their hearts—as the charade progresses. Don't miss it!

Fate takes over in *Winter's Bride* by Catherine Archer, the emotional story of a noblewoman, long thought dead, whose past and present collide when she is reunited with her beloved and overcomes her amnesia. Barbara Leigh's *The Surrogate Wife*, set in the Carolinas in the late 1700s, is about the struggle of forbidden love. Here, the heroine is wrongly convicted of murdering the hero's wife, and is sentenced to life as his indentured servant....

And be sure to look for *The Midwife* by Carolyn Davidson, the heart-wrenching story of a midwife, fleeing from her past, who must care for the newborn of a woman who dies in labor. The midwife and the child's stern father marry for convenience, yet later fall in love—despite the odds!

Whatever your tastes in reading, you'll be sure to find a romantic journey back to the past between the covers of a Harlequin Historicals® novel.

Sincerely,

Tracy Farrell
Senior Editor

Please address questions and book requests to:
Harlequin Reader Service
U.S.: 3010 Walden Ave., P.O. Box 1325, Buffalo, NY 14269
Canadian: P.O. Box 609, Fort Erie, Ont. L2A 5X3

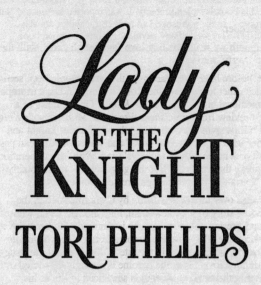

Lady
OF THE
KNIGHT

TORI PHILLIPS

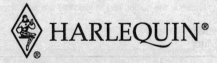

HARLEQUIN®

TORONTO • NEW YORK • LONDON
AMSTERDAM • PARIS • SYDNEY • HAMBURG
STOCKHOLM • ATHENS • TOKYO • MILAN • MADRID
PRAGUE • WARSAW • BUDAPEST • AUCKLAND

ISBN 0-373-29076-4

LADY OF THE KNIGHT

Copyright © 1999 by Mary W. Schaller

Visit us at www.romance.net

Printed in U.S.A.

Books by Tori Phillips

Harlequin Historicals

Fool's Paradise #307
*Silent Knight #343
*Midsummer's Knight #415
*Three Dog Knight #438
*Lady of the Knight #476

*The Cavendish Chronicles

TORI PHILLIPS

After receiving her degree in theater arts from the University of San Diego, Tori worked at MGM Studios, acted in numerous summer stock musicals and appeared in Paramount Pictures' *The Great Gatsby*. Her plays, published by Dramatic Publishing Co., have been produced in the U.S. and Canada, and her poetry is included in several anthologies. She has directed over forty plays, including twenty-one Shakespeare productions. Currently she is a first-person, Living History actress at the Folger Shakespearean Library in Washington, D.C. She lives with her husband in Burke, VA. She would love to hear from her readers. Please write to her at: P.O. Box 10703, Burke, VA 22009-0703.

To the memory of
Brian Russell Cabe
former student, henchman, fellow actor
stage combat partner and
most excellent friend
who loved
Renaissance Faires

Chapter One

"Was ever woman in this humor wooed? Was ever woman in this humor won?"

—RICHARD III

Monday, June 11, 1520
The Field of Cloth of Gold at Val D'Or Between the towns of Guisnes & Ardres, France

Rosie shifted her bare feet on the rough wood of the barrel top, lifted her chin a notch and stared squarely into the face of hell.

Despite the warmth of the evening air, she shivered inside her thin travel-stained shift and torn flax skirt. Apprehension knotted the pit of her empty stomach. Pressing her lips together into a tight line, she tried to ignore the hundreds of upturned faces around her—all male and all staring at her with undisguised lust. They had gathered outside Quince's tent for the express purpose of debauching a virgin—her.

Rosie swallowed, then shook a hank of her tangled hair out of her eyes. She resolved not to allow anyone to see how terrified she was. In a few hours' time, she would be ravished by one of these smirking devils, and so begin her new life as a prostitute.

Standing behind her, bawdmaster Peter Quince slapped her backside with his cudgel. "Smile, wench!" he hissed under his breath. "Show them ye have all yer teeth!"

Rosie stretched her lips into a wide grimace. The noise around the harlots' tent rose in volume. The perspiring customers pressed closer.

"Show us the goods!" roared a drunken voice.

Others cheered and whistled their agreement with the suggestion.

Rosie ignored the sea of faces. Balling her hands into fists, she dug her nails into her callused palms.

Another man raised his voice above the general din. "More light! Let us see if the chit is as innocent as you proclaim."

"Aye," agreed another. "I have forgotten what a virgin looks like!"

Rosie shuddered. Not even Quince knew that she had already lost her maidenhead this past May Day. For an instant, the handsome face of her seducer flashed in her mind. Because of Simon Gadswell and his lying promises, she now found herself up for auction like a haunch of venison. All too soon, she would be sold to the highest bidder. Then she must be very clever with the little vial of pig's blood that she had concealed inside a slit in her waistband. If she did not bleed like a true virgin, Quince would beat her even worse than before.

The bawdmaster held a flaming torch closer to her face. Rosie flinched and prayed that its sparks would not ignite her hair.

"Smile, damn yer eyes!" Quince growled. "I want a good price fer ye."

Rosie bit back the retort that formed on her lips. The bruises from his latest punishment were still fresh on her back. She took a deep breath. A wave of light-headedness washed over her. She had not eaten a crumb since last evening when their boat had finally docked at Calais after a wretched voyage across the Channel. She prayed she would survive this next fortnight and return safely to England.

Rosie tried to distract herself from what she knew was coming. Beyond the ring of torchlight, she saw nothing in the soft blue-black darkness of the summer's night except thousands of campfires that dotted the cloaked French countryside like an army of fireflies.

A raucous voice shattered her brief respite from her unsavory predicament. "Untie her lacings!"

Fifty more took up the cry. "Open her shift! Show us her paps."

Rosie gritted her teeth. The bawdmaster's whores had warned her this would happen and had told her what she was expected to do.

Quince again swatted her backside. "Rosie!" he snarled. "Do it now, or ye will rue this night, I promise ye!"

Rosie's numb fingers fumbled at the tight leather knot that held her shift together. It took her a few agonizing minutes to loosen it. With a grunt of exasperation, Quince reached up and tugged on the garment. Rosie's scant protection slid off her shoulders and down her arms. A low bestial roar welcomed the sight of her bared breasts.

Tears of shame pricked behind Rosie's eyelids. She blinked them back and bit the inside of her cheek to keep from sobbing out loud. In all her nineteen years, she had never felt so alone.

* * *

Observing the scene from the fringe of the crowd, Sir Andrew Ford felt nothing but pity for the poor, half-naked girl on top of a barrel. She blinked several times in the torchlight. Andrew suspected that she was close to crying. Her pale countenance and wide eyes revealed her terror.

A young giant beside Andrew chuckled. "I vow the wench looks the part," Brandon Cavendish remarked to his younger brother.

"A virgin in a brothel tent?" snorted Jack Stafford, the third youth in Andrew's party. "'Tis as rare as a unicorn in London."

"Rare, but not impossible," Andrew mused. He held a clove-studded orange closer to his nostrils to block out the stench of the rogues and knaves around them.

Guy Cavendish cocked his head. "Even if she is a whore, she's a pretty little thing."

Andrew cast a wry glance at his former squire. "How now? Since when have you become a connoisseur of fallen virtue, Guy?"

The golden-haired youth rocked on the balls of his feet. "Life at court has been very…er…instructive, Andrew. And I *am* a knight now," he added. "By the hand of the king himself."

"Ah," Andrew responded. "For two months only. What has happened since April to your vow to honor womanhood? Did you toss it overboard when we crossed the Channel?"

Before Guy could stammer an answer, Jack interrupted the bantering conversation. "To honor *ladies,* Andrew." He pointed to the pitiable object of the evening's entertainment. "Yon minx is not a lady."

"But she could be," Andrew murmured.

Indeed, he could see that the girl was a beauty despite

the dirt on her face and the Medusalike appearance of her dull hair. "With a little cleaning and polish, she could be every inch a lady," he continued.

Brandon chortled. "You are growing soft in the head with your advancing old age, Andrew. That girl is a strumpet, plain as daylight."

Andrew smoothed his crimson velvet sleeve and fluffed the lace at his wrists. "Looks are deceiving," he remarked to his three hot-blooded companions. "'Tis clothes that make the difference between a prince and a pauper—or can turn a whore into a lady."

Brandon pointed at the white-faced girl. "You could never turn her into a lady! A strumpet is a strumpet."

Andrew lifted one eyebrow in mock surprise. "Indeed, Sir Brandon? Perchance you would care to make a wager upon that opinion?"

The elder Cavendish gaped at him. "How now? You can't be serious!"

Andrew inclined his head. "I fear I am, my young friend. I wager that I can take that delightfully wretched creature and transform her into a duchess who will dine at King Henry's feast in twelve days' time."

Guy whistled through his teeth.

Jack draped his arm around Andrew's shoulder. "Oh most excellent jest! Pray tell me, what potent wine have you drunk tonight, old man?"

Brandon gave Andrew a calculating look. "'Sdeath! You are serious!" He grinned. "Then make haste, Andrew. The bidding for your virgin has already begun. What will you wager to shoe this goose?"

Andrew plucked Jack's arm from around the collar of his new doublet. He readjusted his starched collar. "One hundred sovereigns."

Guy choked. Jack roared with laughter.

Brandon held out his hand. "A princely fortune, but I know that you have enough coin to toss away on such tomfoolery. Done, and here's my hand to it. Jack and Guy, witness this bargain."

"Tis reckless folly!" his brother mumbled.

Andrew clasped Brandon's large hand in his and shook it with zest. The young bear's jibe about Andrew's advancing years had pricked his tender self-esteem. "I trust you will earn enough at cards and in the lists to cover your wager, my noble lordling."

Jack chortled. "Ha! If you win, Andrew. But you do not have your bird in hand as yet, and her price is already two angels."

Andrew turned his attention to the auction. "Angels for an angel," he murmured. "Tis fitting. Five," he shouted.

"Seven!" bellowed another.

Andrew frowned. "Ten angels!"

"Twelve!" the other countered.

Andrew craned his neck. "What knave bids against me? I know that voice, yet cannot place the face." He tapped Guy. "Can you see who it is?"

The blond giant made a rude noise in reply. "A sly-crawling cat," he answered. "Tis Sir Gareth Hogsworthy."

Jack clicked his tongue against his teeth. "If he wins the girl tonight, she will be mincemeat by morn. Inflicting pain is his chief delight."

Andrew adjusted his scarlet cap. "Then we shall do an act of mercy by saving the child from him. Twenty angels!" he shouted.

"Thirty!" Gareth answered.

"Thirty-five angels!" Andrew's heartbeat increased its tempo.

Guy blew out his cheeks. "God's mercy, Andrew. Tis a good thing frowns are not arrows. Hogsworthy just sent you a poisonous dart."

Andrew shrugged his shoulders to show his youthful admirers that he did not care. The crowd murmured. Some of the bystanders turned to stare at him. He pretended to ignore them, though his mouth had gone dry. The price for this night of pleasure—even with an avowed virgin—had soared far beyond common sense.

"Thirty-eight!" Gareth bellowed.

Jack elbowed Andrew's ribs. "That's the spirit! You are wearing down the opposition."

Instead of replying, Andrew fingered the money pouch that hung from his belt. He knew he had only thirty angels. "How much coin do you have on you, boys?" he asked in an undertone.

Jack grinned and shook his head. "Five shillings, a few groats and a French ecu. I have a mind to spend them on my own pleasure tonight."

Brandon shook his head. "None but Angel-face—" He winked at his handsome brother. "Lady Luck smiled upon his jousting this afternoon."

Andrew grabbed Guy's arm before the younger Cavendish could punch his brother. "Temper your ire! There is more at stake than your precious vanity, Guy. How much is in your purse?"

The bawdmaster cupped his hands around his fat lips. "The last bid was thirty-eight golden angels. Are there any more bids?"

The poor wench on the barrel looked ready to faint. Guy scowled at his brother.

Andrew snapped his fingers. "Be quick, sluggard! How much?"

"Going once…" the bawdmaster shouted.

"Ten sovereigns," Guy muttered with some reluctance.

"Going twice…"

Andrew waved his silken handkerchief. "Thirty angels and three sovereigns for the virgin!"

Brandon gasped. "You could have bought every wench in Calais for that sum!"

The bawdmaster looked as if he had been struck by lightning, then an enormous gapped-tooth smile split his unshaven face. "Thirty and three it is! Any more bids?" He turned hopefully in Gareth's direction.

Andrew held his breath. Hogsworthy conceded with a hair-curling oath. Andrew relaxed his shoulders inside his padded doublet. He took another whiff of his pomander. "It appears that I have made a purchase," he mused in a calculated offhand manner. He hid his growing excitement from his young companions and their vulgar humor.

The bawdmaster mopped his greasy face with his soiled sleeve. "Going once, going twice, sold to the gentleman in the feathered hat!"

The auctioned virgin peered into the darkness and chewed her lower lip. Andrew found her vulnerability particularly appealing, even though he suspected that the girl was anything but virtuous.

Guy shook his head as he handed his pouch to Andrew. "Methinks today's sun has cooked your usual good sense, my friend."

Andrew grasped the boy's prize money. "Mayhap, but now my wager can begin in earnest. Make a path, Guy. Lead me to my lady fair."

Jack whacked Andrew between his shoulder blades. "Truly the moon has addled your wits, old man! Tis the easiest wager Brandon has ever made. Practically money in his pocket!''

"Aye," Guy agreed over his shoulder as he pushed through the crowd. "But mind you, twas *my* coin that bought the wench."

Andrew inhaled another deep breath of the pomander's spicy aroma. The overwhelming stench of the dense crowd was enough to make a pig gag. "Consider your contribution to my endeavor as an investment, my boy. You may deduct your fee—with interest—from my winnings."

"You are very free with the money you have not yet won," Brandon observed as he elbowed a burly varlet out of the way. "Methinks since Guy paid for part of the wench, he should take his own pleasure with—"

Andrew halted and grabbed a thick handful of Brandon's corduroy jerkin. Even though the twenty-year-old was five inches taller and a good deal stronger than Andrew, the older man knew that his former pupil would never lift a finger against him. "You will keep a civil tongue in your mouth when you speak of yon lady. Do you mark me, jolthead?"

Brandon held up his hands in a show of defeat. "Peace, good Andrew. Put down your hackles. I only jested." He winked at his brother and Jack.

Andrew released him. "Good! If I am to conjure a transformation with that girl, then all of us must begin right now to treat her as a lady. Is that understood by you wooden heads?"

Jack chortled. "Aye! I look forward to turning this dainty sow's ear into a silken purse! I offer myself as her instructor in bed sport."

Andrew looked down his nose at the prattling churl,

despite the fact that Stafford towered over him. "Go hug a swine, Jackanapes."

Jack merely laughed again. "In my own good time, old man."

"Sir Gareth has preceded us. He speaks to the bawd-master and looks as angry as a wet tomcat," Guy remarked in an undertone.

"Then why do we tarry here?" Dropping all show of dignity, Andrew hurried ahead of the trio.

The bawdmaster stank of fried onions, stale sweat and unwashed clothing. Hogsworthy overperfumed himself like a courtesan. Andrew shot both men a withering look of disgust. Holding his brown suede money pouch, he jingled the coins together for dramatic effect.

"Good evening, Master of Damsels, and to you, my Lord Hogsworthy. Is it not a fine night for the procuring of pleasure?"

Sir Gareth's face paled with anger. His thick eyebrows bristled like a badger's. "The slut is mine, you popinjay! I saw her first. I doubt that you possess the fortune you bid."

"Pray do not bleat like a motherless lamb, my lord." Andrew tossed his orange pomander to Brandon. "Hold that, Sir Brandon, whilst I conclude this bit of business."

With a flourish, he emptied his bag on the barrelhead, literally at the bare feet of the girl he had just purchased. He noticed her skin was incredibly filthy. Her toes curled when some of the coins touched her. Andrew looked up to give her a smile of encouragement and he nearly gasped aloud. Upon closer inspection, her breasts proved to be more perfect than he had first thought. Twin peaks of cream rose and fell with a mesmerizing rhythm. His dormant loins sent a flash of heat surging through him.

His awakened reaction to her charms tied his tongue for a moment.

"Count it!" Gareth practically frothed at the mouth.

In silence, Andrew stacked the angels into neat piles. He had the most uncontrollable urge to stroke the lass's bare ankle to see if her skin was as soft as it appeared. As if she could read his mind, she inched a step backward, as far as the diameter of the rough barrelhead allowed.

Gareth's eyes glowed like burning coals when Andrew's money ran out at thirty. "My bid was thirty-eight! She is mine!" He reached for her.

Andrew restrained himself from grabbing the man around his scrawny neck. "You are too hasty, my lord." He produced Guy's pouch. With a self-satisfied smile, he untied the leather strings and drew out three coins. "Tis wise never to keep all of one's fortune in a single place. Three sovereigns."

Gareth fumed with unsavory growls. Andrew noticed that the ragged hem of the girl's skirt trembled, though not a whisper of wind stirred through the enormous English camp. Compassion softened his lust. He congratulated himself for saving the waif from Gareth's brutal clutches.

He slapped the final coin on the golden pile. "Are we square now, Purveyor of Wenches?"

The bawdmaster slobbered his assent. "Take her, my lord. Pleasure yerself as long as ye like."

Andrew cocked an eyebrow at his three companions. "Mark his very words, my young friends. The master says I may have the lady as long as I like. Trust me, knave, I intend to take my time."

"Take all the time ye need," the bawdmaster gibbered. His red-rimmed eyes nearly bulged out of their sockets at the sight of the gold.

Gareth ground his teeth. A thick blue vein throbbed at his temple. "Enjoy the strumpet while you can, Ford, but I will have her yet. You have made me look a fool, and I will be avenged. I swear it on my sword!"

Andrew regarded the enraged man through half-closed eyelids. "You grow tedious, my Lord Hogsworthy. I fear we must discontinue your company. Adieu! Creep back to your kennel." Then he turned his back on the seething man and held out his hand to his prize. He flashed her a warm smile of encouragement.

"Come, fair lady. Tis time we quit these rude surroundings."

Chapter Two

Rosie jumped at the sound of his voice. Never had she beheld anyone so garishly dressed as the man who had just paid a king's fortune for the dubious privilege of taking something that she no longer had.

Her new master was clothed completely in scarlet and gold from the great wealth of nodding yellow plumes on his crimson hat to the toes of his bright red leather shoes. His thigh-length scarlet doublet was trimmed with yards of golden lace. His shirt of ivory silk peeked through the slashing of his full padded sleeves. Panes of gold decorated his red trunk hose and bright yellow stockings encased his muscular legs. The magnificence of his colors put everyone else into dark shade.

Rosie presumed that the gentleman must be a cousin of the king. She wondered why he had chosen her, when he obviously could have had his pick of finer quality ladies.

Then she looked into his face. His mouth, with fine full lips, drew apart in a smile that lit up his clean-shaven countenance. Laugh lines crinkled at the corners of his hazel eyes. His nut-brown hair, shot with streaks of silver, waved over the collar of his short red cape. Rosie's heart skipped a beat. Even though he was past his prime, the gentleman was still very handsome by any woman's reckoning.

Quince rapped her toes. "Quit gawking, girl, and attend to yer business with this lord. 'E don't want to wait until doomsday to swive ye."

The nobleman ignored Quince. He continued to smile at Rosie. "Come, sweetheart, take my hand. I will not let you fall."

His eyes surveyed her in a kindly manner and not with the raw lust Rosie had expected. Summoning all her courage, she placed her hand in his. His gloved fingers closed around hers and he gave her a little squeeze. When she looked into his eyes again, she saw only warmth and approval. A little trill of excitement fluttered in her heart. The doeskin of his gloves caressed her work-roughened palm with butter softness.

Quince shoved her. "Take a strap to the wench, if she don't move fast enough to yer liking," the bawdmaster advised.

Rosie nearly fell on top of the richly clad nobleman. Her new patron tightened his grip to steady her. "Do not be afraid, my dear."

She took a deep breath. "Haint afeared of ye, sir. Methinks ye have paid too much money to do an injury to your goods."

His thick brown eyebrows rose up his forehead. "Well-spoken, mistress. I shall keep your opinion under advisement."

She wasn't sure what he meant by that, but she heard the friendly tone in his voice. She cautioned herself not to take heart from it. All men were deceivers. Holding her skirt with her free hand, she jumped lightly to the hard-packed ground. Giddy from hunger, she wobbled.

She hoped that the gentleman would spare her a goodly supper after he had finished his business with her. She touched the hidden vial of blood to assure herself of its safety, then folded her arms over her bare breasts.

The noble drew closer to her. He smelled of spice and wealth, like someone from God's side of paradise.

"Pull up your shift, sweetheart. There is no need to display your charms to this unworthy assembly," he murmured. His low voice rolled over her like warm honey.

Nodding her gratitude, she gathered the thin muslin around her shoulders. Then her patron looped her arm through his and led her out of the ring of torchlight. The sea of leering men parted before them.

One of the crowd guffawed. "You have bought yourself a pretty posy, Ford! Phew! She reeks like a polecat."

Rosie's temper flared in response. She gritted her teeth.

"Lout!" the fine lord muttered. He patted her hand.

"Save a bit for me!" shouted another.

A third stroked at her as she passed him. "I will look for you in the morning, wench, when you walk with bowed legs!"

She shivered at their lewd catcalls and thanked her lucky stars that she had been purchased by the lord at her side.

"Do not tremble so," he whispered. "I promise I will not eat you."

Rosie tossed her matted hair out of her eyes with a bold show of courage. "Told ye afore, haint afeared. Only—cold." She didn't dare to look at him lest he read the lie in her eyes.

"Ah!" His gaudy plumes danced as he nodded. "You

are correct. Tis a sudden night wind. Allow me to remedy your discomfort.''

He halted, removed his short cape with a swirl, then settled it around her shoulders. Rosie drew the collar close to her face and stroked her cheek against the wondrous material.

"Tis soft like a downy chick!''

He chuckled. "Tis made of velvet. Does it please you, my dear? Are you warm enough now?''

"Oh, aye, my lord. Like toast on a fork.'' She snuggled deeper into its folds. His intoxicating scent clung to the material. "Tis sinful. Methinks the devil himself must wear velvet.''

Someone sniggered behind her. "The wench has found you out already, Andrew. You are truly the very devil of us all!''

Rosie glanced over her shoulder to see who had spoken. Three extremely tall young men loomed in the shadows. One of them winked at her. The naked hunger in his eyes unnerved her. She detected the odor of strong wine on his breath. She pulled the cape closer around her neck.

"Hold tight to your purse strings, my lord,'' she whispered to her new master. "Three great rogues are a-following us.''

Her escort chuckled again. "Ignore the rascals. They love to hear themselves talk.''

The three followers chortled at this remark.

Rosie tugged at the nobleman's arm. "We should flee, my lord.''

He squeezed her hand. "I am humbly grateful for your concern, sweetheart, but tis of no consequence. I fear they are friends of mine.'' He led her into a broad avenue. "This way.''

Rosie glanced around her with growing alarm. Tents, banners and campfires stretched down both sides of the thoroughfare and disappeared into the depths of the night. She had no idea that the English encampment was so large. She wondered how she would find Quince's tent in the morning—not that she was in any hurry to return to him.

"Where are we going, my lord?" she asked as they passed a cluster of more sumptuous pavilions.

The nobleman gave her another one of his heart-melting smiles. His white teeth flashed in the firelight. "To my humble abode."

The three behind them broke into a chorus of riotous laughter. "Wait until you see it, little one," one of them teased her.

Rosie didn't like the way he had said that. She tugged on the gentleman's sleeve again. "Are…are we going to do it there?"

His eyes twinkled. "That remains to be seen," he replied.

The three youths erupted into more boisterous braying.

Rosie's misgivings increased tenfold. "Are they…" She glanced uneasily over her shoulder again. "I mean, are we all going to do it—together?" No wonder the gentleman had paid so much gold for her! She could trick one with her vial of blood, but not four at the same time. Her knees grew weak at the thought.

The most outspoken of the three drew closer. "In good sooth, fair damsel, you are not ours to savor. But—"he flashed her a wicked grin "—if old Andrew tires too quickly, I will teach you to dance a merry tune."

Rosie's protector growled in the back of his throat.

"Mind your manners, Jackanapes. There is a lady present."

Rosie clutched the cape tighter. "Where?" she asked, peering into the darkness. She had never before met a real lady.

The three rogues nearly fell over themselves with laughter.

The gentleman shook his head at them. "Pigs," he remarked to Rosie.

Very soon, they stopped in front of a large double tent. By the light of a bonfire at the entrance, Rosie saw that the canvas walls were painted salmon pink and embellished with gilded ivy. Her patron lifted one of the flaps, revealing a cozy interior, lighted by a wealth of candles in glass lanterns. She gasped with awe at the extravagance, then uttered a little squeal of surprise when the gentleman swept her up into his arms.

He cradled her against his chest as if she were made of the most delicate glass. The warmth and strength of his arms soothed her, though she did not understand why. Her body tingled from the contact. Her fingers ached to stroke his smooth cheek, but she did not dare to take such a liberty. She was nothing but his chattel, she reminded herself.

The gentleman glanced at the trio. "If you plan to come in, boys, doff your muddy boots out here," he instructed them.

Rosie stared at him. "My lord?" His request seemed very odd.

To her further amazement, the three did exactly what he had commanded them.

"Tis old Andrew's conceit, lass," the tallest one explained, as he dropped his boots in a heap by the entrance. "He bought those new rugs before we left London and he is determined to keep them clean."

Her protector nodded. "Just so. Turkish, my dear. Imported on the humped-back camels all the way from the Ottoman Empire."

Rosie had no idea what Ottomans or camels were, but she could tell just from looking at the rugs, that they were the finest things she had ever seen. "If ye want to keep them new, my lord, methinks ye should roll them up, for they will surely grow filthy when it rains here."

The tallest laughed. "She has hit the bull's-eye, Andrew."

"Ah!" The nobleman nodded as if deep in thought. "A point well-taken, mistress. However, be easy in your mind. I have a layer of waxed canvas beneath them." He smiled again at her. "But I am most grateful for your consideration, sweetheart."

Her pulse skittered when he murmured the endearment to her. Rosie quelled the warm feeling. This man was too smooth to be trusted. He meant none of his sweet words. Ducking under the overhang, he carried her inside his pavilion.

Rosie drew in her breath then exhaled slowly. The interior was even more lavish than its rich ground coverings. Rose-pink silk draperies masked the plain canvas walls. The color made the pavilion glow with a soft, heavenly light. A small, but elegantly carved table stood near the center pole. Beside it was a matching armchair with a red cushion covering its seat. A thin wisp of smoke curled from a brass brazier, perfuming the air with an exotic scent.

A second tent of equal size and lavish appointments opened into the first. Rosie could see part of a large bed draped with billowing gauze. Its covers were turned back. Fat pillows nestled against the gilded headboard. Fear swept through Rosie. That bed would be the stage upon which she must act the part of a shy virgin.

The nobleman set her down on one of the wooden stools that dotted the rug. "Keep your feet up for one minute, my sweet," he instructed.

Rosie obeyed, too stunned by her sudden turn of fortune to ask why. Her master opened one of the many chests that lined the walls of the tent and took out a piece of plain muslin. He spread it on the rug in front of her. "There now. Put your feet on that, but do not move an inch off of it. There's a good lass." He stepped back to the center of the tent and regarded her as if she were a horse for sale.

Just then, a boy in his early teens stuck his head through the tent opening. "Good evening, my lord. I did not expect you to return so soon." Then he noticed Rosie. "By the book, what's that?"

Jack replied, "Your master's latest bauble, Jeremy."

One of his companions chuckled. "Tell him the price."

The boy gaped at his lord. "You paid good coin for that guttersnipe?"

Before the gentleman could reply, Jack said, "Not a coin, but an angel. In fact, thirty of them."

"And three of my sovereigns," the tallest one added.

The servant blanched. "For *her?* With all due respect, my lord, have you taken leave of your wits? Why?"

The youths laughed again. Then Jack caught his breath. "Are you so green that you cannot guess why a man buys a wench? Methinks we need to teach you the ways of the world, Jeremy."

The boy made a rude noise.

Rosie huddled deeper inside the cape, despite the fact

that the evening was very warm. She cast a quick glance at her patron to gauge his reaction. She wished they would stop talking about her as if she were a chamber pot. She shook her hair out of her eyes and returned their stares.

The noble lord appeared to take no note of the conversation around him. Instead, he continued to look at her, cocking his head to one side then to the other. He took one of the lanterns and held it up close to her face. Rosie shied away. He winked at her, then he turned to his companions.

"Well, gentlemen, there she is in all her muted glory. By my troth, she is too low for high praise, too brown for a fair praise and too little for a great praise. In short, she is perfect for our devices."

Panic welled up in Rosie's throat.

The gentleman continued, "She has a good figure— once we fatten her up a bit. Hair is a rat's nest. Can't even tell its true color."

Jack made a face. "I counsel you not to touch it, Andrew. The rats may still reside therein."

Rosie murmured an oath under her breath. That flap-eared knave might look pretty but he was a double-dyed churl. Then she realized that Sir Andrew had heard her. She bit her lip.

"I agree with you, sweetheart. Our Jackanapes is a bit rough around the edges," he whispered to her. He took one of her hands in his, studied her palms and fingers then he whistled through his teeth. "Zounds, mistress, what have you been doing with these?"

Rosie curled her fingers to hide them. "Plucking geese, scrubbing floors and washing foul linen, so please ye, my lord," she retorted.

Sir Andrew rapped her knuckles. "And biting your nails, I see."

Humiliated, Rosie sat on her hands to avoid further inspection by the other three who had drawn closer to look at her.

"Methinks she would have a pretty mouth—if she ever smiled," remarked the middle one.

She glared at him. What reason did she have to smile? Any minute now, they were going to ravish her. She held her tongue and prayed that the nobleman would finish his strange examination. She wanted to get the bedding over with before she lost her nerve to hoodwink him.

The serving boy cleared his throat. "May I inquire what does my lord intend to do with this piece of baggage?"

Everyone turned toward Sir Andrew. Rosie's heart pounded against her rib cage.

He unbuttoned his beautiful doublet. "Why, bathe her, of course," he replied. "Tell the pot boys to heat up more water. Fetch the tub!"

Jeremy groaned. "I have just now cleaned it after your own bath."

Sir Andrew removed his coat and hung it over the back of the arm chair. "Excellent! Then you will know exactly where to find it. Be quick, sluggard! The moon begins to wane and we have not yet supped."

Rosie licked her lips. Food! She would bear anything Sir Andrew did to her, if he would only feed her afterward.

Jeremy disappeared with a good deal of grumbling. The three youths settled themselves on the various chests.

Jack chortled. "This will be good sport, Andrew. My thanks for providing us with such unusual amusement."

Under the cover of the cape, Rosie trembled. None of Quince's girls had said anything about entertaining men in a bath.

Sir Andrew rolled up the flowing sleeves of his shirt. The muscles of his forearms surprised Rosie. By his exaggerated mannerisms, she had taken him to be a languid fop. Yet, when he had held her in his arms… She pushed that delightful memory out of her mind. Obviously, her empty stomach played tricks with her fancies.

He cocked an eyebrow at the others. "I fear I must disappoint you, Jackanapes. This much maligned lass must be treated as a lady, therefore she will have privacy while at her bath."

Jack ogled Rosie. "I have seen a good many ladies of the finest quality in their baths. Indeed, I have often joined them."

Sir Andrew snorted. "Not tonight and not with this lady. Tis time to bide your adieus, my lads. Go pester someone else with your rude company and leave me to my pleasant one."

The three moaned in protest. Holding her breath, Rosie prayed that Sir Andrew would prevail.

"Begone at once!" He raised his voice slightly.

The youths roused themselves and padded in their stocking feet to the entrance. They made a great show of struggling to pull on their boots.

"Tis a cruel thing that you do to us, Andrew!"

He planted his hands on his hips. "I have heard that complaint far too often to be moved by you, Brandon. Everything is cruel if it does not suit your fancy. Now, out!"

Jack bestowed a final wink on Rosie. "Remember, wench, if old Andrew goes to sleep on you—"

Sir Andrew tapped his foot. "I hear only a breeze

whistling in my ears and not your words at all. Good night, my Lord Stafford.''

The tallest of the three was the last to leave. For the first time that night, he gave Rosie a genuine smile that held no lechery in it. ''Mark me, lass. Andrew is a good man, despite his peculiar ways. He will treat you well.'' Then he ducked low to avoid hitting his head on the cross pole.

Just as they departed, Jeremy pushed a round wooden tub into the tent. To Rosie, it looked no bigger than the wash tub she had slaved over in the scullery of Quince's bawd house in Bankside. It was certainly too small for her, much less for the two of them. She glanced at Sir Andrew.

''Haint ever had a bath in my life before,'' she murmured.

Sir Andrew opened one of his coffers. ''That is quite obvious, my dear.'' He took out several small bottles and lined them up on the table.

Jeremy poked his head and shoulders inside the tent. He carried a wooden bucket full of water. A curl of steam wafted from it. Without a word Sir Andrew took the bucket, poured its contents into the tub, then returned the bucket to his servant. Jeremy disappeared only to reappear a minute later with another bucketful. Rosie chewed her thumbnail.

Sir Andrew glanced at her. ''You spoke, sweetheart?''

''Ye want to scald me like a goose for plucking.''

Andrew chuckled as he emptied the contents of one of the bottles into the hot water. ''Tis an interesting simile, but I doubt you will cook in this broth. By the time my creeping squire and his minions have filled this tub, the temperature will be merely warm.''

Jeremy reappeared with two more brimming buckets.

Rosie eyed the tub as if it might suddenly attack her. Sir Andrew removed his short gold brocade vest and stepped out of his trunks, leaving him clad only in his shirt, his bright stockings and the most unusual codpiece Rosie had ever seen. Red silk tassels hung from each of its three corners. Sir Andrew noticed her fascination. He cleared his throat.

"Is something amiss?" he asked with a wide smile.

Rosie dropped her gaze to her toes. "Nay, my lord," she murmured. "I was just wondering why ye…that is…what manner of… A pox upon it, my lord! Why do ye truss yourself up like a mummer at a fair?"

Instead of striking her, Sir Andrew threw back his head and roared with laughter. "How refreshing you are in this old world, sweetheart! My attire is all the fashion in Italy and France, though, in truth, many Englishmen would rather die than wear such finery."

Rosie eyed the intriguing apparel. "Then why do ye?"

Sir Andrew sprinkled some shredded herbs into the water before he answered. "Tis my own fancy and conceit, I warrant. And to amaze the ladies. Confess it— aren't you amazed?"

She nodded. "Beyond belief, my lord." She tried not to stare at the dancing tassels. They made her heart skip in the most wanton manner. "Are ye going to do it now, my lord?"

His eyes twinkled with pure mischief. "That depends on what *it* is." He unwrapped a waxy green tablet from a piece of linen and sniffed it with appreciation. "Ah! The finest milled soap this side of Castile."

Jeremy returned with yet more water. By now the tub looked almost too full. Sir Andrew nodded to the boy. "Good! Now away with you, my sprite. Find us something edible in the cooks' tent. Spend an hour, and do not reenter until I call you.''

Jeremy bowed his head, then turned on his heel. He gave Rosie a nasty smirk. "Methinks you are in a fine pickle now, wench."

Sir Andrew pointed to the entrance. "Peace, knave! Such carping is not commendable. Begone! And tie down the flap behind you."

Black terror engulfed Rosie. She was now alone with the man who presumed her virginity. She touched the hidden vial of blood. "Are we going to do it now?" she repeated.

An easy smile played at the corners of his lips. "If it means taking a bath, *you* will do that now. If it means that I take my pleasure with you, the answer is—not yet."

She released her pent-up breath.

He arched his brow. "Take off your clothes," he murmured.

Fury almost choked Rosie. The handsome peacock had lied—just like all the knaves in her life. "But ye said—"

Sir Andrew snapped his fingers, though he continued to smile warmly at her. "Hurry, my sweet, before the water cools."

Taking a deep breath to steady her nerves, Rosie stood up. She was careful not to move off her allotted piece of muslin. She untied her skirt and allowed the ragged garment to fall around her feet.

Sir Andrew cocked his head. "Everything." He opened another chest and took out a comb, a brush and several more bottles.

Rosie wet her dry lips. "What are ye going to do with me, my lord?"

He grinned. "I am going to give you the most thorough scrubbing of your life."

She fumbled with the laces at her neckline.

He straightened up. "Do you have a troublesome knot?"

Rosie blew her hair out of her eyes. "Tis no matter. We can do it with my shift on, my lord."

Slowly he shook his head. "Not in my tub. Now, off with it. Every last revolting stitch you have on."

Rosie pursed her lips. "Ye want me to strip naked with ye standing there a-watching me?" He appeared to ponder the question. She thought she had said it plain enough.

He crossed his arms over his chest. "Aye, that is the very nut and core of it. I do. Perchance, you will recall that I have paid a small fortune for that very privilege, Mistress… *What* did you say your name was?"

She lifted her head with as much pride as she could muster. "Tis Rosie, so please ye, my lord."

He flourished a deep bow. The red silk tassels below his waist swayed with erotic abandon. "I am struck near speechless by your presence, Mistress Rosie. Permit me to introduce myself. I am Sir Andrew Ford, the miracle worker." He bowed again.

Rosie stared at him with a mixture of bewilderment and apprehension. She was trapped alone with a charming lunatic.

Sir Andrew softened his expression. "I do but jest, Rosie. Tis my fashion. Now, for the love of warm water, will you please undress—or shall I do it for you?"

"Nay!" Rosie loosened the bandstring that held her shift together, but she clutched the material to her bosom before it slipped off her shoulders. "I have nothing else on underneath this, my lord."

He held out his hand to her. Cheerful expectation deepened the laugh lines around his eyes and mouth.

"Delighted to hear that, Rosie!"

Chapter Three

A ripple of tenderness crept into Andrew's heart as Rosie reluctantly untied the last lace of her ragged shift, but his feelings changed into unexpected heated ones once she dropped the garment. He sucked his breath through his teeth though he maintained an outward calm.

Rosie's beauty far exceeded his original estimate. In spite of the mud and filth that clung to her skin, she looked like a Venus come to life. Reed-slender, she carried herself with a certain unconscious grace that reminded him of a young willow tree. Rosie squared her shoulders, as if preparing for a battle. This action drew his immediate attention to her firm, uplifted breasts. Below them, her slim waist flared into softly rounded hips. When she noticed that his gaze moved lower, she covered her most private part with her hand. At the same time, she crossed her other arm over her bosom, hiding her tender pink nipples. It was a most unnatural pose for a prostitute, and Andrew found it highly provocative.

His loins stirred and grew hot.

Rosie shot him a wary look. "Is there something amiss, my lord?" she asked in perfect innocence.

Andrew cleared his throat before he trusted himself to

frame a sensible answer. "Nay, my dear." He pointed to the tub. "Hop in quickly before the water has lost all its heat."

Rosie tiptoed across the rug then paused beside the bath.

He smiled encouragement, while his heart raced. "You will not drown, I promise you."

She tossed an unruly tangle of hair out of her eyes. Her full lips twisted into a cynical expression. "I have heard men's promises afore and they proved to be nothing more than chaff on the wind."

Andrew ran his finger around the inside of his collar. "I am not like other men, Rosie. And that is a promise you can trust."

She turned away. Taking a deep breath, she stepped into the tub.

Andrew exhaled. "Excellent! Now sit down, Rosie."

Without comment, she sank into the water. Andrew walked over to her discarded clothing. He pushed the motley garments into a pile with the toe of his shoe.

Rosie stared at him through the snarls of her hair like a cornered rabbit. "What are ye a-doing with my clothes?" she yelped. Her emerald eyes darkened with genuine fear.

In answer he kicked her rags toward the closed tent flap.

She gripped the rim of the tub. Water sloshed over the side onto the rug. "Hold, my lord! Tis all I have in this world."

Andrew gave them another kick. "Good!"

Just then something within their folds crunched under his heel. Rosie gasped and started to rise.

Andrew pointed at her. "Sit back down and soak!"

he ordered in the same tone of voice he had often used on the Cavendish brothers when they had been his pages.

He lifted his foot and examined the bottom of his shoe. Blood dripped onto the clothing. More blood stained Rosie's sorry excuse of a skirt. A grin threatened the corners of Andrew's mouth. An old bawd's trick! So much for the proof of his sworn virgin. Assuming an expression of innocent surprise, he glanced at Rosie. She had turned white under the layer of dirt. He shook his foot. A few crimson droplets spattered onto the rug. "Od's bodkins, my sweet. What do you suppose I have stepped on?"

Rosie ran the tip of her pink tongue across her top lip in the most enticing manner. "Methinks ye have killed a monstrous fat beetle, my lord, and ye had best keep an eye on your bedding in case there are more."

Andrew chuckled and silently applauded Rosie's quick thinking. She would have to use those clever wits in the near future if he was going to successfully pass her off as a lady.

Aloud he remarked, "Aye, my very thought indeed, Rosie. I will instruct Jeremy to henceforth wield his broom with a vengeance." He wiped his shoe on her shift, then kicked the lot under the flap. "Ho there! Timothy!" he called to one of his young servants who hovered outside the tent. "Burn those at once and mind you—there may be a large dead beetle within."

Rosie sloshed more water onto the rug as she started to stand up again. Her pallor had now changed to bright red and her eyes glowed with green fire. "What right have ye got to destroy my things?"

Andrew crossed to the tub in two strides and pushed her back into the water. Then he knelt behind her and whispered into her ear, "You are mine, Mistress Rosie. I own you for as long as I please."

She opened her mouth to say something but stopped when she saw him lathering his hands with soap. With a snort, she turned away from him. Pleased with his command of the situation, Andrew hummed a little ballad under his breath as he scrubbed her neck and shoulders. Rosie said nothing, but his fingers felt the tension in her muscles. Despite the heat of the water and the warmth inside the pavilion, she trembled.

Rinsing her back, he saw a number of purple bruises staining her fair skin. He touched one place lightly and gritted his teeth when she flinched. His mind clouded with anger at the sight of her mistreatment.

He massaged the back of her neck as if she were a child. "Rosie, who did this villainy to you?"

She would not look at him. "'Tis nothing, my lord," she snapped. "Are ye going to do it now with me all soaped up like a greased pig?"

Andrew sighed, and added more oil of roses to the bath water. "Nay, Rosie. I am not going to do anything to you but wash the grime of the ages out of your sweet skin. But, by the rood, I will punish the foul knave who did this piece of mischief. I warrant twas that whoremonger who sold you to me. I will slit the villain's nose."

Rosie hung her head, but said nothing.

He scrubbed one of her arms with a small brush. "That vermin is nothing to you now. You need not fear him."

"Humph!" she retorted. "'Tis easy enough for you to say. You do not have to face Quince in the morning."

"Neither do you, sweetheart," he murmured softly.

Slowly, she turned around. A sheen of tears filmed

over her eyes. Andrew almost kissed away those bitter drops, but he checked himself in time. It would only reinforce her mistrust if he had.

"How now?" she jeered. "Is this another one of your tricks to drive me mad? I pray ye, do not jest with kind words."

Andrew dipped a soft cloth into the water, soaped it, then gently held her chin between his thumb and forefinger while he washed her face. "I swear a solemn oath upon my word as a knight—oh, aye, Rosie, for all my fripperies and silvered hairs, I am a true swordsman—I swear that I do not make sport of you."

Her lips hardened into a thin line. "That is a pretty promise, my lord, and as solid as smoke."

He tenderly wiped the soap suds from her cheeks. "Mark me well, Rosie. I paid enough money for you to last a lifetime—both yours and mine. As of this night, you are bound to no man but me. You will never return to that abominable villain again, I promise."

She stared at him searching to find a falsehood in his eyes. Then she wrinkled her nose. "I will believe you when pigs sprout wings, my lord."

He chuckled. "You never can tell, my dear. Pigs are uncommonly intelligent. Sometimes they surprise us."

Rosie almost smiled. Andrew yearned to kiss her lips, but the voice of prudence warned him in time. This girl was a skittish colt. He knew he must exercise great restraint and patience to win her trust, especially if he wanted her cooperation to turn her into a lady within twelve days. He picked up a jug from the floor.

"Bend over and close your eyes," he instructed.

Rosie's expression immediately hardened. "A blister on that sweet tongue! I spy your deceit, my lord. Fir~

you make me half believe you, then you show your true colors!''

Her sudden mood swing caught Andrew off guard. "'Sblood, Rosie, what brought on this tempest of fury?''

She glared at him. "Myself, my lord! Ye tell me that I should not fear ye, then, in your very next breath, ye tell me to bend over and close my eyes while you use me like a dog. I am a puling fool to have believed your honey words!''

Andrew beseeched heaven for patience. He sat back on his heels and held up the jug for her inspection. "I must wash your hair, Rosie, or else the whole bath will be for naught. I merely asked you to bend your head over so you will not get soap in your eyes.''

She studied his face for nearly a full minute. Finally she nodded. "So please your lordship. I had forgotten that ye *own* me.''

Andrew opened his mouth to defend himself, but instead he decided to seize the moment of her docility. He filled the pitcher and poured it over her hair. She screamed like a scalded cat.

Andrew paused. "What now?''

She hunched her thin shoulders. "Tis mickle wet!''

He chuckled. "Water usually is. Tis its God-given property. Now close your eyes and hold still.''

She squinted at him through her wet lashes. "Why?''

He poured some pale cream into his palm. "Because this will sting if it creeps into your eye.''

He lathered the wilderness of her hair. Patiently, he worked his fingers through the tangles. Rosie sat very still while he added more soap, then more water. The ̇ent of roses grew stronger after each rinse.

̇ndrew discovered that he was enjoying himself. He ̇e way her wet locks tended to curl around his fingers. He caressed her neck and behind her delicate ears. He traced his finger down her bowed spine. She shivered under his touch. Andrew brought himself up short. *Attend to your business.* He soaped her tresses a fourth time.

"Ye have done that already, my lord," she sputtered.

"Aye, and I will do it again, if tis necessary." He poured several more jugfuls over her.

As the last of the soapy water ran down her back, her dull grayish hair turned into an ash blond. He whistled under his breath.

"What?" She patted the top of her head. "Have I gone bald?"

He smoothed her crown. "Nay, I have discovered a rare beauty."

"M...me?" she asked with an incredulous voice.

He smiled into her brilliant eyes. "Aye, my sweet. I will show you anon." He cleared his throat again. "But first you must attend to your personal needs." He handed her the scrubbing cloth and the diminished chunk of soap. "Wash your paps and your...ah...nether area. Tis not proper for a gentleman to perform that service."

He levered himself onto one of the stools and watched her as she continued her ablutions. He could not remember the last time he had grown so hot at the mere sight of a beautiful wench. He welcomed the pleasurable ache that he feared he had lost with the lusty days of his youth.

Rosie wrung out the washcloth. "Water's getting cold."

Her words snapped Andrew out of his erotic reverie. He pulled himself together and hoped she would not notice the physical change in him. He opened another chest and took out several pieces of clean toweling for her and his blue silk brocade dressing robe for himself. He put on the robe first before turning around to hand her the towels.

"You may get out now, Rosie, and dry yourself off with these."

She took the towels. "Ye look flushed, my lord," she observed.

"Tis the heat. France is quite warm for this time of year."

She turned her back to him, then stood up and stepped out of the tub. Andrew collapsed into his armchair. He could not believe Rosie's transformation. Her skin glowed like pink roses floating in a bowl of cream. A little rivulet of bathwater meandered down the hollow of her spine and disappeared between her softly rounded buttocks.

His mouth went dry as he watched the drop's sensuous journey. He wished he were twenty years younger.

Someone scratched on the tent flap. "My lord?" Jeremy called through the canvas. "I have returned with your supper."

She glanced at the entrance with a sudden spark of interest. Andrew shot to his feet. He would not allow that young coxcomb of a squire to spy Rosie in all her naked glory. "One moment!"

"Food!" Rosie inhaled the aroma of roasted fowl with closed eyes. A radiant smile touched her lips. The sight of her bliss nearly undid all of Andrew's good intentions toward her.

He moved quickly behind Rosie and took the towel from her limp fingers. He dried her with considerable speed. She tried to squirm away from his vigorous ministrations.

"Soft, my lord! First ye cook me, then ye flay me. Ouch!"

Andrew murmured soothing nonsense. Rosie's loud protests subsided into small kittenish sounds. He gentled his touch, patting her across her shoulders, down her lovely back and around her delicious bottom. He enjoyed touching her soft curves through the damp cloth. Giving Rosie this bath had been worth every groat he had paid that abominable villain.

Rosie leaned against him and rested her head on his shoulder. Her damp golden hair smelled of roses and almonds. Andrew slipped his arm around her waist. He suspected that she would not protest if he chose to take her straight to his bed. He glanced at the linen bedcovers that were turned down so invitingly. After all, it was what she expected him to do.

Andrew steeled his resolve and banished the tempting idea before it grew to full flower in his imagination. He had never used his wealth to buy either a man's good opinion or a woman's favor, and he refused to begin now. He hugged Rosie as if she were a beloved daughter—the child he had never had. He reminded himself again that he needed her goodwill to win his madcap wager.

Just then Rosie looked up at him. The candlelight made her green eyes luminous. "If ye do it now, I will get your fine bed all wet."

Andrew put his hands on her shoulders and gave her a little shake. "Rosie, my sweet, we are *not* going to swive now."

She regarded him with that soul-plumbing stare. "Ye want to," she observed in a soft tone. "I can see it in your eyes. Am I not clean enough for ye yet?"

Andrew framed her lovely face in his hands and traced

her high cheekbones with the pads of his thumbs. "Aye, Rosie. You are as clean as an angel's wing, but I have other plans for you."

She stepped away from him and drew the damp towel tighter around herself. "Ah, ha! Now I begin to understand. Ye have different tastes. I have heard that there are men who like to hear a girl scream in pain afore they are aroused. Trust me, my lord, I will scream this bloody tent down to please ye, but…" She paused, gulping for breath, then folded her hands as if in prayer. "I beseech ye for the love of God do not beat me."

Her plea took him aback. How could she say that when he had already told her how much he hated to see the bruises on her young skin? "Rosie, I have no intention of beating you, nor do I wish to hear you scream. That behavior is not to my taste either. Trust me. Please?"

Rosie lifted her chin. "Then what are ye a-going to do with me now that I have no dirt and no clothes?" She took another step backward, narrowly missing the tub of dirty water.

The poor girl looked like a hunted doe. Instead of trying to placate her fears with more words, Andrew turned to the nearest coffer, opened the lid and drew out one of his plainer shirts.

"Will this garment suffice for the time being, my lady?"

Rosie caught her lower lip between her teeth. "Haint ever been a lady, but that is the finest-looking shirt I ever did see."

He waved it back and forth. "Tis yours, Rosie. Take it. Put it on."

Like a spark of summer lightning, she reached out and snatched it from his fingers. In one fluid movement, she dropped it over her head as she let the wet towels fall to the rug. The hem fell just above her dimpled knees. Andrew tied the neck laces high above her collarbones.

Rosie ran her hand over the ivory lawn material. "Tis like wearing a spider's web," she whispered. "Haint ever had so fine a shift."

Andrew resisted his latest impulse to kiss her. Instead, he draped his red cape over her shoulders to ward off both the night chill and his squire's lusty gaze.

Then he stepped to the middle of the tent and bellowed, "Are you still out there, Jeremy?"

"Aye, my lord," the boy replied, "together with your cooling supper."

Andrew winked at Rosie. "Well, maltworm! Bring it in!"

A cloud of succulent aromas followed the squire into the tent.

Rosie nearly swooned when she smelled the delicious mixture of roast chicken, warm yeast bread and a cinnamon-spicy scent that she couldn't quite place. It smelled heavenly. Her stomach rumbled with her hunger. She longed to snatch the huge covered platter out of the boy's hands, but Andrew intercepted her and guided her to a stool.

Jeremy cast her a quick glance through the shaggy fringe of his dark bangs. His jaw dropped. Rosie pulled the cape across her bare knees.

Sir Andrew took a comb and began to pull it through her tangled locks. "Mind the platter, clodpate," he growled at the speechless boy. "I much prefer to take my supper off a table than off the floor."

Jeremy gaped at Rosie. She returned his penetrating stare.

Sir Andrew chuckled while he worked on a particularly stubborn snarl. "You remind me of a goggle-eyed turbot, Jeremy. Have you never seen a lady with her hair unbound before?"

The boy swallowed. "Not like her," he muttered.

Rosie stiffened. The young churl was making fun of her predicament. She glared at him. "I may not be a lady, but haint ever been a mermaid either, so ye can put your watery eyes back in your sockets, boy!"

Sir Andrew patted her shoulder. "Well-spoken!" he whispered into her ear. Then he continued to torture her scalp.

Jeremy stepped closer and peered at Rosie as if she were a creature from the New World. "Tis the same wench as before?" Disbelief spread over the boy's face.

Rosie whispered a tavern oath.

"The very same lady indeed!" Sir Andrew worked on another tangle.

"Haint ever been a lady," Rosie muttered, then she squealed. It felt as if he had ripped off half her scalp. "Pray, my lord, I beg ye stop! Are ye a-trying to make me bald?"

He massaged her tender skin. "May I be boiled in a suet pudding if I ever inflicted such a dire punishment upon you, my dear. Jeremy!" he snapped at the transfixed youth. "Attend to your duties! Set the table for two. Use my silver gilt service."

Jeremy slid the platter onto one of the nearby chests. Then he opened the coffer next to it and took out golden plates, goblets, eating utensils and folded pieces of white damask. He set all these items on the table, and arranged them in a pattern. Rosie couldn't understand why her master waited so long before eating. The food must be half-cold already.

She twisted on the stool. "I pray ye, my lord. Leave my hair in peace. Let us eat now."

Sir Andrew clicked his tongue against his teeth. "You must be patient, Rosie. Patience is a virtue, you know." He continued to work with her tresses as if he had all the time in the world.

She eyed the tempting tray and fumed at his delay. "Haint ever had a virtue," she muttered under her breath.

Sir Andrew chuckled. "How now? What about the virtue of chastity? Remember, I paid a great deal for that particular virtue."

She shifted again on the stool, then rubbed the side of her nose with her forefinger. "Aye, my mind mistook that for a moment."

"Of course it did," he agreed in a soothing tone of voice.

Her lie made Rosie feel sick.

Jeremy poured red wine from a large clay jug into a silver pitcher. The polished metal gleamed in the candlelight. Then the squire shook out one of the cloths, folded it in the artful shape of a swan, and placed it on the table. When he noticed Rosie's attention, he made an exaggerated display of his surprising skill with the second snow-white cloth.

She hid her amazement behind a look of disdain. She didn't want this green stripling to think that she had no idea why he had wasted his time to make two such fantastic shapes. She would rather eat a swan than look at one. From under the tantalizing cover of the tray, Jeremy extracted a small bowl of salt and a larger bowl filled with assorted fruits. He put the salt on one end of the table and the fruit on the other. Finally, he wedged a beeswax taper into the golden candlestick, and lit it.

Rosie had never seen such a lavish table setting. The squire lifted the cover from the platter with a flourish. The supper's delicious aroma filled the air. "Tis a torture," she moaned.

Sir Andrew chuckled. "Tis merely combing your hair."

"Nay! That!" Rosie pointed to the steaming dishes on the tray.

He stopped his painful occupation with her locks, and placed his hands on her shoulders. "When did you last eat, Rosie?" he whispered.

"Yesterday after we landed in France, but twas only some stale bread crusts." She glanced at him over her shoulder. His hazel eyes returned her look with a heart-melting warmth. She forced herself to ignore the confusing feelings that stirred within her. "We had a dinner of tripe at a public house in Dover, but the journey over the water was too rough. I puked it all away afore we were even out of sight of land. God shield me, twas a hellish trip."

Sir Andrew put down the comb and brush on a chest. "Then I shall not make you wait any longer." He stood and held out his hand to her. "Come, Rosie, tis now or never."

Rosie groaned. *Now* the perfidious rogue had finally decided to debauch her! Just when she could almost taste the princely banquet set before her. Her empty stomach roiled with fear. Sir Andrew would soon discover her deceit, and she would never taste a mouthful of that delicious-looking supper. She stared at his hand, then at his grinning face. She cast a farewell glance at the roast chicken.

"Where do ye want me to lie down, my lord?" she murmured.

Chapter Four

Sir Andrew's smile broadened, making him look even more handsome than before. "Tis not yet time for bed, Rosie, but for supper, if it would please you to join me."

With a great sigh of relief, she jumped up so quickly, she knocked over her stool. Andrew restrained her before she could lunge for the food.

He tucked her hand firmly within his. "A lady does not charge the groaning board like a battering ram," he admonished her.

Jeremy smirked, though he was wise enough not to look Rosie straight in the eye.

Anger mixed with her hunger. "Haint a lady! And I am perishing for want of food. Is it your cruel jest to make me grovel for your pleasure?"

Sir Andrew chuckled in the back of his throat, though he still held her tight within his grasp. "My pleasure is to escort you to the table."

Rosie tugged at her pinioned arm and shot him a frustrated look. "I can get there well enough on my own. In sooth, I can get there a good deal faster than ye, my lord. Tis but two short steps away." The aroma of the roasted fowl enveloped her. "Let me go, for sweet charity's sake!"

Andrew checked her second lunge. "A lady is led in a docile and demure fashion with downcast looks."

She blew a damp curl out of her eyes and glared at the pigheaded gentleman. "Told ye afore, haint a lady."

He planted his feet on his red-and-blue patterned rug, and gripped her arms. She lifted her chin and glared at him.

The laugh lines around his eyes crinkled in a maddeningly delightful way. "Attend upon this most important point, my dear. If you desire to partake of the delectable victuals that my good squire has procured for our enjoyment, you *will* act like a lady. *That* is my pleasure. Tis what I paid good coin for. Now, what say you?"

Rosie suppressed her immediate inclination to tell him exactly what she thought of his delusions. Instead, she decided to humor his whims while the food was still warm. She drew herself up and tossed her wild hair over her shoulders. "Then lead me to yon table, my lord, if that's what pleases ye. But, prithee, do it quicklike."

Sir Andrew beamed at her as if she had just said something clever. "Your dulcet voice is a delight to my ears, even if your words are a bit rough around the edges. Let us repair to our feast—*my* lady." He cocked his head and grinned at her.

Rosie almost corrected him again, but she closed her mouth at the last split second. This stubborn lord would only argue the matter further while the food congealed in its sauces. Andrew led her to a folding chair, then he stepped behind it and gestured for her to sit. Rosie eyed the sway-bottom leather seat and wondered if it would fold up with her inside of it.

She twisted her fingers behind her back. "I do not know what ye want me to do." She eyed the tempting dishes arrayed before her.

He gave her another one of those melting smiles. "You thank me very prettily, and allow me to push the chair closer to the table."

Rosie cleared her throat. "Thank ye kindly, my lord." She didn't move. Her mouth watered.

Behind her, Jeremy snickered.

Andrew leaned over the back of the chair and whispered, "Rosie, you are supposed to slide in front of it and sit down when you feel the seat touch the back of your knees."

Rosie wiggled her nose as she regarded the flimsy-looking thing. She didn't trust Sir Andrew. This could be a daft prank. He would pull the chair out from under her and laugh when she landed on her bum. She didn't trust him an inch. He grinned at her and waited. No one uttered a word. The lure of the tantalizing supper grew stronger. Rosie's stomach growled out loud.

"Trust me," his lips mouthed the words.

Flinging her usual caution to the wind, Rosie took a deep breath and did as he had instructed. To her surprised delight, he seated her exactly as he had said he would. Once she was in place, he went around to the other side of the table where Jeremy seated his master in similar fashion. Rosie reached out to wrench a plump leg off the golden chicken, but Sir Andrew clasped her hand in midair.

He clicked his tongue against the back of his teeth. "We say grace first and thank the good Lord for this bounty."

Rosie snorted. "Why? He never did cook it."

Jeremy gasped while Sir Andrew merely raised his

brows at this bit of blasphemy. She curled her fingers
into a fist to keep herself from attacking the chicken.

"Have you never prayed before a meal, Rosie?" her
patron asked.

She decided to tell the truth. This peacock of a gentleman should learn something about poverty. "Twas
more like a-praying *for* a meal, and the Lord did not see
fit to listen much to me."

Sir Andrew's face lost some of its mirth. His eyes
glistened. "Then we shall make our thanksgiving mercifully brief." He folded his hands and bowed his head
without waiting to see if Rosie did the same. "Lord God,
we thank you for this food and for the good company
who share it. Amen," he murmured quickly.

"Amen," Rosie breathed with relief. She reached for
the chicken leg again, but Sir Andrew caught her hand
once more. Rosie nearly swore at him, but bit her tongue
instead.

"A lady is always served her food," he instructed
with a grin.

She wanted to scream the tent down. "Haint ever been
a lady and haint ever been served!"

The frustrating lord nodded as if she had spoken a
grain of pure wisdom. "Then Jeremy will serve only me
and you can watch me eat." With his free hand, he
snapped his fingers. The squire lifted the roasted chicken
out of Rosie's reach, carved several large portions and
heaped half of it on his master's plate.

Her lower lip quivered. "Ye said I could eat if I sat
like ye wanted me to and if I said grace," she muttered.
"Ye are no better than any other deceiving man even if
ye do wear finer clothes."

He caressed her hand. The action warmed her despite

her anger. "If a lady desires to partake of a meal, she is served," he repeated with the tenacity of a billy goat.

Rosie swallowed her last shred of pride. "So serve me then."

Sir Andrew smiled, then leaned over his mound of food. His lips brushed against the back of her hand. Rosie inhaled sharply at the contact. Her pulse quickened. She felt she might swoon. With a gentle squeeze, he released her. She hid her hand in her lap. Her skin burned with the imprint of his lips. When she glanced at him, she was startled to see a smoldering intensity darken the hazel of his eyes. Then the raw look disappeared and his usual smile returned.

Rosie was only dimly aware that Jeremy had spoken to her. Having no idea what he had asked, she merely nodded. All the while she stared at her host as if she had never seen him before. What spell had he cast upon her with such a simple gesture that it made her forget her hunger—except for more of his touch?

Sir Andrew's mouth twitched. "Eat your supper, my dear," he suggested in a husky whisper.

The poor girl gasped when she looked down at her plate. Jeremy had piled it high with the other half of the roasted capon, a wedge of cold mutton pie, a large slice of soft white cheese over which he had spooned the honey-mustard sauce and a side dish of spiced peaches. Rosie lost the disturbing pallor in her face as she fell to eating with both hands. The capon's lemon glaze ran down her bare arms to nearly her elbow before she stopped its journey with a quick lick of her dainty pink tongue.

Andrew opened his mouth to instruct her in the proper use of her untouched napkin and the pearl-handled fork that lay by her plate. Then he checked himself. Plainly, the child was starving. Etiquette lessons could wait. He cursed himself for teasing her. He should have realized that the whoremaster would not have wasted his own coin to feed his wenches when there were rich gentlemen like Andrew to do it for him.

He drained the smooth claret and beckoned his squire to refill his goblet. Had the evening turned intensely hot or was it the wild creature opposite him that made the air seem thick with tension and his clothing uncomfortably tight around his tender parts? He had no idea what had prompted him to kiss Rosie's hand, nor did he understand why the experience now made him feel like a callow youth green-sick with his first love. Andrew was too jaded for such childish feelings. He had kissed a hundred ladies in his day and few of them had ever made his heart leap into his throat or his blood pound against his temples. Obviously his discomfort was due to the headiness of the French wine and the close perfumed air inside the pavilion.

Rosie looked up from her feast, her complexion now as rosy as her name. She licked her fingers clean of the honey-mustard sauce. "Is there something amiss with your food?"

Andrew merely shook his head. How could he tell her that her fresh-washed beauty had stolen his appetite for food? She fully expected him to rape her at any moment. His honest admission would only confirm her worst fears.

He dipped a sliver of capon into its sauce and ate it before answering. "Your presence has given me much food for thought, sweetheart. And, in truth, I ate overwell at dinner today."

She cast him a shrewd look. "Methinks I spy disapproval all over your face, my lord. What have I done wrong now?''

He shifted in his chair while he strove to think of some acceptable answer. This chit was too clever by half if she could read his expression so well on such short acquaintance.

He cleared his throat. ''A lady eats with small mouthfuls so that her cheeks are not puffed out like a squirrel at nutting time.'' He sipped his wine and expanded on this safer theme. ''Ladies do not pounce upon their food as if it would disappear before they could taste it, nor do they discourse with their mouths full.''

Rosie swallowed her spiced peach. Then she remarked in a low tone, ''Ladies and their gentlemen know there will always be another dinner for them to enjoy. Poor folk do not. Tis the difference between yourself and me.'' She picked up the capon's wing. ''And haint ever seen so much food in one place afore, so pardon my appetite.''

He inclined his head to her. ''Your philosophy smacks of the Greco-Roman—eat, drink and be merry for tomorrow we die.''

Rosie furrowed her delicate brows, then looked over her shoulder at the grinning squire. ''Does Sir Andrew always speak with such a mickle mouthful of words like that?'' she asked Jeremy.

The boy attempted to look solemn as he nodded.

Rosie returned her gaze to Andrew. Her green eyes sparkled in the candle's light. ''Methinks you are happier to dine on your speech than your food, my lord, so can I have your cheese?''

He stared at her for a moment, then he burst out laughing. ''You will be ill if you eat too much rich food all at once.''

She twirled her fork. "Haint ever," she remarked as she skewered the cheese on his plate.

Rosie could not remember ever eating to the point of bursting. When Jeremy offered her a selection of thin sugar wafers she waved him away, just as she had observed Sir Andrew do. She sat back in her chair and patted her full tummy with the satisfaction of an overly fed kitten. She closed her eyes with a sigh of contentment. Surely this was how the angels in heaven felt all the time.

Sir Andrew snapped his fingers. "Wake up. We have work to do."

Rosie winced inwardly. Now was the moment of reckoning. She steeled herself for the coming battle. At least, he had fed her well. She would always be grateful for that. She opened her eyes slowly. "My lord?" She hoped her voice did not sound as nervous as she felt.

Sir Andrew produced a silver coin from his clothing and tossed to his squire. "Clear away these dishes and yourself, my boy. The lady and I have a need for some privacy."

Jeremy caught the money with one hand. He winked at Rosie when he removed her silver plate. "He's a kind man," he told her in an undertone. "So do not disappoint him. Be generous with your favors."

Rosie glared at the boy. "Ye mind your business and leave me to mind mine," she whispered back.

Sir Andrew took a long drink of his wine, then wiped his mouth with his napkin. He smiled at her as he did so. Rosie's heart tumbled over. She felt like a rabbit caught in a velvet trap. To hide her unease, she picked up her own untouched napkin, shook out its artful folding and followed Sir Andrew's example. His smile broadened as he watched her.

"You are a quick study, my sweet," he remarked. "Let us pray that you will continue to be so."

Rosie chewed her fingernail. How was she going to play the part of a virgin when her vial of blood was now only a stain on the sole of his shoe? She stared at the claret in her goblet and wondered if she could trick him with that. Probably not. Sir Andrew struck her as a very clever man, even if he was somewhat addled in his wits.

She drank more of her wine. The bedding might not be too bad if she were a little bit woolly-headed. "Whatever ye say, my lord."

Sir Andrew snapped his fingers again. "Be off, sluggard!" he told Jeremy. "And mark you, guard my plate well and see that you return no later than the midwatch and with most of your faculties intact."

The boy hefted the large tray filled with the leavings of their meal onto his shoulder. "Aye, my lord, and a merry good evening to you. A very merry one indeed!" With another wink at Rosie, the squire disappeared through the tent flap. The pavilion suddenly seemed a great deal larger to Rosie.

"Where do ye want to do it, my lord?" she asked in a small voice.

Sir Andrew slammed the flat of his hand down on the tabletop. His goblet rattled. "Od's bodkins, Rosie! You try a man's soul to the very nub! Understand this—I am not going to take my carnal pleasure with you tonight or any other night."

She sat up straighter. "Your pardon, my lord, but if ye are not in the mind to swive me, then what do ye want me for?"

Sir Andrew drew his chair closer, then he rested his

elbows on the table. "Do not draw hasty conclusions as to my natural desires and appetites, my dear. I am as lusty as any man would be when in the company of such a beauty as yourself."

She rubbed the side of her nose. The gentleman had obviously drunk more wine than she had thought if he now called her a beauty. Perhaps he had drunk so much that he couldn't...perform. "Ye talk in riddles, my lord. I am not much good at riddling."

He chuckled. "Then I will speak plain. I enjoy making love with a woman, but I prefer not to *buy* the lady's favor."

Rosie narrowed her eyes. "Then why did ye pay a bloody great fortune for me just to drown me and feed me?"

His smiled widened. "Because I need your help, Rosie. I have made a great wager with one of those young lions whom you met earlier. I have told them that I will turn you into a proper lady within twelve days and that you will be so perfect a gentlewoman that none shall be the wiser. What say you to that?"

All the breath went out of Rosie. She opened her mouth to tell him he was moonstruck, but no words squeaked forth. Instead, she hiccuped.

He reclined against his chair back and looked even more pleased with himself. "Aha! I perceive that you have grasped the full import of my words. Sip some wine slowly, sweetheart, and twill cleanse you of that bothersome annoyance."

Rosie needed no urging. She wished she could dive into the bottom of her goblet and never come up again. Sir Andrew Ford, Esquire, was stark, staring mad.

He shook his head and clicked his tongue. "Slowly, my dear. Ladies do not gargle in their drink."

"Haint any kind of a lady," she mumbled between sips.

"But you can be," he whispered. His silky voice held a challenge. "Will you help me, Rosie?"

Not trusting herself to look into his beguiling eyes, she replaced her goblet on the table with deliberate care. Her mind spun like a whirligig out of control. If she said nay, he would toss her back to Quince in a heartbeat, and he would probably demand his money back. Quince, in his turn, would beat her, then sell her again. She recalled the sea of leering faces and shuddered. The next lord who took her could be considerably worse than this affable lunatic.

Rosie toyed with a droplet of wine on the tabletop as she pursued her deliberations. Her protector would lose a fortune to those laughing striplings, not to mention losing the respect of that sneering squire of his, if she did not play the part he asked. Despite his odd behavior, Sir Andrew seemed a good man and he deserved better than what she could give him.

"Well, Rosie?" he murmured, his wonderful voice soft and low.

She ignored the strange fluttering in her stomach. He had offered her a business proposition, not his heart. She hunched forward and plopped her elbows on the table. Their faces were only inches apart. He smelled of wine, sweetmeats and an intriguing exotic scent that was his alone. He raised his dark brows with silent inquiry.

"And what do I get?" she asked with bold directness.

One brow rose even higher. His eyes widened with his surprise.

Rosie hurried on before he had time to grow angry. "Ye say ye need me to help ye reap a bloody great fortune. What do I get in return?"

Sir Andrew folded his hands and looked up to the sloping roof of his tent as if he prayed to the Almighty for advice. "What would you like?" he finally asked. "Ribbons? Laces? A new gown?" He tapped the plate of tempting marchpane between them. "More sweet-meats?"

She shrugged away his limpid offers. "I was given ribbons and sweets once before and it came to nothing. That reeky coxcomb tricked me even though he wore pretty clothes and smelled so clean." She pushed Simon's lying handsome face out of her memory.

Sir Andrew cocked his head. "How now? And what, pray tell, did this rascal trick you out of?" he purred.

"My—" Rosie stopped herself before she blurted out the fearful truth. Her presumed virginity was the only ploy she had. "Something that was mine to give and not his to take."

"Ahhh!" Andrew nodded as if he understood exactly what she meant. "So if you do not require fripperies and sweets for your reward, what do you have in mind?"

She took a deep breath. "Profit. Ye pay me a part of your winnings so that I can be my own self and beholden to no man. Tis what I want."

"Independence." His expression changed and became more sober. "I perceive that you are a woman of business, Rosie. Therefore, allow me to make you this offer. I will put a penny into your account for every lesson of mine that you learn correctly."

She licked her lips. "I be a fast learner, my lord."

He gave her a look of faint amusement. "And I will take away one penny for every mistake you make. Are we agreed?"

She felt as if he had dropped an icicle down her back.

"Fie upon it, my lord! I cannot help making mistakes. Haint ever seen a lady close up."

His full lips quirked with humor. "Very well, I will grant you three errors. After that, one penny gone." He whistled to illustrate her new fortune flying out of his tent. "Now, are we agreed?"

Rosie crossed her arms over her breasts. "Hold, Sir Andrew. How will I know if I have a penny or not? I see no pennies on the table. I will not be cozened with your flowery speeches."

He tapped the side of his nose with his forefinger. "A good point."

He pushed back his chair and rose. He padded across the rug to another one of his chests, opened it and rummaged through a great quantity of clothing. Rosie craned her neck to see what he was looking for. He had more clothes in that one box than her whole family had ever possessed. At last, he withdrew a slate and a thick piece of chalk. He kicked the lid shut, then returned to the table.

"This is your account, Rosie," he said, tapping the slate. "Whenever you have earned your wage, I will make a stroke on it like so." He drew a fat line. "If you lose a penny, I will erase it—like so." He smudged the line with his thumb until there was nothing left but a splotch of chalk.

Rosie said nothing, but she eyed the account board. No one had ever taken her so seriously, nor even acknowledged that she was good for anything except as a drudge or a whore.

He propped the slate against a stack of books on a side coffer. "We will keep your account here, so that you may peruse it—that is, look at it—whenever you wish. Do my terms meet with your approval?"

She could only nod. Excitement welled up within her. The future opened before her like a flower-strewn high road.

"Aye? Then let us shake hands upon it." He held his out to her.

Rosie wiped her greasy fingers on the front of her shirt, then gave him her hand. In formal silence, they shook upon their bargain, but afterward he refused to let go. Instead, he turned her hand over and studied her palm and nails like a blacksmith before shoeing a horse.

He clicked his tongue against his teeth. "Rosie, nail biting is a nasty habit. I will take away a—"

She tensed and curled her fingers into a ball. She hadn't even earned a penny yet, and he already threatened her with debt. She knew she should never have trusted him.

He looked at her annoying amusement. "I shall take away a *halfpenny* for each infraction."

Rosie tried to snatch her hand away from him. "Infrac...what?"

He chuckled. "For each time you bite your nails."

She gasped. "I be out a shilling's worth afore this night is gone!"

"Ladies do not chew on their nails, Rosie."

"Haint a lady," she reminded him, twisting out of his grasp.

His eyes gleamed in the low candlelight. "Not yet, but by all that is holy, you will be!"

Chapter Five

The hubbub of the great English encampment settled into muted revels as the night reached its midpoint. Andrew saw that Rosie fought to keep her eyes open, but the lure of Morpheus fast overwhelmed her. From what she had told him, it had been a hellish day for the lass. The hours of anxiety together with the large supper and the quantity of wine she had consumed had finally taken their toll. Still, she forced herself to stay awake in an effort to preserve the virtue that he knew had already been taken from her. He gave Rosie full marks for the effort, and vowed to add an extra penny to her account.

Rosie's head bobbed. She desperately needed her sleep. He had a full day planned for her on the morrow. He smiled to himself. He could not remember passing such a enjoyable evening as this one for a long time— especially when he had no intention of bedding his fair company. He sighed over his self-imposed denial. Truly, the pretty creature was extremely enticing.

Rosie blinked and yawned without bothering to cover her mouth. Andrew shook himself from his pleasant reverie. He stood, stretched, then yawned loudly for her benefit.

"What be ye a-doing?" she asked in that velvet-edged voice of hers.

He drank in her sweet tone. Rosie had no idea how seductive she sounded, especially when laced with wine. "Preparing for repose," he replied in a forced, light-hearted manner. "Going to bed—and so should you, my dear."

Her upper lip curled back. "Aha! Just like a man! Ye make lovely promises one minute then take them back with interest the next."

Andrew furrowed his brow. He had no clear idea what Rosie meant or why her mood had changed once again. He was far too tired to begin another argument with her now.

She gripped the edge of the table. "Ye told me that ye did not buy a woman for your pleasure, yet now ye be a-talking about going to bed."

Andrew groaned inwardly. He thought he had settled this particular sticking point already. "To sleep, Rosie. Perchance to dream. Tis been a most fatiguing day, though I admit that you have made the evening stimulating." *Much too stimulating.*

He ambled toward the four-poster bed that Jeremy had prepared. The swans-down pillows had been plumped just the way he liked them. The sheets of softest lawn had been sprinkled with lavender water to discourage both fleas and odors of the night. A coverlet of mint green taffeta lay folded at the bed's foot. Taken altogether, his makeshift bedchamber beckoned with irresistible invitation to his tired body.

Rosie struggled to her feet and gripped the center tent pole to steady herself. "Ye are a-going to sleep?"

He yawned. "Aye, tis my sole intent at this particular moment."

She blinked like an owlet. "Then where do I go?"

Andrew lifted one of the lanterns and shed its light into the second chamber's far corner. "There." He pointed to Jeremy's truckle bed.

Rosie closed her eyes and sagged against the pole. Andrew moved closer in case she collapsed, but she rallied before he touched her. Without a word, she scurried to the cot, pulled back the cover and tucked herself between the sheets.

"Sweet heaven!" She sighed. She burrowed as far down as the straw mattress allowed her. "Tis a wonderment, my lord!"

He knelt beside her. "Clean sheets?" he inquired.

She rolled her eyes. "Haint ever *had* sheets, my lord."

Andrew shuddered inwardly. He really had to do something about her butchery of the king's English but it could wait until dawn. Then Rosie looked up at him and actually smiled.

The unexpected sight nearly overthrew all of Andrew's high-minded principles. He felt as if he had been struck by a bolt of lightning. He thanked assorted guardian saints that neither one of the hot-blooded Cavendish boys nor the lust-driven Stafford had seen that smile of hers. There would have been blood on the rug by now and it would not have come from Rosie's pathetic ruse. He leaned over her.

Her smile fled. She stiffened and cringed as if she expected to be struck. Her bee-stung lips compressed into a tight line. Andrew reversed his lustful intentions. Instead, he planted a chaste kiss on her forehead.

"God give you sweet repose, Rosie," he murmured in a husky voice that barely cloaked his passionate urgings. "Sleep well and safely. I swear upon my honor as a knight, no harm shall come to you."

Her shoulders relaxed. A glimmer of her smile returned. "And to ye, my lord." Then she turned over onto her side and closed her eyes.

With a whisper of regret, Andrew rose, blew out the lantern and made his preparations for his own slumber. He poured some rose water in the basin of his portable washstand—a device of his own invention—and rinsed his face and hands. The cool ablutions did little to quench his inner fever. After he brushed his teeth with a peeled stick from an elm tree and polished them with a piece of tooth linen, he went around the tent and blew out the rest of the candles. The campfire outside the entrance bathed the interior of the pavilion with a golden glow. He shook out a spare pallet for Jeremy—whenever the scamp decided to return.

Andrew shucked his dressing robe, then he pulled his shirt over his head and tossed it over a coffer. He loosened his codpiece, stepped behind a painted screen and made use of his new close stool. It was as elaborate as the one Great Harry himself had for his most personal needs. Ever since Andrew had inherited his late wife's fortune, he had indulged himself in all the finest accoutrements of gracious living. Yet in the depths of the night, he admitted to himself that all his refinements and luxuries had not filled the yawning emptiness in his life.

Returning to his sumptuous bed, he sat on the edge of it, and peeled off his dusty, sweat-soaked hose. He balled them up and tossed them beside his shirt. Jeremy would take care of the laundry in the morning. For all his put-upon airs, his squire was a good lad, though Andrew missed Guy. Now that the younger Cavendish had become a knight, he no longer had to wait upon Andrew's every whim. Yawning, he stretched his arms over his head and basked in the freedom of his nakedness.

He heard a small, muffled giggle behind him. He looked over his shoulder. Rosie's eyes twinkled from the depths of her little bed.

He felt a flush steal up his neck and around his ears. He blessed the darkness and wished it were darker still.

"Methought you were asleep," he muttered, jumping into his bed.

"With ye a-splashing and grunting like a hog in a mud wallow?"

Andrew pursed his lips. "I marvel at your eloquent description of myself, dear Rosie. Have you been acquainted with many hogs in your short lifetime?" Her unappealing appraisal stung his vanity.

She had the gall to giggle again. "One or two, my lord, but methinks ye are the best of the lot."

He fumed in the luxurious sanctuary of his gilded bed. "I give you thanks for your kind words," he growled.

"How old are ye, my lord, if ye do not mind me asking?"

Injury to insult! "Eight and thirty years since this Shrovetide." He laid down amid his flock of feathered pillows and pouted.

"Ah!" The chit was mercifully silent for a moment, then she said, "Ye should not let those minions of yours call ye an old man, Sir Andrew, for ye have a good strong body that gives the lie to your years."

A ridiculous warmth flooded Andrew. He grinned in the darkness. What an intelligent girl he had acquired! Rosie obviously possessed an innate sense of good taste.

He cleared his throat. "Ladies should not observe a gentleman when he disrobes, Rosie."

She snorted. "Haint a lady—yet! Good night, my lord."

Andrew blew her a kiss. "Good night, sweet Rosie," he whispered.

Despite his fatigue, he discovered that he could not sleep. Rosie's even breathing told him that she had at last slipped into the healing grace of slumber. He laced his fingers behind his head and stared into the blackness of his silk-swathed ceiling.

Rosie danced through his thoughts like a maddening sprite. In his imagination, he heard her smoky voice and her sudden silvery laughter. Since he could not banish her from his mind, he turned his powers of concentration fully upon his latest acquisition.

It was already evident that she had teased a new vigor in his body. He sighed. Too evident. He would have to watch himself in the coming days if he was going to have her full cooperation. Any dolt could tell that she had been ill-used by men in her past. He swore to himself that he would try to make her future much more pleasant, even if it meant denying himself the pleasure that was his by right of ownership.

Andrew rolled onto his stomach and punched his pillows into a mound. Rosie had surprised him with her quick wit. True, she was entirely uneducated, but her natural instincts proved to be razor-sharp. He could tell that she would be an apt pupil. His hopes rose. It was not the money, but his pride that was at stake. He chuckled to himself when he imagined how Brandon would writhe when Andrew unveiled his little bit of mummery at the king's banquet. Let the young cockerel sweat out the consequences of his rash gamble for a few days. Then, when he had learned his lesson, Andrew would return his losses to him.

Then there was Rosie. Andrew curled on his side. Was she really only a gleaning from the gutter? His observation differed. There was something about her that hinted of better blood—something familiar that he couldn't quite recognize. Her face was too fine and delicate to be that bred from a mere peasant. Her complexion, kissed by the sun, reminded him of the petals of a flower. And her hair!

Andrew threw off his sheet, swung his legs over the side of the bed and got up. He fumbled for the tinderbox on his bedside table and after a few moments, lit his candle. Jeremy had not yet returned. Wastrel!

Holding the candle aloft, he crept around the foot of the great bed. The light fell upon Rosie. Her hair cascaded over the white pillowcase in a tumble of sun-kissed curls. Andrew knelt and touched the nearest one. Pure silk under his fingers. His loins stiffened and grew hot. He cursed himself for his weakness but did not move.

He continued to stroke the soft curl as he imagined all the delicious possibilities that making love with Rosie would present. Her veil of hair would clothe him as it enticed him. He longed to bury his face in her fragrant tresses. To bind himself with them. To taste their strands, to die—

The tent flap opened and Jeremy stumbled inside with a whispered oath. His load of cleaned supper plate clattered to the floor. Andrew stood up quickly and blew out the candle before the squire got a good look at his master's rejuvenated body.

"Silence, churl!" he whispered to his tipsy squire. "I have only just now soothed her to sleep."

Jeremy giggled like a wench. "And was she easy to leap upon, my lord? Did you have much good cheer?"

"I'll leap upon you, you quirt, if you do not stop that damnable bleating, and I warrant you, the experience will bring you no cheer at all. Get you to bed!" He pointed to the pallet by the entrance.

Jeremy half sat, half fell onto it. "Your pardon, my lord," he mumbled as he pulled off his jerkin.

Andrew climbed back into his own bed. "Granted, but not a word to the young lady on the morrow or you will rue it forty days, I promise you."

"Aye, my lord," Jeremy yawned. He lay down still half-dressed. "I am right glad that she pleased you." He ended with a soft snore.

Andrew shook his head at the general folly of youth. "That she does," he whispered to himself. "She pleases me well."

Tuesday, June 12

Angry voices pulled Rosie from her slumber. From habit, she curled tight into a ball and pretended that she still slept even though she was now fully awake. Then she realized that the voices did not belong to her foster parents, nor was she shivering under the eaves of their cottage in Stoke Poges. A white sheet smelling faintly of lavender covered her and the morning's sun bathed the interior of Sir Andrew's tent with a soft glow.

"Surely ye have done with her by now, my lord. Tis near the dinner hour," Quince whined on the other side of the canvas wall.

Rosie shivered despite the warmth of her bedding. She pulled her sheet up to her chin.

Sir Andrew chuckled. "By my troth, I have barely begun taking my pleasure with Mistress Rosie, and you said to take all the time I wanted."

Quince stammered, "B-but another gentleman has already paid me a pretty penny for her. He waits for the wench now."

Rosie chewed on her thumbnail. She couldn't go back to Quince. She had never done much praying before, but now her lips framed a silent plea to heaven for deliverance.

"That other gentleman's name had better not be Cavendish or Stafford," Sir Andrew remarked in a dark tone.

"Nay." Quince's whine increased. "Tis a very insistent lord named Sir Gareth Hogsworthy, and methinks his patience is shorter than gunpowder."

Rosie slid deeper under her covers. She remembered the man from last night because he reminded her of her foster father. She instinctively knew what sort of a beast Sir Gareth would be. Heaven help the woman who fell within his sadistic grasp.

"And what did Sir Gareth pay you for the attentions of the fair damsel?" Sir Andrew inquired. Danger lurked in his voice.

Quince hesitated. Rosie guessed that the bawdmaster was calculating a greater profit. She wanted to cry out a warning to Sir Andrew, but her sense of self-preservation silenced her.

"Twenty gold ryals, my lord," Quince finally replied.

Ten times Quince's highest price! Sir Andrew would never pay it. Rosie moaned into her pillow. Her sweet holiday from reality was over.

Then she heard someone swear softly inside the tent. She opened her eyes and peeked over the covers. Jeremy stood with his back to her while he listened at the closed entrance. He held a naked sword in one hand. By his stance, Rosie realized that the boy knew how to use the weapon.

"The devil take you, master of flesh!" Sir Andrew raised his voice.

Rosie cringed. She pushed back her covers and searched for another way out of the tent. They would have to catch her before any man could have his cruel way with her.

"Jeremy!" Sir Andrew bellowed. "Fetch my purse!"

The squire turned around and saw Rosie. She froze, barely daring to breathe. Jeremy unlocked a brass-bound trunk and lifted out a brown leather pouch. From its shape and size, Rosie guessed it contained a fortune.

The boy curled his lips at her. "You must have pleased my lord past all remembrance, wench," he whispered with a rough edge to his voice. "Sir Andrew has never spent so much money on a woman before except his wife." With that, he batted the flap aside and strode out.

Rosie didn't know whether she felt flattered, appalled—or hurt. Sir Andrew hadn't mentioned anything about having a wife. Rosie had assumed he was a bachelor. She should have known better. What a deceitful devil he was! Of course a rich and handsome lord like Sir Andrew would be married, and he probably had a castle filled with children as well. She cursed her naïveté, then cursed herself even more for caring. What was he to her but a slim respite from the hell of her life? What was she to him but a whore with whom he would play an outlandish jest upon the king? Why did she care?

Just then Sir Andrew entered his tent. He was dressed most informally in a clean lawn shirt with a wide band of lace at the cuffs and his hose were decorated with green-and-white stripes. He whistled as he tossed his purse from one hand to the other. When he spied Rosie, he broke into one of his heartwarming smiles.

He swept her a deep bow. "Good morrow, my lady!"

Rosie's heart hammered against her ribs and a brief shiver of excitement rippled through her. The rogue looked even more handsome by daylight, especially in those tight hose. She gripped a large handful of her sheet and pretended indifference to his greeting.

"Quince cheated ye," she retorted. "Ye will be the laughingstock of the venders afore noon."

Sir Andrew dropped his money bag back into his strongbox and locked it. He grinned at her over his shoulder. "I am already the laughingstock in a number of places both high and low, my sweet. One more or less is no matter to me. Besides, the price is a trifle compared to the value of the merchandise." He threw a meaningful glance at her.

Rosie stared at her toes. She wasn't too sure what he had just said, but she presumed it was a compliment. His breezy manner confused her.

He crossed the rug, and held out his hand to her. "Come, Rosie. The day has begun and we have much work to accomplish."

With a sigh, she allowed him to help her out of the bed, though she was perfectly able to do it herself. Perhaps this was part of being a lady.

Andrew pointed to a screen set at an angle against one side of the tent. Unicorns frolicked amid pink roses and blue cornflowers on its painted panels. "You may wish to relieve yourself."

Rosie wrinkled her brow. "Do what?"

Jeremy snickered as he laid out a basin of warm water, several small towels and a wicked-looking razor. Sir Andrew frowned at his squire, then he leaned over and whispered what he had meant into Rosie's ear.

She sighed with relief. "Why didn't ye tell me afore? My bladder's fit to burst." She practically ran behind the screen. She heard Jeremy's unrestrained laughter which was followed by a sharp rebuke from her patron. She stared at the apparatus in front of her for several long moments, deathly afraid to touch it. Then she poked her head around the side of the enclosure.

"Tis a cruel trick ye have played on me, Sir Andrew."

He was seated in one of the folding chairs and his face was covered in a white frothy lather. Jeremy stropped the razor on a piece of leather.

Sir Andrew licked some of the soap from his lips. "How now, Rosie?"

She pointed behind the screen. "Tis a great chair fit for the king and not for...for... Tis padded in velvet! Are ye daft?"

Jeremy started to chortle again but stopped when his master growled in the back of his throat. Sir Andrew then smiled at Rosie, his bare lips surrounded by a cloud of white cream. If she hadn't been in such immediate distress she would have laughed at the sight.

"How very discerning of you, my dear! Tis an exact copy of the king's personal close stool. If you lift the seat, you will discover a hole and a chamber pot for your immediate needs. I promise you will find the experience quite comfortable."

Screams of frustration crowded her throat. "Ye want me to sit on that velvet thing and—" She stopped when she saw Jeremy's grin widen.

Sir Andrew shooed her away with his hand. "Have a little faith and trust, my dear. Give it a try. I am sure you will understand what is required. Alas, I fear propriety forbids me from demonstrating. Go to, go to! And you, sir knave! Lay on with that razor but mind your strokes. My face is not a quintain.''

Rosie ducked back behind the screen and followed Sir Andrew's instructions to the letter, much to her great relief and surprise.

''Bliss,'' she announced when she reappeared.

Sir Andrew did not move nor speak while his squire ran the razor's keen edge up his throat. Rosie crept closer to watch. When the boy had completed the task, he wiped his master's face with a warm towel, then patted a few drops of oil on his smooth cheeks. A scent of exotic spices filled the air. Sir Andrew pointed to his comb and a wide hairbrush.

''Tidy your hair, Rosie. Ladies do not go abroad with sleep knots in their tresses.''

Rosie picked up the brush and ran her fingers through its thick bristles. ''Haint a—''

Sir Andrew held up his hand for silence. Both Rosie and Jeremy looked at him with expectation. What was wrong now? she wondered.

''Let us begin with your first and most important lesson, Rosie. *Haint* is not a recognized word in the English tongue, save among certain types of lowlife that you have recently abandoned. You will banish that foul sound from your mouth this instant. Say 'I have never.'''

Rosie gripped the brush. ''Pray, what happens if I forget?''

Sir Andrew pointed dramatically to the slate propped against his books. ''Then I will deduct one—''

''Aw-uu,'' she wailed.

''Halfpenny each time that you do,'' he continued.

Rosie narrowed her eyes. ''Ye be a cold-blooded fish!

I will never make a sixpence in a month of Sundays, let alone ten days!''

Her rebuke only amused her tormentor. ''While we are on the subject, you will also banish the word *ye*. Tis out of fashion. The proper word is *you*. Pray, remember that.''

Pushed to the limits of her endurance, Rosie drew in a deep breath, then exploded. ''*You,* my lord, are the most cold-blooded fish that ever I did see on a market day, and furthermore, *you* prattle like a...a jackdaw in love with his own croak!''

Tossing all caution aside, she pointed to Jeremy who had turned red in the face from stifling his mirth. ''And *you! You* are in the worst rank of manhood, for *you* are only half-done!'' She crossed her arms over her heaving breasts. ''There now, my lord. Does my pretty speech please *you?*''

Chapter Six

Sir Andrew's brows rose almost to his hairline while Jeremy looked like he had been hit on the head with a shovel. Rosie wanted to laugh at both of them, but realized that she had gone far enough already. Perhaps too far, but she could not recall her angry words now.

Then Andrew burst into laughter. He clapped his hands as if applauding a fine performance by a juggler. "Bravo, my dear! You have won this round! Mark you, Jeremy, you and I may be nimble with a sword or lance, but this fair lady jousts with speech and a marvelous wit. She speaks daggers and every word stabs the soul."

The squire merely glared at her. With quaking knees, Rosie waited for Sir Andrew to deliver a blow across her rash mouth. Instead, he took up the slate and drew three thick lines upon it.

"Behold, three pennies earned before you have even brushed your hair." He pointed to his chair. "Sit!" he commanded.

She slid into place. Sir Andrew took the brush from her slack fingers and began to draw it through her tangles.

"Second lesson—from now on you will consider

yourself a high-born lady. You will think like one, talk like one and act like one.''

Rosie scratched the bridge of her nose. ''Methinks your fancy is the child of an idle brain,'' she murmured. The even strokes of the brush soothed her injured pride and stormy temper. She leaned against the back of her chair and closed her eyes.

''Aye,'' he murmured as he worked through her hair, ''but there is method in my madness.'' He stepped around and regarded her. ''By the book, Rosie! You are as fair a flower as any in King Henry's court. I forbid you ever to allow your tresses to fly wild again. Twould be a sin against the goddess of beauty.''

A hot flush stole over Rosie's cheeks. She looked down at her hands clasped in her lap. ''Not so neither, my lord,'' she mumbled. His kindness made her feel even more ashamed of her outburst.

Sir Andrew grinned. ''My words to the letter.'' He snapped his fingers at Jeremy. ''Attend me, sluggard! The green doublet—at once!''

His squire blinked, cast Rosie another quick glance, then scuttled to one of the larger coffers. He withdrew a long bundle and unwrapped its unbleached muslin covering. Rosie blinked when she saw the elegant coat of forest green velvet, its wide sleeves slashed with panes of cinnamon-colored satin. Gold edged the neckline. Alternating panes of green velvet and brown satin on the knee-length galligaskins matched the jacket.

Jeremy shook out the garments. ''The sun is still below its midpoint, my lord, yet the day waxes hot. Methinks you will find this too warm.''

Sir Andrew shrugged. ''Aye, but knowing that everyone else in this accursed valley will be equally uncomfortable gives me a measure of cold comfort. You note how we are slaves to fashion, Rosie?''

She could only nod in agreement. She watched with a mixture of shock and fascination as he tied three little golden bells to the points of his white, satin-covered codpiece. When he had finished, he wiggled his hips to make them jingle.

Spying her interest, he jingled them a second time. ''Pray give me your honest opinion, Rosie. Do my accessories please you?''

A dozen answers crowded her tongue, none of which she dared give voice. Finally she replied, ''Past all words, my lord.''

Sir Andrew clapped and rubbed his hands together. ''Excellent! I go to visit a lady and she will expect a gladsome appearance.'' He stepped into his breeches that Jeremy held for him. The bedecked codpiece stood out even more alarmingly against the green velvet.

An unexpected dart of envy pricked Rosie. She brushed her hair with short, hard strokes. No wonder Sir Andrew had not bedded her last night! He had a mistress who liked expensive clothes and bells in unusual places. Why should that matter to Rosie? She did not want Sir Andrew as a lover, but as her means of escape from her past.

Sir Andrew thrust his arms into his doublet. While his squire fastened the gold-and-pearl buttons, he cocked his head at her.

''How now, my sweet? Your face looks like a rain cloud.''

Rosie swiveled away from his gaze. ''Tis nothing.''

''Ha!'' he roared behind her. She jumped and looked back over her shoulder. Jeremy laid a wide gold chain around Sir Andrew's neck.

He winked at her. "Allow me to divine your displeasure. You think I am decking myself to sport with a lady, do you not?"

Rosie wondered if he could read her mind. She hid her surprise with a dismissive shrug. "It matters naught to me what ye do, my lord. Ye—that is, *you* are free to sport where you will and none can say naught against you. I am merely your chattel and have no say in the matter whatsoever."

"Aha, Jeremy, I was correct! Yon frowning sprite thinks I will have a bit of morning's pleasure afore our dinner," he remarked.

Rosie pretended to ignore him, but her jealousy festered.

Sir Andrew crossed to her side. Lifting her chin with his fingers, he forced her to look into hazel eyes that twinkled with merriment. "I give you thanks for your concern, but I have no such plans. I am going to visit Lady Mary Washburne, a cheerful lass whom I have known since she was in leading strings. I was in her brother's service. Lady Mary takes great delight in all manner of singing, dancing, masking, games—and disguising. If I am my most charming to her, mayhap she will lend me some of her gowns and fripperies."

Rosie furrowed her brows. "Ye—I mean *you* seek to disguise yourself as a woman?" She had been right to think he was addlepated.

Both men laughed. When he caught his breath, Sir Andrew replied, "Nay, Rosie, I am not inclined in that direction. The gowns are for *ye!*"

"You," she corrected him. Then she realized what he had said. "You are daft! No lady would part with so much as a shift for the likes of me. We peasants are a foul and gamy lot, or haven't you heard that tale?"

He caressed her chin with the pad of his thumb. "Oh, aye, but you are a lady now. I washed away the farmyard last night."

Rosie sighed. "Twill take more than soap to do that, my lord."

He leaned closer. "You have hit the nut and core of the problem, my dear. Most excellent wench! Tis why I must cozen a gown or two for you. You cannot go abroad clothed in just my nightshirt—fetching though you look in that scant attire."

She rubbed the side of her nose. "What am I to do while you are gone, my lord?" She hoped he would suggest that she eat something.

Sir Andrew grew serious. "Do not go outside," he warned her. "Lord Hogsworthy is not a gracious loser, and he may try to abduct you by force. Jeremy, I hold you bound to protect my lady, and for entertainment..." He lifted a large green leather-bound book from the pile on his coffer. "Stand up, my dear." When Rosie did so, he balanced the book on the top of her head. "You may while away the hour by walking up and down with my songbook on your head."

She crossed her eyes trying to look at it while not dropping it. She dare not tell him that this idea was the silliest suggestion he had yet proposed. "Tis heavy," she muttered.

He nodded with a grin. "Aye, tis a weighty tome, I warrant you, but tis filled with many a light and winsome air. And, my dear Rosie, the book is very expensive. Mind that you do not drop it."

Rosie stiffened. "May I ask why I am a-standing here like a bloody trained bear with this blessed book on my head?"

He chuckled. "Tis to help you with your posture. Now walk—go to."

Rosie took a hesitant step. The book slid off to one side. Jeremy caught it before it hit the ground.

Sir Andrew rubbed his hands together. "Excellent! I see that you two will work well together. Rosie, do not look at your feet when you walk. Stare straight ahead and pull back your shoulders. There's a good lass. A penny if you can do it upon my return."

Rosie hefted the song book. "Tis a mickle heavy, my lord. Surely balancing it is worth two pennies." She gave him a smile that she hoped would sweeten his decision.

He laughed in a deep jovial way. "Rosie, you will make a better businesswoman than a lady if I am not careful. Tis agreed. Two pennies if you can traverse my rug without a fall."

Rosie smiled with true joy this time. "Thank ye— *you,* my lord."

Sir Andrew clapped a hand on Jeremy's shoulder. "And my squire will instruct you in the proper form."

It was the boy's turn to goggle. "Me, my lord? But I have the soiled clothing to deliver to the laundress, and your armor to buff and—"

Sir Andrew shook him a little. "Most importantly, you have my sweet lady Rosie to guard, to guide and to cherish in my absence. And you *will* behave as a proper gentleman to her or I will flay you by inches. Are we understood, maltworm?"

The squire's cheeks turned a mottled red. "Aye, my lord."

Sir Andrew caught up a green velvet sack cap and smoothed the white feather that adorned its gold embroidered headband. "Delighted to hear that, my boy.

And now, my fair lady, I bide you adieu until dinner time. I leave you to the tender mercies of my good squire who will *gladly* be your slave until my return.''

At the entrance, he executed a flourishing bow to Rosie and the fuming Jeremy. ''Smile and be of good cheer, my chicks. God has sent us a fine day wherein we will roast ourselves. Fare thee well!'' He lifted the tent flap and disappeared, whistling a cheery tune.

Rosie and Jeremy glowered at each other.

''You heard my lord. Put the book on your head and walk,'' the squire growled. ''And mind you do not drop it.''

Without giving her another glance, he went over to Sir Andrew's great bed and began to straighten the bedclothes. When she was sure he couldn't see her, Rosie stuck her tongue out at him.

''Ye are supposed to help me to learn this tomfoolery.''

Jeremy plumped one of the pillows. ''The word is *you* not *ye,* and I have my duties to perform. So do you, so shut your mouth and attend to your work.'' He punched a second pillow with vehemence before arranging it against the gilded headboard.

Rosie watched him while he completed the bed making. Pointedly ignoring her, he then picked up a clothes brush and proceeded to work on the crimson doublet that Sir Andrew had worn the night before.

''You have not taken a step,'' he remarked.

Rosie put the book on her head, squared her shoulders, stared at one of the hanging lanterns and lifted her right foot. The book wobbled. She paused, then moved her left foot. The book teetered, then slipped off. She caught it.

Jeremy snickered. "Mayhap you have a pointed head," he suggested.

Rosie held the book close to her as if it would shield her from the squire's open hostility. "Ye do not like me much, do ye?"

He looked up at her. "Say 'you' instead of 'ye,' and perchance I will give *you* an answer."

If the songbook had not been so expensive, Rosie would have thrown it at him. "*You* hate me, don't you?"

Jeremy looked her up and down as if she were a piece of bog slime that had crawled into his life. "Well aimed for such a jade as you. But to answer your question, as long as tis Sir Andrew's fancy to pretend that you are a lady, so will I. But once he has grown tired of the game, then I will treat you as you really are—a guttersnipe."

His blunt words hurt her far more than she had expected. She bit her little fingernail. "How now? The pot calls the kettle black?"

Jeremy put down the doublet and brush on the center table then stood. Though he was younger than she, the youth was taller by several inches. Rosie sensed a raw strength that the boy kept barely in check.

"Exactly who do you think I am, wench?" he growled.

Rosie gripped the book tighter. "One like me. We both serve Sir Andrew. I attend to his mad fancies while *you* empty his slops!"

Jeremy balled his hands into fists. Rosie braced herself, and prepared to ward off his blow with the book. She had had many years of experience defending herself from her foster father's insane rages.

Jeremy jutted out his chin. "Is *that* what you think a squire is?"

Rosie took one step backward. "Aye, you are a body

servant to your master. You wash his clothes, dress him and serve his dinner. How does that make ye any better than me?''

He gave her a half smile. "You have never met a squire before?''

"Oh, aye, squires are a dozen a farthing at a goose fair.''

Instead of growing angrier, Jeremy softened his stance. "Do you even know what an apprentice is?''

Rosie narrowed her eyes with suspicion. "'Course I do,'' she answered warily. "Tis one who learns a trade from a master.''

Jeremy nodded. "Aye, you have hit the mark. A squire is an apprentice knight. In five years or so, I hope to win my spurs.''

Rosie giggled. "Ye hope to learn how to fight from Sir Andrew?''

"Aye, tis a privilege and an honor to be his squire. Sir Andrew is one of the finest swordsmen in England.''

Rosie could not control her burst of laughter. "Tis a rich jest, Jeremy! Methinks the only blade Sir Andrew has mastered is his eating knife.''

The squire took a step closer to her. "Watch your tongue lest it sting you. My lord is as great a knight as any in the king's court. And none can match him on the archery range.''

Rosie held her ground. She refused to let this quirt frighten her. "Tittle-tattle! Tell me, squire, is there anything that this perfect knight of yours cannot do? Has he no faults?''

The boy's pretty face transformed itself into a cold mask of anger. "Sir Andrew is adept in all manner of things, except—in truth, he does not ride well in the joust. But my lord sits upon a horse far better than *you,*

I warrant. His horsemanship is no matter to me. I am proud to serve him and to learn from him. He was sword master for both the Earl of Thornbury's sons as well as my Lord Stafford. Those three knights have already won many prizes here. One day I hope to be as good as they.''

A little bell of warning rang in the back of Rosie's mind. ''Are all knights gentle-born?''

Jeremy nodded gravely. ''They are indeed.''

She took a step backward. ''Are you?'' she whispered.

He drew himself up then gave her a little bow. ''You have the honor to address Jeremy Arthur Metcalf, eldest son and heir of Sir William Metcalf, the undersecretary to His Grace, our good King Henry VIII.''

A sudden trembling seized Rosie. ''Send me straight to hell,'' she moaned more to herself than to Jeremy. She turned away from him and grasped the center tent pole for support. She chewed on her thumbnail. What a fool she had been! Why hadn't Sir Andrew told her? A sob escaped her lips before she could catch it.

''Why are you crying?'' the boy asked gently.

''Haint crying,'' she sniffed, trying to stop herself. ''I never cry!''

Jeremy circled around the pole, then knelt so that he could look up into her face. His former cold expression changed to concern. ''Forgive me, I did not mean to frighten you.''

She wiped her face with her sleeve and turned away from his pitying looks. ''Haint afeard. Only weaklings are afraid of blustering boys. Ye took me by surprise, tis all. I had thought that we were alike—both servants. Now I find I am truly alone—once again.''

Jeremy's eyes mirrored her pain. ''Where did you come from, Rosie?''

She gave him a sour grin. "From God—or so I have been told, but I do not think so. A most ungentle fortune placed me in that goose yard." She lowered her lashes to hide the painful memories of her childhood.

"I was a ward of Saint Giles' Church in Stoke Poges. The priest found me a-wailing on the altar steps and clutching a gold sovereign. He gave me to Mistress Barstow since she had just lost her own babe to a fever. Her husband was glad enough to have the money, but he refused to give me a last name. He said I was spawned in sin. Tis why I am just plain Rosie. I never had a comfortable life like you do. Old man Barstow sold me to Quince for five bloody shillings. How much is *your* life worth, Sir Jeremy?"

The boy scrambled to his feet. His face had lost all its color. "I am not yet a knight, Rosie, so just call me Jeremy." He offered her his arm. "And I will be your supporter, if you will give me leave."

She was too startled by his sudden offer to make any objection. Instead, she took his arm. He balanced the heavy book on her head.

"Chin up, Rosie. Look straight ahead and take small steps."

Together, they crossed the ornate rug in silent concentration. After a successful return trip, she glanced at the boy out of the corner of her eye. "My thanks, Jer…Jeremy. And, I swear…haint a strumpet."

He returned the barest whisper of a smile. "You should say 'I am not a harlot.' And time will tell the truth of that tale."

She answered him with a desperate firmness. "I *am* not a harlot—not now, not ever. I vow I will die first."

Chapter Seven

Lady Mary Cavendish Washburne laughed merrily. "Hoy day, sweet Andrew! Methinks this is the maddest prank of your career yet! Are you sure you have not overindulged in wine so early in the morning?"

Andrew smiled at her amusement. So far, his visit had gone very well. "Nay, Mary, I am as sober as a cleric in the confessional."

The lady arched one of her fine eyebrows. "Oh? Our priest often has a tipple or two before shrift. I suspect that is the only thing that keeps him sane while listening to all our sins, offenses and negligences." Another gale of infectious laughter interrupted her further observations.

Andrew mopped his damp brow with a fresh cambric handkerchief. The air was stifling inside Lord Washburne's dark blue canvas pavilion. He quaffed some of the cool ale that Lady Mary's handmaid had served. Thus fortified, he steered the conversation to his purpose.

"I assure you that I am quite serious, Mary. In eleven days, I will escort Rosie to the king's farewell banquet and all the court will think she is a well-bred lady. My lass has already proven to be an apt pupil, though I admit she is sadly lacking in a few essentials.''

"Such as a noble birth, an education in the rudiments of etiquette, a knowledge of dancing and so on?'' Lady Mary giggled behind her fan.

Andrew cleared his throat. "Rosie sorely needs the proper clothing, and thereby hangs my tale.''

"Aha!'' Mary's blue eyes twinkled with mischief. "Exactly what items does she need? Pray, Andrew, try to be specific.''

He shrugged in mock helplessness. "Tis simple. Rosie requires everything from the skin out.''

She stared at him with rounded eyes. "Dare I ask what the poor thing is wearing at this very moment?''

"One of my nightshirts.''

Mary's laughter again rippled through the thick, hot air. "How utterly scandalous!''

Andrew flashed a mild leer. "Exactly,'' he purred.

He forced himself not to dwell on the ravishing memory of Rosie's slim body scarcely hidden by the thin material of his shirt. He must concentrate on his goal. Later, he would allow himself the pleasure of watching Rosie at her toilette. Perhaps another bath would be in order. It was such a hot day. He had especially enjoyed bathing her last night. What a fine pair of ripe breasts Rosie had—

Lady Mary swatted his knee with her fan. "Stop woolgathering, Andrew! By my troth, you have not heard one word I just said!''

He chuckled with guilt and crossed his legs. "You have caught me out, Mary. I crave your pardon.''

"I *could* provide what your little lightskirt needs—''

Andrew interrupted. "Rosie might not be as pure as an angel, but she is not made for sporting tricks.''

Mary cocked her head. "Oh, ho! Does the wind blow in that direction? Is that a love light I spy in your eye?"

He shifted on his stool and wished that Mary had not been gifted with a quick intelligence. "Rosie is merely my employee. I have promised to pay her a percentage of my winnings."

Mary continued to eye him with a knowing look that made him feel very uncomfortable. He swigged more of his ale.

"You are too sure of yourself. God's teeth, Andrew! Tom will skin Brandon alive when he learns that the boy has wagered a fortune."

Andrew dismissed the Earl of Thornbury's wrath with a wave of his hand. "I do not intend to beggar the boasting scamp. I merely desire him to wriggle upon my hook for a little. Ever since he was knighted, our Brandon has taken to swaggering like a rooster in the henhouse. He needs to be taken down a peg or two."

Mary nodded. "You speak the truth, but upon my soul, tis no game that you play with your wench." She poured more ale into his mug. "You have become quite dense in your dotage, my dear. Tis this—*you* may be playing a game, but what of your Rosie? Tis her life and fortune that you juggle. For all your conceits, you are too chivalrous to mock even a harlot."

Her observation made him squirm. "I have no intention of mocking the child," he replied almost primly. "You may not believe this, but I have treated her with the utmost respect." *So far.*

Mary fanned herself in silence for a long moment. Outside, a persistent bee droned against the canvas wall, perhaps drawn by the sweet smell of the ale. "What happens afterward?"

Andrew wiped a droplet of the brew from his lips with his handkerchief. "After what?"

She rolled her eyes toward heaven. "After the feast, after the tents have been folded and put away, after there is nothing left but the trampled earth. Will your Rosie be one more broken flower tossed away on this Godforsaken plain when you leave?"

Andrew's gold chain seemed to grow heavier around his neck. "She will go back to England, I expect. She is English after all."

He had not given much thought to what would happen to Rosie after the wager had been won. Returning her to Quince was out of the question. Beyond that, Andrew didn't know. His mind had been filled only with the challenge. He felt a little uncomfortable, and he resented Mary for introducing the subject.

She shook her head. "Oh, Andrew, you did not used to be so dull of wit. You expect this poor mite to go back to the stews of Bankside and to bless you for giving her a glimpse above her station?"

He fumed under his velvet cap. Why had cheerful Mary suddenly turned into such a scold? "I will see to her welfare. Trust me, Mary."

A glint of her natural good humor returned to her eyes. "I cannot wait to meet this wild meadow rose who has entrapped you in her briars."

He snorted. "I fear you are mistaken this time, Mary. *Nothing* catches me unless I will it."

Her lips twitched with suppressed mirth. "We shall see. Tell me, how tall is the girl? Will any of my gowns fit her?"

Andrew thought back to when he had held Rosie close against his chest. A wave of pleasure washed away his ill humor. "She is just as high as my heart," he murmured.

The lady arched her brow again in the most annoying fashion. "What an interesting observation and choice of words." She tapped her cheek with her fan. "It appears that she is too small for my things, but methinks she would fit Marianne's quite well."

Mary got up and went to the rear of the tent where a row of large chests stood open. She rummaged through one, and tossed clothing on a nearby cot. "That daughter of mine ordered so many things for this trip that she has forgotten half of what she brought."

Andrew rocked back on his stool and beamed as the pile of pretty gowns, petticoats, chemises, stockings, hanging sleeves, smocks, French hoods and veiled headdresses grew. He had to admire both Marianne's taste in finery and her mother's indulgence in the girl's whims. He hoped that Marianne's future included a wealthy and generous husband.

Mary topped the glittering array with a hoop farthingale and an exquisite pair of red slippers. "There! Twill do?"

Andrew nodded and resisted the urge to rub his palms together with glee. Mary had a way of asking for return favors at inconvenient times.

"Methinks that your daughter will be most displeased when she notices that her wardrobe has shrunk," he observed.

Mary folded the assortment into neat bundles. "I doubt it. Marianne has spent these past four days hanging on the railings at the tournaments and mooning over every knight under the age of five-and-twenty. Twill be a month of boring Sundays before she notices that anything is amiss."

He chuckled. "Then tis well that she is cousin to my three hellions, or you would have a great deal to give you sleepless nights."

Mary smoothed a cloak of gray wool. "I leave *that* worry to her father. Twas his idea to bring her to France in the first place. Shall I accompany you and help you bear this load?"

Andrew stood. "My thanks, gracious lady, but I am still able to muster enough strength to carry these few fripperies."

She broadened her smile. "Then I shall be free to help your young mistress into her new clothes."

He shuddered at that suggestion. "Again, my deepest gratitude overflows its bounds, but alas, I must decline your kind offer. Rosie is shy, skittish like a new colt. I will dress her myself—to give her confidence."

A gleam of amusement played in Mary's eyes. "This is news indeed! Methought you were more adept at *undressing* a woman."

In one swift move, he scooped up Rosie's new wardrobe. "I am a man of many talents, Mary. And you must admit that my sense of fashion is renowned. Rosie will be as well-laced into her gowns as you are yourself." With a bow, he started to back out of the tent.

"Oh, Andrew!" She called after him.

He swore to himself. She had that teasing expression on her face that often boded some unforeseen trick. "Aye, you minx?"

She giggled like a girl on May Day. "I *do* so like your bells."

He could not help swaggering a bit. His silver bells responded with a merry jingling. "I wore them expressly for you."

"Tush, you prattling peacock!" she bantered, though she blushed. "You wore them for Rosie, didn't you?"

He continued to smile while inwardly he cursed Mary's unerring sixth sense. "My goal in this life is but to please the ladies," he replied with a jaunty air. "All of them!"

He winked at his childhood friend, then fled from her before she wheedled anything else out of him. The heavy, humid air of the midmorning felt cool on his brow after the hell he had just endured inside the Washburne pavilion. Gripping his precious gleanings a little tighter, he whistled a ribald tavern ditty as he wove his way through the camp. He couldn't wait to dress Rosie in her borrowed finery.

His pleasant thoughts evaporated like mist in sunlight when he drew closer to his own establishment. Sir Gareth Hogsworthy, in company with some of his weaseling minions, clustered outside the pink tent. In the shivering tones of a smooth-spoken serpent, the disappointed lord chilled the hot June morning with his threats. A sizable crowd of curious squires, lackeys, household servants and grooms, together with a few interested members of the nobility, had gathered around in a wide circle. More gawkers ran to join them lest they miss all the excitement. Andrew noted two points in his favor: his tent flaps were closed and tied tight on the inside to the point of puckering, and guarding the entrance on the outside stood the most reckless of all his former pupils, Jack Stafford.

"You trod a slippery path, you cur-bred potboy!" Gareth blustered directly into Jack's grinning face. "Stand aside! I will claim the jade *now!*"

Jack merely chuckled. "Go to and fill another room in hell!"

Gareth turned a darker shade of fury. He bared his teeth at the blond giant. "I'll make a sop in moonshine of your sluggish brains!"

Jack yawned elaborately, then he turned to the swelling rabble and addressed them. "Mark how sour this gentleman looks! Like a lemon long spoiled. In truth, I cannot bear his presence without suffering from heartburn an hour later."

The audience guffawed with appreciation. Andrew realized that the crowd's approval would encourage Jack to taunt Hogsworthy into a dangerous corner, unless the boy was checked by a cooler head. Andrew sighed and wished he weren't so encumbered with his gaudy burden at the moment.

"In fact," Jack continued in a breezy tone, "I have seen far better faces in my time than this gentleman before me. Look you, good people, see how red my lord grows. In faith, methinks his garters are too tight!"

Andrew groaned as the crowd applauded Jack's witticism.

Gareth hooded his black eyes. "Out of my way, dunghill!"

Jack folded his arms across his broad chest. "Did he say dung?" he asked the mob. "Good, I am glad my lord has broached that noisome subject, for I intend to tread him under my heel into a mortar, and daub the walls of my privy with him."

Gareth knotted his right hand into a heavy fist and reared back to deliver a bone-crunching blow. Andrew shouldered his way through the mob. At the same time he raised his voice.

"Good morrow, Lord Hogsworthy! What tomfoolery is this so early in the day? Pray forgive the folly of this youth. I fear our Jack is not the flower of courtesy at this early hour.''

Gareth wavered for a moment, torn between his intent to flatten the young knight or to get what he had come for. Andrew seized the man's hesitation to plant himself between the two.

''Your wit has grown stale, Andrew,'' Jack whispered behind him. ''Let me prick this hog some more. It entertains our countrymen far better than a mummer's play.''

Andrew answered out of the side of his mouth. ''Chill your anger, Jackanapes. Tis too hot for a fray.''

Gareth dropped his hand, though he still maintained his aggressive stance. ''Methought you were cowering inside your pretty pink tent, Ford. I am much amazed that you had the courage to sally forth where the hellish sun could burn that soft skin of yours. Ha! But I see you have been shopping!''

He pawed through Andrew's pile of colorful silks and satins, then pulled out a green gown and held it up for the crowd to see. ''By my troth, do you prance around in this attire for your own amusement? Or do you entice your pretty Cavendishes with a wanton's feathers?''

Andrew's common sense clouded with hot anger.

Jack choked. ''I will saw him in half with a rusty razor!'' he roared, much to the delight of the mob.

Andrew stomped on the boy's foot to silence him. Then he snatched Marianne's dress out of Gareth's sweaty hands. ''Speak quickly, tedious fool. Why has an ill wind blown you against my doorstep?''

''The wench,'' Gareth growled. ''You have toyed with her long enough, Ford. I thank you for preparing the way for me. She should be well opened by now—at least, I think that is what you have been doing with her. Looking at you, tis hard to tell.''

Andrew curbed his natural impulse to flatten the knave.

"Hold your tongue, Gareth! Why should I allow myself to give way to your rash choler? Do you think I am frightened when a spoiled child whines? Should I tremble because of your slanders? Not so. Methinks your words have gone up in smoke—back home to the devil, your master.''

Gareth opened and closed his mouth like a stickleback fish tossed on a riverbank, but no sound came out. Andrew pressed his advantage.

"In fact, I cannot devise a name too unworthy or ridiculous to fit you. Furthermore, you have an undressed, unpolished, uneducated, unpruned, untrained and unconfirmed sense of fashion. By my troth, you have butchered all your buttonholes!''

The crowd whistled and applauded Andrew's witty retort.

Gareth jutted out his chin and snarled, "I have paid good money for the chit and I demand my satisfaction!''

Andrew shook his head with mock sorrow. "Then I fear you have misspent your fortune in a bad business venture. Speak to the bawdmaster, not to me. Tis he who holds your purse. Only this morning, I paid him twice over last night's sum. The lady is mine until I say nay. Now remove your presence from my threshold, and good day to you.''

Gareth took a step forward. Jack drew his sword and pointed it over Andrew's shoulder. "A fool and his money are soon parted, eh, my lord?'' Jack taunted. "What else do you want to part with this morning? Your long nose—or the jewels that dangle between your legs? Tis all one to me.''

Several of Gareth's henchmen took hold of their leader's shoulders and pulled him back.

''God's teeth! I will bury you in the sand of the tilt-yard,'' he sputtered.

Jack dipped his blade in agreement. ''I look forward to the pleasure, my lord. Name the day and hour.''

''Twill be your last day on earth! And, you Ford, you will *wish* you were dead before I am finished with you!'' Hogsworthy spat on the ground at their feet before turning away.

Andrew drew in a deep sigh of relief as he watched the irate man push his way through the snickering crowd. His cohorts followed after him like a ragged pack of whipped hounds.

''Put up your sword, Jackanapes. Tis all over but the drinking. Methinks Sir Gareth will have a ringing head before the supper hour.''

Jack rammed his blade back into its scabbard. ''How could you let that stretched-mouthed villain insult you so shamefully and in public?''

Andrew gave him a world-weary look. ''When I was as green as you, I would have gladly welcomed any opportunity for a fight. Since then, I have learned a good many painful lessons. Now I find that I can bear a knave's insults far better than his bruises. In faith, I have grown quite fond of my blood, and I prefer to keep all of it safe inside me.''

Jack grimaced. ''Then heaven shield me from gray hairs and soft brains! I did not need your help just now. I can fight my own battles. I will make Hogsworthy rue this morning.''

Andrew grasped the young fool's shoulder and shook

it, wishing he could shake some sense into Jack's head as well. "Never underestimate Gareth Hogsworthy. He is a well-seasoned jouster and not above cheating his opponents. Consider this if you wish to live long enough to celebrate your twenty-second birthday."

The younger man looked at Andrew, then at the ground in silence. Andrew relaxed. Jack could be foolhardy at the worst of times, but he possessed a good mind when he chose to use it. He prayed that Jack would heed his warning and allow his anger to cool.

When Jack looked up again, he flashed a boyish grin. He patted the clothing that Andrew still held against his chest. "So, tell me, my venerable teacher, what pleasant sport have you been doing today? Did you win all this finery off the back of some innocent but willing lady?"

Andrew assumed an injured air. "Methinks a long soak in a tub of salted herring would do you wonders, Jackanapes. This wardrobe was honorably obtained from Lady Mary Washburne. Tis for my Rosie."

Jack laughed. "I am not surprised! I warrant Lady Mary is now your confederate in your game. Does she approve of your latest whimsy?"

"She will keep an eye on me," he replied.

"And does Lady Alicia also know of your plan?"

Andrew rolled his eyes with true horror. The mother of Brandon and Guy would descend upon him like an avenging angel. "I pray that the good Countess of Thornbury is both deaf and blind for the next two weeks."

"Amen to that," Jack agreed.

Chapter Eight

Behind the curtain of rose silk that Andrew had drawn to give her some privacy, Rosie stared at the incredible pile of clothing that covered his large bed. She gently ran her finger down the bodice of a peach colored damask gown. Never had she felt anything so rich. She chewed on her thumbnail, then caught herself. Sir Andrew would take away one of her precious pennies if he spied her indulging in her "nasty habit." She wiped her hands on the nightshirt she still wore, then ventured to pick up a white chemise made of the sheerest lawn. How could she possibly wear such a fine garment?

On the other side of the flimsy wall, Sir Andrew cleared his throat. "How goes it, Rosie?" he asked with a cheery note.

"If you need any help, Rosie, I am your man," Jack offered. He could scarcely disguise the hunger in his voice. "I am well acquainted with the ins and outs of a lady's apparel. In truth, I am the very champion when it comes to disrobing a woman." He chuckled.

"Go to the devil, Jack," Sir Andrew suggested in a mild tone.

Emboldened by the protection of the concealing bit of

silk, Rosie stuck out her tongue in the direction of the lecherous young lord.

"Rosie?" her protector called. "Is something amiss?"

"Haint ever seen the like of all this, my lord."

He clicked his tongue against his teeth. "Rosie, mind your vocabulary. Repeat after me. 'I *have never* seen the like of all this.'"

Jack chortled again. "Hoy day! Twould be easier to teach a pig to dance than to school yon strumpet into a lady. Your wager is already in Brandon's pocket!"

Rosie swore under her breath at Jack, then cleared her throat. "By my troth, Sir Andrew, I swear that I *have never* seen such goodly clothes, and, by my troth, Sir Jack, I *am not* a strumpet!"

Both men laughed. Goblets clinked as they poured wine into them.

"Well-spoken, my dear!" Sir Andrew called through the curtain.

His compliment gave her courage. Taking a deep breath, Rosie drew off Andrew's nightshirt. The men on the far side of the curtain lapsed into a breathless silence. The little hairs on the back of her neck tingled as if she were being observed. Covering her breasts with the shirt, she looked behind her to make sure that the gentlemen had not pulled aside the drape. Her silken shield still hung in place.

Quickly, she dropped the chemise over her head. The hem fell to her ankles. She tied the lacing around her neck, creating a soft ruff just under her chin. Next she chose a pair of thin, cream-colored stockings and pulled them on, fastening them with red silk garters.

On the other side of the curtain, Jack sighed. "How

can you look so cool, old man?'' he asked. ''I am twice
as hot as I was before now.''

''Patience, my boy,'' Sir Andrew replied. ''Tis a virtue you lack in profusion.'' He raised his voice. ''The
bum roll goes on next, my dear. Tis that thing that looks
like a sausage. It ties around your waist.''

Rosie again glanced over her shoulder. She could
barely make out the men's shapes as they lounged in
their chairs. Jeremy's vague shadow hovered near the
pavilion's entrance. She held up the padded roll.

''To be sure!'' she called to Sir Andrew. ''I'll look
like a weaver's distaff in this,'' she added to herself. She
wrinkled her nose as she tied the cumbersome thing in
place. Then she stared at the bewildering mix on the bed,
not sure what came next.

Sir Andrew coughed in a manner that indicated he
wanted her attention. ''I believe you will need the corset,
then a petticoat.''

Rosie whirled around but saw through the silk that the
lords had not moved. How did Sir Andrew know what
she was doing? She put her hands to her hips and encountered the thick bum roll instead.

''If ye be so wise tell me what does this corsey thing
look like?''

Jack stood up. ''Allow me to show you, sweet daughter of Venus.''

Rosie backed away from the curtain until the bum roll
thumped against the footboard of the bed. ''Your pardon,
Sir Jack, but I was not a-speaking with ye, but to Sir
Andrew. Ye stay right where ye be.''

Sir Andrew chuckled. ''Bravo, Rosie! You have taken
the wind out of my young friend's sails for he has no
breath left to speak. A corset goes around your bust and
regrettably flattens your very fine breasts.''

She found the thing in question and eyed it with even more disgust than the bum roll. "Who thought up this piece of torture?"

Sir Andrew gave a deep sigh. "The gods of fashion, I fear, and we poor humans must toil in abject slavery to their decrees."

She fitted the uncomfortable cage around her and began to lace it up. "What is the point of a woman's breasts if they are flat, I ask you?"

"By the book, the girl has hit the right nail upon its squared head. My very thoughts exactly, Rosie!" Jack replied. "I say, let us dispense with corset, bum roll and the whole lot!"

Rosie paused in midlacing. "Does that mean that Sir Andrew must give up his bells as well?" she asked.

"His what?"

A light, silvery jingle answered Jack's question. The younger man laughed and called for more wine.

"Pull tighter, Rosie," Sir Andrew advised.

The hairs on the back of her neck tingled again. "How do ye know what's what?" she asked.

He chuckled. "I am a man of many skills, Rosie. Now hurry along or twill be midnight before you are dressed to meet the day."

She stared at the silken drape while she chewed on her little fingernail. Perhaps Sir Andrew was a wizard. That thought caused goose bumps to rise on her flesh. And yet, he was kind, and did not consort with a brindled cat nor did he have dried dead things hanging from his tent pole. Rosie remembered the witch woman who lived in the woods outside of her village. Many a time her foster father had threatened to sell her to that old hag. Rosie made the sign against the evil eye, then she pulled her laces tighter.

"I can scarce draw a goodly breath," she complained.

"Excellent!" Sir Andrew remarked.

She chose the plainest of the gowns. Even so, the bodice of the dark green taffeta was embellished with burgundy satin ribbons. Pretty golden rosettes danced around the square neckline. The tight sleeves fit almost as if they had been made just for her. Then she realized that she had encountered an insurmountable problem. She chewed on her thumbnail again while she contemplated what to do next.

"Rosie!" Sir Andrew barked. "If you dine upon your fingernails one more time, I shall deduct a full sixpence from your meager earnings, and you do not yet have a sixpence to your abbreviated name."

Rosie snatched her thumb from her mouth. The man was a devil!

Sir Andrew rose and crossed the rug until he stood next to the curtain. Rosie saw the toes of his green suede shoes peek under the bottom of the silk hanging. "I believe that you now require the services of a lady's maid, my sweet. As there are none available, allow me to be your humble servant. Come forth and I will lace up your back. Have no fear. You wear twice as much now as you did last night."

Jack snickered. "Whoever heard of a shy harlot? Come out, Rosie, and let me be your undoing!"

She clutched the long opening of the gown with both hands. "Hain…I am *not* a harlot!" she shouted.

Sir Andrew placed his palm against the curtain. "Pay no mind to my Lord Stafford. I fear he is given too much drink, too much sport and far too many late nights. Do you want me to come in there…with you?" he asked, almost shyly.

Rosie gave herself a shake. She had faced worse

things than a drunken churl in her lifetime and probably would face a good deal more in the future. She would not give either man the bloated satisfaction of knowing her fears. She kicked the curtain aside, tripped on the hem of the pale green underskirt and nearly fell headlong into Sir Andrew's arms.

Though taken by surprise, he caught her and turned her around in one smooth movement. "Hold quite still, Rosie, and twill be done."

Jack poured himself more wine from the pitcher on the table. "You are a killjoy, Andrew," he sulked. "I could have trussed her up as well as you."

"Humph," Sir Andrew replied as he pulled Rosie's laces tight. "You begin to grow tedious, Jackanapes. Go bash someone's head in the tiltyard. You need the practice. Better yet, go find your cousins and bash in their heads. I warrant they have been up to no good."

Jack downed his wine in a single gulp. "You speak the truth methinks. Lady Olivia cast her net for Guy after the joust yesterday and methinks he did not wish to wriggle free save in her bed last night."

Sir Andrew swore under his breath. "Tis a pity that Guy is so young and has not yet learned the difference between a jay and a turtledove."

Jack shrugged. "At least, he was warmed last night, while I went to my poor pallet alone. Is that not a sad tale, sweet toothsome Rosie?"

She cast him a cool glance down the bridge of her nose. "I have heard sadder ones than that, my lord."

Sir Andrew gave her laces one final tug. "*Touché,* Jack!"

He turned Rosie around to face them, and swept a stray lock of hair from her eyes. His gentle touch made her shiver with pleasure. He bowed over her hand as if she were the queen herself. Then he flashed her a quick wink. Warmed by his approval, she smiled at him in return.

Sir Andrew swept his arm in a wide arc. "There now, my friends, behold a fine lady, newly minted. What say you?"

Jack raked her with a hot gaze. "She looks good enough to feast upon, old man. Let's unwrap this pretty package and have a merry time."

Sir Andrew glared at the younger man. "Out of my sight, weasel!"

Instead of taking offense, Jack merely laughed. He replaced his goblet on the table, saluted Rosie with a leer, and then strode out the open entrance. "Fare thee well, graybeard!" he called over his shoulder.

Once he was truly gone Rosie relaxed. Jack made her extremely nervous. She did not trust him an inch.

Sir Andrew snapped his fingers at the silent squire. "Well, Jeremy? Speak! I require your opinion. What do you think of my lady?"

The boy wet his lips. "In God's truth, she is passing fair, my lord, and I would not have believed it if I had not seen it happen."

His words and the enraptured look on his face gave Rosie a measure of delight. She straightened herself with as much dignity as she possessed. "Tis true, my lord?" she asked her employer.

The warmth in his hazel eyes answered her before he spoke. "Aye, little Rosie. Come, see for yourself." He pointed to a large mirror that was propped between two chests.

Lifting her layers of skirts out of the way, Rosie shuffled across the rug to take a closer look. A stranger with a halo of sun-kissed hair stared back at her from the glass. The discomfort of the constricting clothes fell away as she drank in her reflection. She had never seen herself except in a pool of water and never in such glorious finery. She touched a rosette and the girl in the glass did the same.

"'Tis witchcraft!" she breathed, tilting her head to one side, then the other. Her image moved as she did.

Sir Andrew came up behind her and chuckled as he looked into the glass over her shoulder. "Nay, Rosie. Tis merely the skill of the Venetian who made it. *You*, however, are a thing divine—and you look every inch a gentlewoman." He filled the tent with his laughter. "By Saint Peter! This wild conceit of mine is really going to work!"

Rosie touched the glass with her finger. The thing must tell the truth for Sir Andrew looked the same in it as he did in person. She touched her cheek, then her hair in wonderment. "I look pretty," she murmured.

Sir Andrew leaned closer and whispered in her ear. "More than that, my sweet. You look like a lady."

His warm breath tickled her neck and made her feel a little light-headed. She started to thank him but the words died on her lips. Instead, she snapped her mouth shut as she stared past her reflection and into the pink bower where she had changed her clothes. Her happiness veered sharply to anger. She glared at her grinning employer.

He lifted his brows. "How now, Rosie?"

"You!" Fury almost choked her. "You are a...a false-faced villain, my lord! You lewd rascals were a-spying on me the whole time. Aye! And laughing at me out of the sides of your mouths, I'll warrant!"

Sir Andrew showed no contrition. Instead, he grinned all the more. "At least, my lady has not abandoned the proper usage of the king's English,'' he remarked to Jeremy.

Rosie wished she dared to box his ears, but her common sense held her in check. ''Twas a vile trick to play upon me. Methought ye were a magician who could read my mind!''

''Nay, Rosie.'' He took her face in his hands and caressed her cheek with his thumb. ''I am merely a man in the company of a pretty lass.''

Her ill humor melted away as ice in sunlight, though she tried to hold on to it for a little longer. How could anyone stay angry at such a charmer when he smiled so warmly and touched her with such tenderness? She thought he might kiss her. He had that look in his eye. She moistened her lips in unconscious expectation and even rose a little on her toes.

Instead, Sir Andrew chuckled, then released her. ''I beg your forgiveness, my sweet. Twas not intended, but when we beheld you as the good Lord made you, well, we thought twould be a sin against beauty to turn away. Forgive this old fool for his whim, my dear.''

At that moment, Rosie would have forgiven him every crime on earth. ''You are not so old, my lord,'' she remarked while her heart hammered against the confines of the corset, ''so do not let that coxcomb Stafford tell ye otherwise.''

Sir Andrew glowed at her words. Then he took up her slate and made a bold stroke upon it. ''You know how to flatter a gentleman, Rosie. Tis a lesson many ladies have not yet learned.''

Though she could not count in a book-learned manner, she could see that the number of her pennies had grown. Sir Andrew moved to the far side of the tent and beckoned to her. ''Let us see you walk, my sweet.''

Rosie shuffled a few steps, then stopped. She knew she must look like a tortoise. "Tis nigh impossible! I cannot move with all this cloth and wire wrapped about me. Nor can I raise my arms to my shoulders. In faith, I can barely breathe. How does anyone run in such heavy attire?"

His eyes twinkled with merriment. "Ladies do not run at all."

Rosie wrinkled her nose. "Then tis no wonder that ladies are pregnant all the time," she observed.

Jeremy exploded in a fit of laughter. Sir Andrew joined him. "You are the very soul of wit, my dear," he said when he had caught his breath. "I must remember that one. Twould amuse the Earl of Thornbury."

He clapped his hands. "But to business! Jeremy, take my lady's arm in yours and be her supporter. Rosie, lift your skirts a little with your other hand. Nay, do not display too much leg or you will attract company of the wrong sort in no time. Jeremy! Mind your eyes and not the lady's ankles. Rosie, lower your skirts just so." He demonstrated.

Rosie did not dare to giggle, though out of the corner of her eye she spied a smirk hovering on Jeremy's lips. She pinched his arm. The boy instantly became the model of gravity.

Sir Andrew waved his hands in the air as if he conducted a band of minstrels. "Rosie, head up, shoulders back! Good! Now then, my ducklings, take one step forward. Nay, Rosie, do not look at your feet. They are Jeremy's concern. Her feet, you ass, not your clodhoppers. And another step. Better and better! Jeremy, escort the fair damsel around our humble dwelling. Rosie, chin up, eyes downcast."

"Why?" she called over her shoulder as the squire

steered her around the tent pole. "How can I keep my head up if you want my eyes down, and why should I keep my eyes down if I am not supposed to look at my feet? What am I supposed to look at?"

"Nothing and everything!" Sir Andrew replied.

"Do not confuse the matter by asking him questions," Jeremy advised her, "or we will be walking in circles the whole day."

"Excellent!" applauded Sir Andrew as they rounded the pole once more to face him. "Now curtsy for me."

Rosie sent a quick look of appeal to the squire. The boy stared straight ahead. "Haint ever curtsied afore," she muttered.

Sir Andrew cupped his ear. "What was that, my dear? Did I detect a slight lapse in your vocabulary?" He reached for the slate.

Rosie gasped as she watched him erase one of his marks. "Oy! Haint fair!" she yowled.

He rubbed out another stroke. Two pennies gone in less than a minute. Sir Andrew might be a gentleman but he was a coney-catcher, all the same. Rosie despaired of ever keeping so much as a groat.

Sir Andrew fanned himself with the smudged slate. "Would you care to revise and repeat your last two statements, Rosie?"

"Say it properly," Jeremy pleaded. "Or we will never eat dinner."

"Haint had breakfast yet," Rosie whispered back.

Jeremy winced. Sir Andrew cocked his head and held his finger above another chalk mark.

She pursed her lips, then said slowly, "I *have not* eaten any breakfast. I *have never* curtsied afore and I think it is not fair that you take away my money when

I *haven't* even seen the color of it yet, so please *you*, my lord."

He chuckled softly. "You do indeed, my lady."

He quickly gave her back the three pennies he had wiped away and added one more. Then he put the slate on the table and stood before his stiff couple. "When a lady does reverence, she puts her feet like so." He turned his toes out so that they faced in opposite directions, one foot slightly ahead of the other. "Then she bends her knees like so."

Rosie giggled. "With respect, my lord, ye look like a blessed frog."

Sir Andrew straightened immediately and assumed a more manly pose. "I have no idea if frogs or any other denizens of cow ponds enjoy a particularly beatific state, Rosie, but tis no matter to me at all. *You* are the one who must look like your frog. Now!" He pointed to her and then to the slate with a meaningful look.

"Do it!" muttered Jeremy.

Rosie took a deep breath, gripped the boy's hand and squatted. The squire yelped.

"She's digging her nails into my skin like a cat, my lord!"

"Tush, tush, my boy," Sir Andrew crooned. "What is a little pain when tis perfection that we seek? Rosie, downcast eyes, if you please. One does not stare into the face of the king."

She wobbled. "What king?"

Sir Andrew extracted his handkerchief and waved it like a banner. "Why, I speak of our sovereign lord, Henry, eighth of that name. By the grace of God, king of England, Ireland, Wales and sundry parts of this blessed France that we now stand upon. And *you*, my dearest duck, will do him reverence in eleven days' time when I escort you to his banquet. Surely you have not already forgotten?''

Rosie collapsed to the rug in a heap of green skirts. Jeremy lost his balance and crashed down beside her. ''Fire and brimstone, my lord! Ye never said nothing about the king! We will both end up in Newgate prison house if he ever claps an eye on me dressed up in these borrowed feathers and a-curtsying to him!''

Her employer merely smiled all the more. ''I fear you have made a few incorrect statements, my sweet. First of all, if it please His Grace, I will find myself residing in the Tower of London. *You* will be in Newgate.''

Rosie squeaked with horror at the thought.

''In the second place, you will not be wearing those particular garments that now grace your lovely form. You will be swathed in far costlier raiment when you meet the king.''

Rosie chewed her little fingernail and moaned in the back of her throat. Why hadn't Sir Andrew been more specific when he had explained his wager last night?

''Rosie! Stop biting your nails!'' He erased a chalk mark from the nearby slate. ''Where was I? Ah! My third and final point—your curtsy. It lacks a certain…flair. Jeremy! Help the lady to her feet and let us do it once again.'' He held up his hands. ''Not a word, my chicks. Not even a peep, or twill be the ax for all of us!'' he added with a dramatic dark note.

''Your master is stark, raving mad,'' Rosie whispered to the squire as he pulled her upright.

The boy swallowed hard. ''Tis Sir Andrew's pleasure to entertain many fantasies. Pray that this is merely one of them.''

''Amen to that,'' she replied in an undertone.

Sir Andrew winked at her, then motioned for her to

crouch like a frog again. "Excellent!" he exclaimed after her third try. He drew a very large mark on the slate.

She decided to ignore Sir Andrew's threat about meeting the king. If she could earn pennies for bobbing up and down like an apple in a tub of water, she would not question either her lord's sanity or his future plans. It was her future that most interested Rosie, and each new stroke on the slate brought her one step closer to her independence.

At long last, Sir Andrew declared himself satisfied with her progress. Just when she thought she could take off the tight gown and relax, he announced that it was time to go for a walk.

"Stir up a hearty appetite for the delicious repast that Jeremy will procure for us whilst we dally away the next hour," he said.

Rosie gulped. "What if someone should recognize me as one of Quince's girls, my lord?"

She didn't want Sir Andrew to become the laughing-stock of the entire English encampment on her account. In spite of his daft ideas and gaudy taste in clothes, he was a good man—far too good for her.

He shrugged away the idea. "Let the lady use your clogs, Jeremy. Twould be a blasphemy to besmirch her new slippers with the foul dust of France."

The squire dropped a pair of heelless wooden shoes in front of her. She nudged one with her toe.

Sir Andrew raised an eyebrow. "What now, Rosie?"

"Haint ever—" She stopped, then corrected herself before he could touch the slate. "I *have never* worn shoes before, my lord," she said.

Utter disbelief etched his features. "Not even in the winter?"

She shook her head. "I tied rags around my feet on

the coldest days. I am used to walking on a rough road.''
Unlike you, my tender-footed lord.

He dismissed her past discomfort with a flick of his
lace-ruffed wrist. ''Then tis high time to change all that,
my dear. Slide those things on and we shall be off! 'Ods
Bodkins!''' He struck his forehead with his hand. ''Your
beauty has so blinded me that I have become quite be-
fuddled.''

He crossed the rug in three long strides, pulled back
the silken curtain to his inner chamber, then looked
among her new clothes.

''Aha!'' he crowed with delight. In one hand, he held
a green coif with a gauzy white veil hanging down the
back. His other hand waved a pair of kid gloves the color
of fresh butter. ''As much as I enjoy your exquisite
tresses, Rosie, propriety dictates that they must be covered in civil company. And the gloves are to hide the
fact that you have plucked a multitude of fowls in your
recent past, and that you bite your nails.''

Before Rosie could protest that the additions were too
much to wear on such a warm day, her employer had
clapped the headdress on her head and stuffed her hair
within the veil. He tossed the gloves in her lap and stared
pointedly at them, then at the slate. Rosie saw it would
be useless to argue with him. Moreover, she did not want
to lose another penny now that she was finally ahead.
With a sigh of resignation, she wiggled her fingers into
the gloves. All the while, she wondered why ladies
would allow themselves to be stuffed, prodded and
poked into such uncomfortable attire. A gentlewoman
might look fashionable on the outside, but she suffered
within. Finally, Rosie thrust her feet into the heavy clogs
and attempted to stand up. Jeremy had to assist her. She

swore a colorful tavern oath under her breath. Unfortunately, Sir Andrew's sharp ears heard her.

"Tsk, tsk," he remarked, smudging out not one but two of her precious pennies. "Ladies never swear—and certainly not with the flavor of Cheapside."

Rosie bit her tongue. She was no lady and would never be one, no matter what Sir Andrew wanted. Goose girls were as far from the halls of Whitehall as the devil was from heaven. No amount of baths or rich clothing was going to change that fact. Sir Andrew might as well hand over his purse to Brandon Cavendish right now and save himself a packet of trouble.

He took her hand in his and smiled into her eyes. "Alas, fair lady, why do you look so sad? We are merely going for a morning's stroll, and not to an execution."

She wanted to rebuff him for his own good, but when he looked at her like that, her knees grew weak and her sensible objections evaporated. She licked her dry lips.

"Speak for yourself, my lord. As for me, I feel like the headsman awaits me yonder. Methinks soon all the world will know that I am not to the manor born. I pray you, sir, do not subject yourself to waggish jibes and foul insults on my poor account. Let us stay in here where tis safe."

He caressed her cheek as if she were a kitten. "Fear not, sweet Rosie. I will tell you a little secret. Men seldom look at a whore's face. Tis only her body that they want, and once they are done with her, they forget all entirely. You are safe now—with me."

He patted his bonnet and adjusted his ornate sword on his hip. His little bells rang merrily. "Besides, in your new finery and clean face, you look quite different. Heigh-ho, and we are off! Step lively, Jeremy! We expect our dinner in an hour's time. Come, my dear Rosie.

Let us walk about and I will show you how real ladies and gentlemen deport themselves.''

With a grand flourish of farewell, he led Rosie out into the sunshine and into a world that far surpassed her wildest dreams.

Chapter Nine

Even though the hazy sun of the forenoon beat hotly down upon her and a roguish wind stirred up the dust, Rosie forgot all the discomfort and heat the moment her eyes adjusted to the glare. It had been dark when she arrived in France scarcely two days ago, and she had been too tired and miserable to take an interest in her new surroundings. Now, looking around her for the first time in the light of day, Rosie could not believe her eyes.

Sir Andrew chuckled as he tucked her hand in the crook of his elbow. "There now. What thinkest thou?"

Rosie could barely blink, afraid that she might miss something or that the splendid sight would disappear in a cloud of golden smoke. "Tis a dream of paradise, my lord."

On all sides, as far as she could see, a great tented city stretched across the vast treeless plain known from ancient times as the Val D'Or—the Golden Vale. Now the grand name had come to life. Everywhere Rosie looked was the glitter of gold. Many of the round pavilions were painted with such a bright golden color that it dazzled her eyes when she looked upon them. Other tents were brilliant-blue, strawberry-red, green-striped, yellow-striped, tawny-colored and snow-white. All, like Andrew's garish rose-pink pavilion, were decorated with festoons of red and white roses, tendrils of glossy green ivy that wound its way up one side and down another, blue cornflowers intertwined with scarlet poppies and yellow-eyed white daisies. Every flowery detail had been painted by artists with cunning skill.

Rosie turned a full circle, being careful not to move too quickly lest she fall in the wobbling clog shoes. "There must be hundreds and hundreds of these grand dwellings," she marveled. "Even the meanest tent here is finer than any house I have ever seen."

Her companion beamed at her. "Aye, Rosie. Before you is spread the cream of all English society. Cardinal Wolsey's clerk of provisions confided to me that there are more than four hundred of these canvas huts—and that is only on the English side of the valley. The French have put on an equal show in their encampment beyond the tilt field. We must be equal in all things or else someone might take offense." He cocked an eyebrow. "Mark you, Rosie, our sovereigns are not at peace. They adapt themselves to these unusual circumstances, but they hate each other very cordially."

Jewel-colored banners fluttered in the hot wind above nearly every pavilion. Griffins, lions, stars, maces, roses, bulls, dragons and other marvelous creatures sported across the bright silks.

"Coats of arms, my dear." Sir Andrew answered her silent question. "They announce whose abode lies underneath. For instance…" He pointed to his own pennant of light-blue. "Do you see the silver swan upon yon azure field? Tis my very own device. I am the silver swan."

Rosie thought the vain, self-satisfied bird was a very

appropriate symbol for the glittering gentleman, though she did not voice her opinion in case he might take offense.

Sir Andrew pointed to the modest blue-striped tent next to his. ''Our good neighbor is Sir Jeffrey Brownlow—a hearty jouster if ever there was one. Yesterday, he nearly decapitated his French opponent. You will know Sir Jeffrey by the great brown bear on the golden field. And over there...'' he indicated a red-and-gold tent across a narrow lane ''...is Sir Tobias Emerickes, my chief opponent at the archery range, and his Lady Jessimond. You will notice that those regrettable heads on the sable field bear marked resemblance to goats with spikes in their heads. Tis Emerickes' idea of unicorns.''

Rosie giggled. The poor beasts really did look like they suffered monstrous headaches.

Sir Andrew waved his hand in a third direction. ''If you wended your way among those rather pedestrian groups of shelters, you would come upon the entire Cavendish family. They have at least a dozen tents of various sizes and degrees. Together they make up their own village, so to speak. You will know them by the ferocious wolf's head on a red background. Beyond them is one of the large cook tents provided by our esteemed Cardinal Wolsey so that we poor souls will not starve on this barren waste.''

Rosie nodded, and prayed that she could remember half of what Sir Andrew had said. Her attention wandered away from the tents to the inhabitants. Even the servants who emptied the slops in the trenches that ran behind each row of pavilions looked dressed for a feast. Their masters were almost beyond description.

Rosie ogled at a lady who passed and nodded to Sir Andrew. She was dressed in several shades of green taffeta with her overskirt and flowing sleeves made of burgundy velvet.

"By my larken, my lord, look there! Is she a duchess?" She wondered if she was supposed to curtsey to such a rich-looking personage.

Sir Andrew grasped her outstretched hand and pulled it down to her side. "Pray do not point at Lady Eleanor Foxmore, sweet Rosie. Tis ill-mannered. She is not a strange creature from the New World on display at a fair, nor is she a duchess. Her husband is a gentleman usher to the king. Furthermore, ladies never point—they indicate."

"Oh." Rosie lifted her hand to chew her thumbnail, but tasted the leather glove instead.

Sir Andrew quirked an eyebrow as a reminder. "Even though the slate of your account is not at hand at this exact moment, I have a prodigious memory and can recall your lapses at will. Be advised."

She rubbed her nose while she tried to decipher what he had just said. "You mean you'll take away my pennies even outside your tent?"

He flashed her a toothful grin. "Exactly, my dear!"

Just then he pulled her aside as a great black warhorse trotted past them. The animal and his rider were both decked in dark-blue satin shot with golden stars. An incongruous bouquet of gold satin roses decorated the horse's beautiful flowing tail. A pair of panting greyhounds wearing collars of gold chains raced behind their star-studded master.

"You are amazed?" Sir Andrew murmured in her ear as they watched the glittering knight continue on his way down the broad avenue.

Rosie paused a moment while she considered her answer. She knew he wouldn't like it, but she would speak her mind anyway. "Amazed—and disgusted, my lord."

He cocked his head. "How now? Do we stand too near the jakes' trench? Avail yourself of my pomander." He offered his clove-studded orange that hung from a gold chain at his belt.

She shook her head. "Nay, my lord. I have smelled far worse in London than I do here. Tis hard to explain."

He patted her hand as he conducted her down the avenue behind the receding knight and horse. "I have a good ear and all the time in the world, dear Rosie. I yearn to know—what particularly disgusts you—besides the proximity of the blessed French?"

She searched her vocabulary for the right words, while walking very carefully to avoid a disastrous stumble in her uncomfortable shoes. "Tis all this display of wealth, my lord," she finally replied. "The rich clothes. The gilded tents. Even the dogs are sleeker and better dressed than the mayor of Windsor. Tis a waste!"

Sir Andrew considered her opinion for a moment, then turned to her with a mildly perplexed look in his eye. "Come again, sweetheart, for you have lost me in that last turning of your thoughts. What is so wasteful—except perchance Emerickes' sorry excuse for a unicorn?"

How could Sir Andrew be so dense? He had struck her as one of the few intelligent men she had met. She pulled him to a stop in the middle of the roadway. "Look about you, my lord. Do you see anyone curled in a corner, gray and gaunt for the want of a crust of bread? Do you see a family of children blue to the skin because they lack clothes to wear in the winter? Where are those poor souls who are plagued with open sores that turn your stomach to look at them? Where are the shambling houses that have only half a roof to keep out the rain?''

At each question, he grew more uncomfortable. ''I agree that we are temporarily freed from such doleful sights. Tis the king's holiday time. The only beggars here are French. Unfortunately we shall have to return to our own in a fortnight.''

She wanted to hit him. ''Are ye blind, my lord? Or is your head merely thick as an oaken post?''

''Hold, wench!'' He fixed her with a stern glare. ''You forget to whom you speak.''

Distracted by her anger, she dug her fingers into the ornate material of his sleeve. ''Nay, Sir Andrew Ford, I have not forgotten where I came from, but methinks you have. Who paid for these lavish amusements and fripperies that I see on every side—even on the horses and dogs?''

Understanding suffused his handsome features. ''Ah, I spy your meaning.'' A red blush stole up his neck from his tight collar. ''The king's treasury pays for the king's appointments.''

She gave him a withering smile. ''And who puts good coin into the king's treasury? Nay, you need not answer that, my lord, for we both know that it comes out of the mouths of the common folk of England. Why, for the cost of that banner with the ridiculous unicorn, a family such as mine would have bread for the entire winter. One of those chains that grace yon dog would buy a wealth of blankets to warm every child in Stoke Poges. That, my lord, is the waste.'' She lowered both her voice and her eyes. ''I hope that our good king does not roast in hell for his vanity.''

Sir Andrew leaned over and whispered in her ear. ''Speak gently if you speak of Great Harry, little angel, or else you may find your wings clipped in the grim Tower of London.''

Though his words frightened her, she could not resist a final sally. ''Methought you said I was too low for the likes of the Tower. Methought I would be sent to Newgate.''

His frown disappeared with a grin. ''You are truly a wonder, Rosie, and I will pledge myself to keep you out of both, or die in the attempt.''

He must be jesting, she thought, for her experience had already taught her that no one would lift so much as a little finger to save her skin. She was about to deny his idle promise, when a weeping girl dressed in the clothes of a handmaiden practically flew out of a nearby pavilion and fell into Sir Andrew's arms. She was followed by a very grand lady whose beauty was marred by the anger of her expression.

''Slut! Beetled-headed fool!'' the noblewoman screamed at the quaking girl. She boxed the maid's ears. ''That veil you tore cost more than you are worth!''

Sir Andrew stepped between the two women and grabbed the lady around her waist before she could strike again. ''Hold, Olivia! What is amiss? Your frown blots your legendary beauty, my love.''

A change like a ripple across a still pond came over the lady. Her whole body seemed to soften and her dark eyes took on a warm, coquettish look that Rosie neither liked nor trusted.

''Why, Andrew! Tis been too long since I was last in your arms.'' Lady Olivia slipped her hands around his neck and swayed her hips against his. ''Surely you could stop awhile and renew our acquaintance?''

Rosie watched the scene with astonishment. In her short but educational time under Quince's bawdy roof, she had often witnessed such displays of wantonness, but never in the broad daylight, never outside in a public place and certainly never done by a gentlewoman of quality and good breeding. Rosie sniffed with disapproval and envy. That bedecked jade had no business to take such liberties with her patron.

At least, Sir Andrew had the decency to look surprised. He favored the woman with a thin smile as he pried her fingers out of his hair. "Have done, Olivia. I am no longer your spaniel." Then he turned her around to face Rosie. "I have the distinct pleasure to introduce you to my Lady Ros…Rosalind. Lady Rosalind, this *gentle* creature is my Lady Olivia Bardolph."

Rosie blinked at her new name, then she noticed his free hand making a downward motion. *He wants me to curtsey to Madam Wildcat!*

Biting back her urge to stick out her tongue at the shrew, Rosie gathered her skirts in her hands and made a small bob without pitching nose-first into the dust. Sir Andrew rewarded her first public test with a wide smile. The warmth of his approval made Rosie's heart sing.

Lady Olivia barely noticed her or the hapless maid who had skittered around the far side of the tent and disappeared. The lady gave Andrew a seductive smile that left no mistake what was on her mind. "You are truly a heartbreaker, Andrew," she purred, rubbing against him like a cat. "I found myself alone last evening. What do you think of that?"

He chuckled as he stepped away from her. "Methinks you mismanaged your time, Olivia. Or did your lover of the moment grow cold? As for me, I was otherwise…engaged." He shot another heart-melting smile at Rosie.

Her spirits soared with elation. A part of her reveled

in his open admiration of her, but another part of her—
her common sense—chided Rosie and reminded her that
Sir Andrew was merely playing his role. He did not care
an oyster for her personally. She was only a goose girl
who had been ill-used by an esquire's son and sold for
a whore.

Lady Olivia leveled a penetrating stare at Rosie. The
girl shivered under the other's scrutiny. She was sure
Lady Olivia could see straight through her flimsy disguise.

The lady curled her lip. "She's a pretty little thing, I
warrant you, Andrew, but I am amazed. Your advancing
years must have dulled your taste. Anyone can see the
child is dressed in dreadful fashion."

Rosie looked down at her lovely gown and the pretty
rosettes that decorated it. How dare this shrew make
remarks about her clothes or Andrew's age? A heat
flooded her cheeks.

Andrew took Rosie's hand in his and kissed her
gloved fingers. "I much prefer a fresh daisy from the
meadow than a hothouse flower that is beautiful to look
upon but, alas, has no…perfume. And if you find me so
ancient, my dear, mayhap you should amuse yourself
with greener stock."

Lady Olivia laughed without mirth. "I have already
taken your advice, Andrew my heart. Since we have
been in France, I have sampled the joys of both the
young Cavendish knights and found their youth…
stimulating. And their cousin Jack Stafford?" She fluttered her lashes in a mock appearance of rapture. "Oh!
The appetite of that boy's eye—and other parts—did
scorch me up. La, Andrew! *Four* times in one night! I
was quite worn out with pleasure."

Sir Andrew's hold on Rosie's hand tightened as the

lady taunted him with her shameless conquests. His smile turned frosty. "Youth must be served, lady, and I am glad that you serve it so well. Good day." He gave her an abrupt bow and pulled Rosie away before she could attempt another curtsy.

Once out of sight and hearing of the shameless Olivia, Rosie tugged on Andrew's sleeve. "So is *that* how a lady should act, my lord?" she asked with a sneer. "That woman is no better than any of the strumpets in Southwark. The only difference is their wardrobes."

He arranged his features into a pleasant smile once more. "I quite agree with your astute assessment, my dear. Lady Olivia Bardolph is a polecat of the first order."

"Were you her lover, too?" she asked. She felt she must know.

He coughed behind his hand before answering. "Tis not a proper question for a lady to ask a gentleman."

"Haint a lady," Rosie mumbled under her breath, "and neither is she."

Andrew cocked his head. "I am a little deaf when outside in the sun. What did you say about being a lady, Rosie?"

She started to repeat her observation, but stopped herself before the whole of "haint" escaped her lips. She wrinkled her nose then retorted. "I *am not* a rump-fed lady."

Andrew nodded. "You are quite correct, my dear, but the words *rump-fed* should never issue from a lady's mouth. Prithee amend that mistake in the future."

As they passed a large gilded tent, their way was blocked by a long procession of servants. Each one carried two buckets of steaming water. Rosie wondered what it was that they could possibly be cooking. The sounds of a lute, pipe and tabor wafted from inside the tent. The music was accompanied by off-key singing—and splashing.

Sir Andrew chuckled as he looked skyward at the banner waving over the revels within. ''Methinks the Master of Cheviot is entertaining a merry crew of rascals.''

Rosie didn't understand why her escort appeared so amused. ''Tis early in the day for a carouse.''

''Tis near the dinner hour, but we are in France, dear Rosie, and so all usual custom is out the window—or washed away in the bath.''

''How now, my lord?''

Before Sir Andrew could reply, the lead serving boy pulled open the tent flap to reveal the most amazing scene within. Three large wooden tubs stood side by side just inside the entrance. Each tub was filled to the brim with water, and splashing each other merrily were three couples, a pair in each tub. There was no doubt in Rosie's mind that the bathers were ladies and gentlemen for they wore lavish hats or headdresses bedecked with feathers, colored ribbons and jeweled pins. More gold and precious stones hung about their necks. Other than those accouterments, the revelers were completely naked.

A long, thin board, covered with a gold-fringed cloth, lay along the length of the tubs, creating a most unusual banqueting table. The couples sat on opposite sides of the board and feasted off small silver roundels and drank from silver goblets. Another flock of servitors hovered behind their masters and refilled the trenchers and vessels as fast as they emptied. Rosie's mouth dropped open. The couple in the middle tub were more engrossed with fondling each other than with eating the delicious repast before them. The nearest gentleman looked up from his plate of pink shrimps and gave Sir Andrew a broad grin of welcome.

"What ho, Ford! Come join us. By the time you and your sweet lady have divested yourselves of those too confining garments, my Lord Rothbury and his mistress will have moved to yon bed for further sport. Plenty of room. Come, wash away the dust of France with us!"

Andrew squeezed Rosie's hand by way of warning her not to say a word. Then he executed a deep bow with many a flourish of his hand. "Sir Griffith, you do me a great honor to invite us to join in these pleasant pastimes with such good company. Alas and alack, I fear my lady and I must decline. We are late for an appointment, and twill never do to keep royalty waiting. I thank you for your offer of such joyful hospitality but beg to be excused. Another time, perchance?"

The pink-skinned man chortled, then lifted his goblet and toasted Sir Andrew and Rosie. "Fare thee well, Andrew, and that little dainty morsel by your side. You don't know what you are missing, does he, my duck?"

With a grin full of mischief and lust, Sir Griffith reached under the water. The lady opposite him squealed with surprise and glee, then threw a strawberry at her partner. Water sloshed over the rim of their tub, soaking the canvas flooring.

"I wish you and your guests much good cheer," Andrew replied pulling Rosie away. Ribald laughter answered him as the tent flap was lowered, shielding the further antics of the party.

Rosie could not believe what she had just witnessed. No one in her experience had ever dined in the nude. "Is *that* why ye love bathing so much, my lord?" she asked him.

He flashed her a look of naughty innocence. "Nay,

my sweet, my purposes are honorable. Cleanliness is next to godliness?''

Rosie cocked an eyebrow at him. ''God was nowhere near that tent.''

Sir Andrew laughed at her remark.

''In Quince's house, when the girls entertained their clients, at least they did it behind curtains and not in the middle of a thoroughfare. Pray tell me, my lord, for I am slow to learn, is this…sport another fashion for noble ladies?''

Sir Andrew saluted a passing noble before he answered. ''Nude dining is a pastime enjoyed by many,'' he remarked in an offhand tone of voice. He did not look at Rosie.

She jerked his elbow to get his attention. ''Have *you* ever enjoyed it?'' She had the sinking feeling that he most certainly had.

Sir Andrew fanned his flushed face with his handkerchief. ''I have a number of pastimes that I enjoy, my sweet. We need not concern ourselves with them at the moment. Let us continue our—''

Rosie interrupted him. ''The truth, my lord. Have *you* ever bathed naked as a jay with that peevish Lady Bardolph?''

Chapter Ten

Though Andrew had always prided himself to be a worldly-wise gentleman of pleasure as well as refinement, he found himself at a loss for words. Never before had he blushed to admit an amorous fling. Of course he had dallied with Olivia Bardolph—in and out of beds, baths, meadows and even once in the garderobe of Greenwich Palace. Why should he be embarrassed to tell Rosie, of all people? What was she but a shade this side of harlotry herself?

Yet, looking into her emerald eyes now filled with fiery sparks of indignation, he could not bring himself to admit it. For some unfathomable reason, he wanted to keep Rosie's good opinion of his character. She had to trust him, or else she would not win his wager. But in his heart of hearts, Andrew knew that was not the reason why the truth stuck in his throat like a piece of dry toast.

He was saved from his predicament by a young girl who ran headlong into him from behind. Andrew caught her before she careened into a pile of horse dung.

"It seems that women are falling all over you today,

my lord,'' Rosie observed dryly. ''Does this happen often?''

The elfin child flashed them an enchanting smile. *''Pardonnez-moi, monsieur et madame!''* Despite her obvious haste, she executed a beautiful curtsy. ''I crave your pardon, sir, but I am on a great adventure.'' She glanced over her shoulder.

Rosie grinned at the delightful sprite. ''Can you understand her, my lord? What is she speaking?''

Andrew hunkered down and brushed some of the dust and straw from the child's ruby-red skirt. ''She is French and she is having an adventure.'' He returned the little girl's smile. ''And what is such a young lady doing alone among the English, I wonder?'' he asked her in French. ''And where are you running to?''

The child rolled her huge purple eyes. ''Oh, la, la! I am not running *to* anything but *away* from my bodyguard. Pah! If he catches me he will take me straight back to our pavilion, and Pappa will be so angry, he will make me stay inside there forever. You would not want that to happen to me, eh?'' She cocked her head.

Andrew tried to maintain a serious demeanor. ''Have you not heard that the English are monsters and have no manners? Are you not afraid to be among us?''

The little girl giggled. ''Pah!'' She snapped her fingers. ''I am well protected. See?'' She pointed to a small crucifix that she wore around her neck. ''And I am not finished having my adventure yet. I am looking for the fountain that spouts wine. Do you know of it?''

Andrew nodded gravely. *''Oui,* but, my little one, it stands just outside the English king's residence. Are you not afraid he will see you?''

The child shook her head. *''Mais, non!* I am so little

that no ever notices me—except Gaston.'' She made a
face. ''And he only notices me when I am *not* there.''

''Celeste!'' A deep-throated roar filled the air.

The little maid ducked her head. ''*Ma foi!* I speak his
name and Gaston calls. Oh, please, kind *monsieur,* do
not tell him you have seen me. Give me a little longer
to enjoy my freedom. And, please, where is this marvelous fountain? I *must* see it!''

Andrew chuckled. ''The fountain is straight up that
avenue.'' He pointed. ''But you may wish to take the
roundabout route so that the furious Gaston does not find
you.''

Celeste threw her arms about Andrew's neck and gave
him a hug. ''I am forever in your debt, *monsieur.*''

''Celeste!'' The furious Gaston sounded much closer.

Celeste bunched her skirts in her hands and dashed
toward the nearest tent. Then she halted, whirled back
to Andrew and Rosie, dropped another flawless curtsy
and disappeared around the pavilion. Andrew stood and
took Rosie's hand just as a large muscular man with an
enormous moustache appeared around the corner.

''Say nothing,'' Andrew whispered as the man ap-
proached them.

She gave Andrew a quick nod. ''Since I didn't understand a word, I have nothing to say.'' She gripped
Andrew tighter.

The man halted before them. *Jesu, he is a brute!* Forc-
ing a smile, Andrew nodded his head. ''And a bright
good day to you, my man,'' he greeted the monster in
English.

The burly Frenchman returned a sneer to Andrew,
then spoke in rapid French. ''Have you seen a little girl
with black hair in a red gown?''

Andrew pretended he did not understand the language

in order to give the child a little more time to effect her escape. No wonder she ran! "I am sorry, but I do not understand what you said. Never could wrap my tongue around all those blessed vowels."

The Frenchman narrowed his eyes and started to open his mouth to speak, but Andrew hurried on in English. "Ah, you need not say a word, good man, for I know just what you are thinking. You would like to cut my heart out for being such a stupid fellow, no? But there you have it. A dismal lack of education. What can I say?" He shrugged.

The other man's answer rumbled up from his throat. "Bah! You are an imbecile in velvet. I would spit on you but I do not have the time, nor the spittle to waste on such a stupid man as you! Bah! A pox upon you, you goggle-eyed carp!"

Though Andrew fumed at the ruffian's bold presumption, he maintained his outer calm. "And the same to you, my friend." He gave the Frenchman a wide smile and another little bow. "If we meet again, I pray twill be at sword point!"

The Frenchman lumbered away in the wrong direction, bellowing "Celeste!" every other step. Andrew glanced at Rosie and noticed that she had turned a little pale under her light tan. He patted her arm. "Tis nothing, my dear, but a great windbag. Pay him no mind at all. The little lass will have a few more minutes to enjoy her adventure."

Rosie gave herself a little shake. "I suppose that next you will tell me the little French girl is also a lady?"

He nodded and smiled with the pleasant memory of the child. "Aye, one in training, I must admit, but she had beautiful manners."

His companion snorted in a very unladylike fashion.

"Ha! She is in training all right—she has already learned how to make a man chase after her."

Andrew looked at Rosie with a new respect. "You continue to astonish me, sweetheart. There is more inside that pretty head of yours than I first thought."

Clapping and cheering drew their attention to one of the many open patches among the pavilions. There, a troop of Spanish acrobats tumbled, capered, and walked on their hands to the amazement and astonishment of the growing crowd.

"Oh, look!" Rosie whispered with awe as one of the entertainers juggled several wicked-looking daggers and an apple. At the conclusion he severed the apple in mid-air. "That is the most marvelous feat I have ever seen!" She clapped her hands with joy.

Andrew smiled at her exuberance. Then it occurred to him that he had not heard her laugh with such abandon. He glanced at her and again he experienced the feeling that she reminded him of someone he had met. Andrew racked his brain to think whom she resembled. *Twill come to me in the dead of night.*

The roar of a second crowd drew them to the other side of the patch. A cockfight had been in progress but two young knights had supplanted the roosters and were rolling around in the dirt, pounding each other for all they were worth. This action amused the ladies and their lordly escorts even more.

When Andrew moved closer for a better look, he was surprised to see it was the Cavendish brothers. Their colorful satin doublets were torn beyond repair and their hose were rent into rags.

"By the rood!" Andrew swore. "Leave them to their own devices for half a day and they proceed to kill each other! Guy! Brandon! Desist!"

Rosie covered her mouth to hide her laughter. Andrew grew even more angry. What sort of an impression did the wench have of the nobility when their sons rolled in the mud for the amusement of gawkers? He spied Mark Leyland, Brandon's new page. He snatched the child out of the way of the flailing fists and feet.

"What began this fray?" he asked the boy.

The seven-year-old rolled his eyes with excitement. "My master called his brother an angel."

Andrew groaned, then explained to Rosie, "From youth Brandon has taunted Guy for his beauty. Methinks tis fed by envy, but no matter. The worst thing you could say to Guy is to call him Angel-face."

"It appears that Sir Brandon is getting the worst of it now," Rosie remarked with an unashamed giggle.

Andrew squatted down to Mark's eye level. "And just why did Sir Brandon say this to Sir Guy?"

The little rascal puffed himself up with the importance of his information. "Sir Guy asked how could my master do such devilish things at night with the daughter of a French vintner. Sir Brandon called him a spying arch-angel. Sir Guy made no answer but hit him instead. Tis a marvelous good fight, do you think, my lord?"

Andrew cursed the two lackwits under his breath. Several Frenchmen, who stood nearby, shouted rude observations of the Cavendishes' fighting abilities. Unfortunately for them, both Brandon and Guy spoke French as a second tongue. The two giants stopped their personal quarrel and turned to the French interlopers.

Brandon wiped the dirt off his face. "How now, my lords?" he asked in flawless French. "You speak a brave show. Would you care to couple your bold words with action? My good brother and I will be glad to relieve you of some of your teeth."

One of the visitors looked like he might bolt, but his companion stepped forward. "*Oui*, English dog. Twill be my pleasure."

"Go to! A Cavendish!" Andrew shouted encouragement to his former pupils. No Frenchman alive could best his boys.

Soon there were four men whacking and pounding each other while the crowd cheered and made many wagers over the outcome.

Rosie tugged on Andrew's sleeve. "I suppose *this* is how a true nobleman behaves?" Her words dripped with mocking mirth.

Andrew mopped his perspiring brow with his handkerchief. He winced when he saw the disdain on her face. "The lads are merely practicing their knightly skills," he murmured.

Rosie shook her head with a sneer. She pointed to the Cavendishes who made mincemeat of the opponents. "For *this* you are called our betters? For *this* we common folk should grovel in the dirt before you? I thank you for this most educational stroll, my lord. I have learned mickle much about the ways of fine ladies and gentlemen. Do you think I should now practice how to swear and fight? Or how to lead good men astray by using my body in a wanton fashion? Shall I bathe in the nude three times a day in the middle of the road? Pray tell me, good Sir Andrew, is there anything *else* I have missed?"

He bestowed on her his widest smile, though her every word stung him like a whiplash. He took her hand and led her away from the brawl. "Aye, my sweetest Rose. Once again, you have hit the mark. We are missing our dinner. Come!"

* * *

With a terrible roar, Sir Gareth Hogsworthy backed his henchman against the palings of the practice tiltyard. Again and again he rained blows of his blunted broadsword against the splintered shield of his opponent. Young Walter Ormond sank to his knees in the soft sand and tore off his practice helm. His pale face ran with sweat.

Dropping his sword, the stripling held both his arms in front of his pimple-pocked face. "I yield, my lord!" Ormond whined. "Pray cease! I am worn to the nub!"

Hogsworthy cuffed the puling boy with the flat of his blade. Then he drove his weapon's tip deep into the sand. The sword quivered with the impact. Tossing a curse over his shoulder, Gareth stalked over to the near side of the ring and grabbed the leather water bag out of his squire's hands. He poured the contents over his head, then shook off the excess much like a dog would.

Sir Edward Fitzhugh leaned his elbows on the railing and chuckled. "You fight like a demon today, Gareth," he remarked. "Whose face do you see instead of young Ormond?" He offered his wineskin to Gareth.

The fuming lord helped himself to a deep draught before he answered. "I would that Ford were cowering on his knees in the sand." He wiped his mouth on his sleeve. "I would not have stayed my hand."

Fitzhugh chuckled again. "All for that little bit of skirt?"

Gareth glared at his friend. "God's death! It runs deeper than that. That gaudy-dressed game cock made me look the fool this morning. I'll not bear such slanders. I'll have that knave's gizzard served on a platter. Aye! And I'll make his wench eat it!" He threw his gauntlets and chain mail hood at his squire.

Fitzhugh picked at his fingernails. "As for the girl, get yourself another. There is more than one poesy in the field. Indeed, a goodly stock of gamesome strumpets from every point of the compass have gathered on the fringes of our camp. There is bound to be one that will appeal to your particular tastes."

"The pox infect you, Fitzhugh! I paid good coin for that virgin."

Edward shrugged. "Then split the bawdmaster's fat head in twain and take back your money. Tis a bit late in the day for your wench. She's no longer a virgin by now, I warrant."

Gareth gnashed his teeth. "Tis *that* one I want! Ford snatched her away from me when I had won her fair and square. Now he flouts her under my nose! Did you see them walking together this forenoon as bold as you please? Why, he even has dressed her in pretty rags. I swear to you, I will not tolerate this infamy!"

Fitzhugh fanned himself with his hat. "Then challenge the man."

Gareth took another long pull from the wineskin. He would not admit to Fitzhugh, nor any one else, that he was afraid of Andrew Ford's skill as a swordsman. The man might dress like a peacock, but over the years at court Gareth had seen Ford in action and knew that the knight was a formidable adversary. Now that Ford was growing older, Gareth thought he could beat him but, on the other hand, a defeat at the hands of that popinjay would be worse than this morning's embarrassment.

Then there was that brash Stafford's challenge. The boy fought with a wild recklessness that was downright terrifying to watch. Gareth had no intention of meeting that hothead in the tiltyard, no matter how "cordial" the rules were. Gareth also knew that where Stafford went, his two cousins, the Cavendishes, would be near at hand. Those acorns had not fallen far from the tree of their formidable father, Thornbury. Gareth knew that if he tangled with one, he would tangle with all. The odds were against him from the first. He swore another blistering oath.

Edward raised an eyebrow. "How now?"

Gareth drained the rest of the wine. "We will steal the wench right out from under Ford." He chuckled at that idea. "Twill stew up that old man in his own foul juices. He has always prided himself as an expert seducer. We will say she ran away from him, then proclaim far and wide of his failure to keep even a common whore satisfied. He will come to rue the day he tweaked *my* nose."

Fitzhugh stared out beyond the practice yard. "Aye, a good plan, but how will you effect it? Ford guards her like an old hen with one chick."

Gareth leaned against the railing. "He will have to leave her when he attends the king. I highly doubt that he will parade her under Great Harry's nose no matter what pretty ribbons he ties on her. We will set a man to watch his tent. Meanwhile I will bide my time as if I have forgotten the whole matter. Young Ormond there..." he pointed to his hapless practice partner "—he will make a good watchdog."

Fitzhugh nodded. "In that you speak the truth. Walter is slimy enough to flit between shadows and he possesses no inconvenient morals."

Gareth gave a hollow laugh. *And once the wench is in my hands, I will make her curse the day she ever smiled at anyone but me.*

* * *

Rosie lay in her trundle bed and stared at the canvas roof. She could hear Sir Andrew and Jeremy speaking in low voices on the other side of the silken curtain that separated the sleeping area from the main part of the pavilion. The light of the single lantern cast their elongated shadows against the curtain. The pink color of the silk bathed Rosie's side of the tent in a restful glow.

She yawned without bothering to cover her mouth as her mentor had chided her to do all evening. She stretched her body under the light linen sheet and wiggled her throbbing toes. Her slippers were indeed beautiful to admire but hellish to wear. Her whole body ached. How could walking with a book balanced on her head make her feel so exhausted? Plucking geese and washing brothel house linen was much harder work, but she could not remember when she last felt so tired. No wonder ladies looked pale and pinched in the face!

On the other side of the curtain, Sir Andrew said "haint" to Jeremy and they both laughed. Rosie made a face in their direction. Sir Andrew had spent the long, tiresome afternoon trying to teach her proper speech. The account slate had so many markings and erasures on it by now that Rosie wasn't too sure if she was ahead or behind. She sighed and chewed her fingernail.

Where was this playacting going to lead when all was said and done? What did Sir Andrew's wager with Sir Brandon matter now? Rosie estimated that her lord had already spent twice as much as the money he hoped to win from the elder Cavendish.

"For the blessed challenge of it, my dear," he had told her when she asked him that very question during supper. "In all of Great Harry's court, Sir Andrew Ford is known to be the authority of refinement and good taste. Tis my jest upon them all." He chuckled.

Rosie had plopped her elbows on the table between them and had asked, "And me? Am I merely your jest as well?"

She remembered that he had looked surprised at her question. She had no idea why. It was a perfectly logical thing to ask.

"How now?" He had raised one eyebrow in that highly engaging manner of his. "Do you not like wearing pretty clothes? Or eating good food—like that baked sole you are trying to stuff in your mouth all at once? Break it into pieces, my dear. The fish doesn't mind a bit. And have you lost interest in earning a few shillings for all these pains?"

It had been on the tip of her tongue to ask "Then what?" but she was afraid of his answer. For all his gentle manners and flowery speech, Sir Andrew was like any other man. He would eventually use her for his own pleasure—whatever that may be—promise her the moon, then toss her in the dust of the road. Rosie sat up, drew her knees to her chest and propped her chin on them.

She ought to run away from this mad lark before it went any further. But where to? Certainly not back to Quince—blast his black, penny-pinching heart. She knew now that she would rather die than return to the stews of Southwark. On the other hand, she knew that she could not stay in France once the English went home. How could she manage when she could neither understand nor speak their language? As it was, she was having enough trouble learning how to speak her own.

Sir Andrew laughed again and the sound filled Rosie with a warmth that she had felt last night. He had a wonderful laugh, deep and sensual, that sent ripples of a strange new awareness through her. Just then, he asked for his lute, plucked a few notes on it, cleared his throat

and began to sing a tender ballad. Leaning back against
the plump feather pillows, Rosie closed her eyes and
allowed the sweet melody to wash over her.

Why should she want to run anywhere when there was
a haven of comfort and safety in Andrew's tent—and
also, there was Andrew. She smiled in the semidarkness.
What a fine man he was! So full with life and the joy
of living. He greeted each hour of the day like a new-
found treasure. Despite his long-winded speeches and his
obsession with his wager, he had a gentle touch and soft
words.

No matter how many times she had said "haint" or
broken one of the thousand rules of courtly etiquette,
Andrew never lost patience and struck her as her foster
father had often done. By all rights, he should have
given her back to Quince as a poor bargain—after he
had deflowered her, of course. Her lower lip trembled.
What would he do if and when he finally decided to take
what he had purchased? The man was no lackwit. Would
his good humor finally snap when he discovered that she
did not have a shred of virginity left? She buried her
head in the crook of her elbow.

Tonight he had tucked her into her bed as if he were
her real father—nay, like a fond older brother. Then he
had leaned over and kissed her gently on the forehead.
Rosie touched the place where his lips had pressed
against her skin and sighed. *I wish he had kissed my lips
instead. After all, I did clean and polish my teeth in a
proper ladylike manner.*

Earlier that morning Jeremy had assured her that his
master was a man in every sense of the word. The squire
hinted that Andrew had years of lovemaking experience.
Rosie remembered the way that Lady Olivia had looked
at him—like she wanted to pour honey all over him and

lick him clean. Rosie damned the noblewoman to a very hot clime.

She ran her fingers through her hair. What was so wrong with her? Why didn't she attract Andrew's favor? She had kept her face clean and her hair brushed all day long, just as he had wanted. Wasn't she pretty enough or clean enough for him now?

Rosie, you dolt, you have fallen in love with Sir Andrew. Close up your heart, for he will break it as sure as there are stars in the heavens.

She lay down and shut her eyes against the powerful emotions that struggled within her heart. *I am his chattel and nothing else.* She turned away from his lilting music and covered her ears with a pillow.

I am also the greatest fool in this tent!

Chapter Eleven

Wednesday, June 13

The Countess of Thornbury lifted her wide skirts of popinjay blue fustian and stepped around a large pile of steaming horse droppings. She nodded to several disheveled gentlemen she knew who returned her early morning salutation with a mixture of guilty looks and painful movements. Alicia Cavendish smiled to herself. No doubt she had caught her acquaintances creeping back to their abodes after an all-night carouse. At least, it wasn't one of her sons or their irresponsible Stafford cousin. *Twould be an awkward moment for all concerned.*

Alicia smiled in earnest when she spied poor, overworked Jeremy boiling a large kettle of water outside his master's tent. "Good morrow, Jeremy," she called to the youth. "Is Sir Andrew awake?"

The squire spun around, stared at her and nearly fell backward into the fire. "Lady Alicia!" he gasped. "'Tis early in the day to pay a call." He wrung his hands and cast a quick glance at the closed flaps.

Alicia knew exactly why Andrew's loyal squire looked like a little boy caught with of crock of honey. She circled around the fire. "Since you are preparing Andrew's shaving water, I presume that he *is* awake."

Jeremy planted himself in front of the entrance. He practically quaked in her presence. "Aye, my lady, but he is not yet dressed."

Enjoying the squire's obvious discomfort, Alicia cocked her head and gave him an innocent smile. "Oh? Methought I heard he had a young woman whom he had taken under his wing. Is this not true, Jeremy?"

The boy licked his lips and looked miserable. "Nay…that is…aye, but tis not what you think, my lady."

Alicia pretended surprise. "But what *am* I to think if Andrew has a woman in his tent and yet you say he is not dressed? Come, come, Jeremy. You answer out of both sides of your mouth."

The perspiring squire backed up against the entrance. "My master is not *fully* dressed, my lady. Not for receiving visitors. But he is properly attired in his hose and shirt. Truly things are not what they seem to be."

Alicia chuckled. "I shall be the judge of that. Announce me!"

The youth swallowed. "God shield me," he whispered under his breath. Then he ducked into the tent.

Alicia followed him inside. Twenty years of raising Brandon and Guy had taught their mother to take the advantage of surprise.

Andrew sat on a folding stool with his back to her. As Jeremy had said, he was indeed clothed informally. "No cooperation, no breakfast," he admonished the young girl who stood in the center of his ornate rug with his lute book in her hands and fire in her green eyes.

"How can you expect me to balance this bleeding book on my head when my head is light for want of food, my lord, and how can you—?" She spied Alicia, gasped, then dropped into a perfect curtsy fit for the king, except for the fact that the child was dressed in only a night shift.

Andrew looked over his shoulder. His hazel eyes widened. With the grace of a dancer, he rose and bowed to his unexpected guest. "Lady Alicia, welcome to my humble dwelling. You are abroad early this morning." He flushed a little. "You have trapped me in my lair."

Alicia returned his smile. "Aye, Andrew. Now, do not stand there like a dolt. Introduce me to your charming companion."

He extended his hand to the girl. "Good countess, I have the pleasure to present my protégée, Rosie of Southwark. Rosie, my dear, I have the honor to present you to Lady Alicia Cavendish, the Countess of Thornbury—and the keeper of my conscience."

Rosie swooped another curtsy and clutched the songbook for dear life. "Good day, my lady," she murmured more to the floor than to Alicia.

"Good day to you, my dear," Alicia replied. The poor creature trembled despite the warmth inside the tent.

Andrew snapped his fingers. "Jeremy! A chair for the countess!" To Alicia, he remarked, "Methinks I have overlooked my squire's training in certain areas. He should have given me fair warning of your arrival."

The countess settled herself in the armchair. She took her time to arrange her skirts around her feet. "Do not berate the boy, Andrew. Tis not his fault that I moved faster than he."

Andrew stepped in front of Rosie to shield her from the countess' scrutiny. "Wine, my lady? Or ale? Mayhap some bread with honey? A spiced apple with cream? Strawberries with cream? Pears with cream?''

Before Alicia could reply, Rosie muttered, ''All of them with cream, my lord, for I am perishing with hunger.''

''Rosie!'' he hissed out of the side of his mouth.

Alicia lifted her fan to cover her smile behind its plumes. It was worth going abroad early this hot dusty morning just to see Andrew so flustered. ''I should think that bread, butter, honey and some light ale would be delightful.''

Her host barked to his squire, ''Jeremy, to the cook tent post haste.''

Alicia held up her hands. ''Fetch enough for two, Jeremy. I do so enjoy to have company when I eat.''

Andrew waved the boy out of the tent. ''Be gone, maltworm!''

Thoroughly enjoying herself at Andrew's expense, Alicia again held up her hand to stop the squire's departure. ''And some spiced apples, methinks. Tell me, Rosie, are you partial to spiced apples or baked pears?''

Rosie peeked around Andrew's broad shoulders. Her green eyes were simply enormous. ''Both, so please you, my lady.''

Andrew fidgeted. ''Rosie! Retire and get dressed!''

Alicia chuckled behind her fan. ''Nay, Andrew, you have mistook my purpose and meaning. Tis *you* who must retire—outside, if you please. Twill do you a world of good to shave and break your fast in the fresh air.''

He looked aghast. ''But, Lady Alicia—!''

She shot him a no-nonsense look. Even her grown sons quailed before one of those expressions. It gratified her to see that she had not yet lost her power over her husband's former squire. ''Shoo, Andrew! Out! I did not come to banter pleasantries with you but to have some serious conference with your Rosie.''

Jeremy snickered but his master's glare silenced the boy. The squire bolted out of the tent. Andrew mustered his best smile and bowed to Alicia.

''As you wish, dear lady, but you do realize that I will probably become the laughingstock of my immediate neighbors when they see that I have been routed from my domicile and must content myself to gnaw stale bread crusts under the blazing sun and in full view of every jackanapes who might happen to stroll by.''

Alicia nodded. ''Of course, Andrew. You will survive the experience, I warrant, and will turn it into a jest or two—at my expense, no doubt.''

For a brief moment, his expression grew sober. ''Never would I hold you up to ridicule, my lady. My life upon it.''

His heartfelt loyalty pleased the countess. She promised herself not to chide him too much for he had a good heart, even if his ways were extremely worldly. ''I am glad to hear it. Now, away with you. Rosie, draw up that stool and sit by me. I promise that I will not bite you.''

The girl placed the book carefully on one of the chests. ''Never thought you would, my lady,'' she murmured. She fetched the stool.

Andrew looked at them, then gave a deep sigh of regret. ''Two beautiful women within my own tent, and I must be sent away?''

Alicia smiled behind the feathers again. ''Aye, Andrew. Twill not be for long. Then I shall bore you to death with my company.''

A wry smile wreathed his lips. ''I had thought you might. Therefore, I will go—but not far, lest you might need me for something. Enjoy your breakfast. Rosie, mind your manners.''

She nodded several times. ''Aye, my lord. I will try.''

With another exaggerated bow, Andrew finally departed. Rosie shifted on her seat and twisted her fingers in her lap.

Alicia regarded the nervous girl. ''Methinks that you find yourself in a confusing state and do not know which way the wind will blow next,'' she remarked in a soft voice.

Rosie sighed. ''Aye, tis the nut and core of it, my lady.''

Alicia nodded. ''I can understand that. I was once in your position.''

The girl blinked. ''How now? Begging your pardon, my lady, but you could never have been a harlot.''

Alicia sucked in her breath. Her sister-in-law had not told her the exact particulars about Andrew's latest adventure. She fanned herself while she contemplated this latest tidbit. ''You don't *look* like a whore.''

Rosie shrugged. ''I am and am not, so to speak.'' She wiped her hands on her shift. ''Pray forgive me, my lady. Haint ever spoke to a countess afore. I mean, I *have never* spoke to a countess. Did I say that right?'' Her beautiful eyes begged for approval.

The last shred of Alicia's objections melted like ice in the hot June sun. ''Aye, Rosie, you spoke that right well.''

The girl sighed with relief. ''Thank you, my lady. Sir Andrew would scratch out another penny from my slate if he thought I said something improper.'' She grinned again.

Alicia was too stunned by the girl's smile to ask her

what she had meant by pennies and slate. For a brief moment, Rosie had looked startling familiar.

Just then, Jeremy returned bearing a cloth-covered platter. He placed it on the table next to the women, then lifted off the cover with a small flourish. The mouth-watering aroma of fresh-baked bread filled the air. He poured two mugs of cool ale from the pitcher.

Alicia bestowed a warm smile of approval on the boy. "Splendid, Jeremy. Now go serve your master and keep him happy until I call."

The squire nodded in a respectful manner. "Aye, my lady." He backed out of the tent.

Without waiting for Alicia to give her permission to begin, Rosie grabbed her bread and honey as if it might disappear at any moment. Alicia sipped her ale and nibbled on a strawberry while she watched Rosie devour her breakfast. Alicia's feeling of familiarity grew stronger. Rosie's profile, the tilt of her nose, the way she held her mug—all reminded her of a dear, long-dead friend.

Alicia waited until the girl had slacked her hunger before she continued her questions. "How is it you came to be in the stews of Southwark? Your accent tells me that you were not born in London."

Rosie answered in between bites of a large strawberry. "Nay, my lady. I come from Stoke Poges. My foster father, God rot him, sold me to a bawdmaster for five shillings. Tis more money than he ever saw since—" She stopped suddenly and pressed her lips together.

On the scent of something interesting, Alicia sat up straighter. "My knowledge of the southern part of England is sketchy. Where is Stoke Poges?"

Rosie licked a driblet of cream from her fingers.

"Nearby Windsor town. I can walk there betwixt dawn and dinner."

Alicia gripped the ivory handle of her fan. Fenderwick lay only a few miles from Windsor. Dearest Margaret had eked out her loveless life inside the stone walls of that cheerless estate. "Who were your real parents, my dear?" she asked with an encouraging smile.

Rosie shrugged. "Never knew. Father Gregory found me on the altar steps of Saint Giles' Church at Stoke Poges. He gave me to the Barstows to raise—along with their geese."

Alicia quelled her rising excitement. Surely this changeling waif couldn't be the same child that Margaret had borne her secret lover all those years ago? "And how old are you?" she asked.

Rosie shrugged again. "I cannot count beyond my fingers, Lady Alicia, but my foster mother said she got me at the turning of the century during the harvest time." She made a face. "My foster father said I was a poor harvest for all the trouble I gave him, but he only said that after the money stopped coming."

Alicia felt a little light-headed. She sipped her ale and did a quick calculation in her head. Margaret had confided her pregnancy to Alicia at the court's Eastertide festivities in 1500. Since Alicia was also pregnant with Guy at the time, Margaret found an understanding ear. Alicia had welcomed Margaret's friendship and had even helped to shield her swelling condition from the watchful eyes and wagging tongues of the bored courtiers. Rosie was the right age. "What money?"

The girl rolled a large strawberry in the thick cream. "Father Gregory found a gold sovereign in my hand, or so he said. Every year after that, he found another coin on the altar steps on the anniversary of the day when he had found me. Said it was conscience money from my parents.'' She popped the whole fruit in her mouth, chewed it, and swallowed before she continued. ''The money stopped just when I began to grow my paps. That's when Barstow moved me into the barn. Said I wasn't good enough to live under the same roof with Christian folk because I was a bastard.''

Alicia detected a waver in the girl's voice. A knot formed in her own throat. Margaret had died of a chill and fever in the winter of 1512, having finally succumbed to the neglect and indifference of her cold husband, Gilbert. Her spirit had already died when her lover died of the plague shortly before she had given birth to their daughter.

Alicia sent a joyful prayer of thanksgiving to heaven. After all this time, here was Margaret's lost child—if Rosie truly was. Alicia needed to be sure. She buttered a piece of bread and remarked, ''I know exactly how you feel, Rosie. I am a bastard too.''

Rosie choked on her ale. She stared wide-eyed at Alicia. ''Ye jest with me,'' she gasped. ''Ye...*you* are a grand lady and a countess as well.''

Alicia shook her head. ''Tis true nevertheless. I was born out of wedlock to a great lord and his mistress. The difference between us is that my foster father loved me like a true daughter, and my real father had left me a goodly dowry. I was raised in a goldsmith's shop in the city of York until I wed my husband. We had been betrothed at a young age when my Thomas had not been expected to succeed to the earldom of Thornbury. I am a countess purely through an accident of fate.''

Rosie didn't speak for several minutes while she mulled over Alicia's startling revelation. Alicia wondered what the girl would say if she knew that Alicia's real father had been Great Harry's grandfather, King Edward IV. Some secrets were best left untold.

Rosie swept her hair out of her eyes. "No wonder you are a sight better than the other ladies I met yesterday. You know what it means to work for your bread."

Alicia smiled at her. "Aye, Rosie, that I do." She caressed the fan's feathers with her fingertips. "Prithee, child, lift your hair away from your face for a moment."

Rosie assumed a guarded look. "My neck and ears are clean."

Alicia patted the girl's hand. "I might have a headdress that would compliment your looks perfectly," she murmured. She did not think it would be prudent to divulge her real reason.

Still on her guard, Rosie gathered her blond tresses in both hands and pulled them back, revealing a perfect oval face and the fine cheekbones that whispered better breeding than a goose yard.

"Turn this way and that so that I can see your profile. Have no fear, dear Rosie. Your skin is as clean as milk."

Rosie wrinkled her nose, but did as Alicia requested. The countess stifled a small cry. Though not as tall as her mother, the goose girl of Stoke Poges was the mirror image of Margaret when Alicia had first known her.

"Twill do very well," the countess murmured. "You shall see anon."

Rosie looked directly into Alicia's eyes. "Then ye had best loan me that coif soon, my lady, for I do not know how long Sir Andrew's fancy will last. I could be back in the tent of the Golden Cockerel by tomorrow."

Alicia cleared her throat. "Ah, Andrew—I had forgotten him for a moment. Tell me the truth, Rosie, has he bedded you?"

The girl shook her head. A quick look of regret flitted

across her face. "Nay, my lady, he has acted right proper with me. Oh, I admit to you that Sir Andrew is a little odd in his habits and long-winded in his speech, but he has treated me as…as a little sister." Leaning her elbow on the table, she cupped her chin in her hand. "Tell me true, my lady, am I too ugly for him?"

Her question startled Alicia. Then she realized that the poor child fancied herself in love with him. He had that same effect on most women, especially his late wife. How could Rosie wonder such a thing when she possessed her mother's ethereal beauty? "Of course you are pretty," Alicia hedged. "I am sure many of your… ah…gentlemen have often told you."

The girl blushed and looked at her toes. "If you mean customers in a bawdy house, haint ever…I mean, I have never had any."

Alicia stopped fanning herself. "But methought you said you were a…a…" Margaret would weep without ceasing if she had known to what depths her daughter had been thrown.

"A whore?" Rosie gave her a cynical smile. "Not yet."

Alicia drew in a deep breath. "Pray explain, my dear. Others have found that I am a good listener and do not make rash judgments." *Your blessed mother for one.*

Rosie chewed on her fingernail, then stopped herself when she realized what she was doing. "Sir Andrew thinks I am a virgin. That's why he bought me two nights ago. The truth is I gave myself once to the son of our esquire on May Day." She drew closer to Alicia. "I pray, lady, do not think less of me than you already do. Twas a beautiful day and Simon was so handsome and so nice to me. He bought me sweetmeats and ribbons and he told me that he loved me. He lied, of course.''

Alicia squeezed her hand. "He seduced you." She wished she had the opportunity to throttle the perfidious Simon.

"Aye, in our barn. Twas the only bed I had. Some of the children saw us and told old man Barstow. He caught us." Rosie chewed her lower lip and looked away. "Twas too late for me. I thought Simon would protect me, but he did no such thing, of course. He thanked my foster father for the use of me, then he left without so much as a backward look."

"A puling slug, methinks," Alicia remarked. If Rosie had been their daughter, Thomas would have killed the debaucher on the spot. "Didn't your guardian demand that Simon marry you?"

Rosie shook her head. "Ha! He said he always knew I came from bad blood. He locked me in the grain house for over a week until he sold me to Quince. Said he would have done it sooner if he hadn't needed me to raise his children when my foster mother died."

The countess quivered with repressed indignation. There wasn't a drop of bad blood in Rosie. Her natural parents were gentle born. How dare that lout say such a thing! "I presume he told this Quince you were a virgin?"

Rosie nodded. "To get a better price. Quince thought he got the best of the bargain. He said he expected me to fetch him a fortune here. Tis why he saved me for this trip. Now I am at sixes and sevens. God knows what Sir Andrew will do to me when he finally—"

"He will *not* take his pleasure at your expense," Alicia vowed. "Tis well for him that he has not done so already!"

Rosie only sighed. "Your pardon, my lady, but I can tell you have never wanted for anything. Tis a cloth of a different color for me." Her expression hardened. "I must make my own way since I have no one to protect me. I do what I must in order to live. My wits are all that I have."

Alicia's good heart nearly broke. She wanted to take Rosie in her arms and shield the child from the wickedness of the world, yet she knew that the girl would disdain her pity. For dear Margaret's sake, Alicia must do something, but she had no idea what. In his cheerful, careless way, Andrew was unwittingly creating a person who was neither fish nor fowl. Rosie, by her birth, was already too far above the gutter ever to fall back into it, yet she could not continue her disguise as a lady unless—

Alicia sighed. There was one man who could transform Margaret's waif into the lady she was born to be. All he had to do was to say "aye."

Chapter Twelve

Rosie sopped up the last few crumbs of honey-soaked bread with her finger, then sucked them into her mouth. All the while she observed a curious flow of expressions cross the countess' beautiful face. *She wonders what to do with me.* Rosie straightened her shoulders and waited for whatever would happen next. Both women jumped when Andrew poked his head inside the tent flap and whistled.

"Hoy day, ladies! By your stern looks, tis a serious talk indeed. Have I your leave to come in yet? Tis as hot as hell out here in the sun."

His clean-shaven face was quite red and he dripped with perspiration. Rosie had never seen Sir Andrew look quite so uncomfortable. He mopped his face with his wrinkled handkerchief.

Lady Alicia waved him inside with her yellow-plumed fan. "Aye, Andrew, we have finished—at least for the present."

Smiling broadly, the gentleman swept through the entrance. Jeremy scurried behind him. With a burst of activity, the squire threw open one coffer after another and pulled out a number of items from each. Sir Andrew's

large boxes held the wonders of the world, Rosie
thought. There seemed to be no bottom to them.

"What mischief will occupy you today, Andrew?"
The countess ignored the growing pile of bright clothing
that Jeremy draped across the empty stools and chest
lids. "Do you wait upon the king?"

Andrew held up a beautiful jacket of butter-yellow
and bright-orange. Gold thread trimmed the buttonholes
and edges. "Nay, my lady. I am to demonstrate my skill
on the archery range within this very hour."

He nodded his approval of his squire's selections.
"Mind you, tis a waste of everyone's time and arrows.
The judges should award me the prize at the start. No
one need draw a bowstring in this heat." He grinned.
"All of England and soon France will see that I am the
best shot in the world."

Rosie wrinkled her nose. No doubt this outrageous
boast was merely another one of Andrew's wild jests.
How could anyone take him seriously when he wore
such garish colors? Or such tight hose? Rosie couldn't
help but admire his figure. For a gentleman of leisure,
Sir Andrew had quite strong legs. His thigh and calf
muscles rippled under the parti-color stockings. Her gaze
roved over his tight backside. He radiated a vitality that
drew her to him and made her pulse leap with stirring
excitement.

Lady Alicia smiled up at him with a motherly fond-
ness in her eyes. "Then with your permission, Rosie and
I shall accompany you. Twill be good experience for her
to see what a gentleman does."

"I already know what a gentleman does," the girl
muttered.

Andrew shot her a warning look. He had the ears of
a fox.

The countess stood and beckoned Rosie to follow her into the rear chamber. "Pray wait until we have removed ourselves before you dress, Andrew," she admonished him with a clicking of her tongue.

He chuckled. "I quite agree, my lady. The sight of my manly form would be too much for your chaste eyes. You would swoon within seconds." He held up a codpiece that was decorated with a golden sunburst. "Do you think this would distract my French competitors?"

The lady pushed Rosie behind the silk curtain. "How you do love to hear yourself talk, Andrew!" Then she pulled the drape completely closed.

Rosie felt more than a little embarrassed when she realized that this stately woman intended to play the maid and dress her. "I can tie my laces as well as you, my lady," she protested.

Lady Alicia chuckled. "Not if they go up your back. How your laces are tied tells the difference between a girl who works for her living and a lady who lets others do her work. Suck in your stomach and don't slouch." She pulled the laces of the pale blue dress she had picked out for Rosie.

The girl shook her head at the choice. "Methinks I will get this gown dusty in a trice if I walk about in it for very long. I have no money to pay Lady Mary if the garment is ruined."

The countess pulled tighter, nearly squeezing all the breath out of Rosie. "Tut, my child. My sister-in-law told me that she *gave* you these clothes. They are yours to mend or mar as you please."

"Tis true?" Rosie felt a little giddy and concluded that it must be because she could not draw a deep breath. "Spit in your palm and swear on the moon, my lady," she whispered.

Alicia smiled and nodded to her. Rosie turned her head away so that the kind gentlewoman would not spy the tears that shimmered in her eyes. Tears were a sign of a weakness that she did not want to admit.

Fifteen-year-old Walter Ormond lounged in the deep shadow between the canvas sides of the two large tents diagonally opposite the garish pink monstrosity that Sir Andrew Ford called his home away from home. The stripling curled his lip at the sight of it. No self-respecting Northumberland man would acknowledge such a confection as his own.

The sullen boy shifted his position on the hard-packed ground and wished he had not been so eager to act as a spy for Sir Gareth. To while away the time, he amused himself by catching the droning flies with one hand, then pulling off half their wings. He giggled as he watched the mutilated insects stagger and attempt to fly.

An hour crept by and the day grew more humid. Walter lifted his wineskin and drank a mouthful of the warm liquid. He looked up just in time to see a tall, dignified woman in a blue gown disappear inside Ford's tent. Though he had not seen her face, he recognized the wolf's head emblem that her bodyguard wore. Muttering an oath against his father's nearest neighbor and nemesis, Walter wondered why the Countess of Thornbury visited Andrew so early in the day. That fop had more women hanging about him than the wretched flies around a midden heap.

The next half hour proved a little more interesting. Sir Andrew, dressed in only a shirt and his hose, came out of his tent, sat on an upturned wine cask and was shaved by his pretty-faced squire. Walter had met Jeremy Metcalf once before and the slender-built boy had proved to be made of tougher mettle than Walter had expected. After a severe pounding, young Ormond had learned not to make any sniggering comments about Ford within Jeremy's hearing.

A number of gentlemen who were out to enjoy a breath of morning air before the sun heated the valley like a blacksmith's anvil stopped when they saw Sir Andrew and exchanged loud pleasantries. Sweat trickled down Walter's face. A pox on the lily-livered French and their peevish weather! The boy couldn't wait until this courtly farce between the two kings was concluded. He missed the cool greenery of England and the sharp winds that blew across the moorland near his home at Snape Castle. Walter swore he would boil his guts in fish oil before he ever set foot in France again.

Despite his near-nakedness, Sir Andrew greeted all comers with a jest and a hearty laugh. Walter had always thought the peacock lord soft in his head anyway. He wondered what the wench thought of Ford.

Now *there* was a dainty morsel! A ticklish feeling settled below Ormond's belt when he remembered the strumpet's bare breasts in the glow of the torch light. Sir Gareth had all but promised Walter that he could dally with her once the older man had sated his pleasure. The boy closed his eyes and rubbed himself as he imagined what he would do once he had the jade under him.

When he opened his eyes again, Sir Andrew and his squire had disappeared. The youth pulled himself to his feet. Hogsworthy would have his hide if Walter lost track of the girl's whereabouts. While he eased the crick out of his back, he wondered if he dared to move closer to Ford's tent and to spy within. On the other hand, he had no desire to tangle with Jeremy again—at least not on an even footing. He would get his own back on the squire on a dark, moonless night.

Walter stepped into the full sunlight and squinted his eyes against the sudden glare. He started across the open area between the tent pegs, then the tent flaps moved. The boy had just time enough to duck back in the shade before Sir Andrew emerged, leading the tall lady by the hand. Jeremy and the lady's handmaid followed behind them. The squire carried a longbow and a green leather quiver stuffed with arrows. Two men-at-arms, one wearing Ford's swan livery and the other the Cavendish badge, brought up the rear. Walter watched the company saunter down the broad avenue that led toward the middle of the valley where the tiltyards and archery butts were located. The toothsome whore had been left behind unattended.

As soon as the group was well out of sight, Walter sprinted down the back alley between a row of tents. He leapt over a reeking sewage ditch then he dodged around a large gray tent where stacks of firewood and large tuns of water awaited the needs of a hundred lackeys. Ormond cleared another ditch, equally as foul as the first, ran down a lane of modest pavilions, then drew up in front of Sir Gareth's.

Both flaps were tied open in the hope of catching the last of the morning's breeze. Just inside the entrance, Sir Gareth played at cards with Fitzhugh. By the smug look on Gareth's face, Fitzhugh must have lost a great deal of money. Walter sighed with relief. Since he was already in a good mood, Sir Gareth might reward the boy's message with a coin or two. Walter's debts were a continual sore point with his father.

The youth bowed to Gareth. ''My lord, Sir Andrew

has gone to the archery range with his squire and the Countess of Thornbury.''

With a pleased smirk, Gareth fanned out the cards in his hand so that his companion could see them. Then he gave Walter his full attention. ''And the wench?''

''She remained behind, my lord. Alone.''

''Guards?''

''None, my lord. Mayhap Sir Andrew does not value her much.''

Gareth chortled to Fitzhugh. ''Ho, my friend! Put away that peevish look. My luck has turned again in a widening gyre. I spy good entertainment before the noon hour strikes.''

He stood so quickly that he overturned the small table, scattering the cards and mother-of-pearl gaming pieces to the ground. Without a backward glance, Gareth strode out of his tent with Walter panting close behind him. Fitzhugh followed at a more dignified pace.

''Stand on watch,'' Gareth growled to the boy when they neared Andrew's pavilion. Then, the lord slipped inside.

Perspiration beaded on Walter's forehead. He had no desire to confront one of the Cavendish brothers nor their insufferable cousin if one of them should happen to walk by. Each minute crept by like an hour.

''A thousand devils take you!'' Gareth erupted from the tent and snatched up Walter by his collar. ''The wench is gone!'' He shook the boy like a rag poppet, then threw him to the ground.

Walter wiped the swirling dust out of his eyes. ''I did not see her go, my lord,'' he whined.

Gareth kicked him. ''You puling mealy-mouth poltroon! Did you think she would still be dressed in rags and filth? Not with Andrew Ford as her keeper. He has cleaned her up and dressed her in fine feathers. How many women did you see accompany him?''

The boy scooted out of the range of Gareth's boots. ''Only the countess and her maid.... Oh!'' He realized his mistake.

''Aye, you clodpate! Ford hoodwinked you! But *why* has he spent a fortune on this whore? That is the question.''

Fitzhugh ambled out of the tent's shadow. ''Perchance Lord Satin Britches dabbles in a double-dealing scheme, Gareth,'' he suggested in a gritty voice. ''Ford has always been a sly trickster.''

Gareth stroked his chin. ''Aye, he bears watching. Come!'' He turned on his heel and strode down the avenue.

Walter scrambled to his feet and limped after the two lords. He rubbed his thigh where a hard knot already formed from Gareth's boot. Ten minutes later, they entered the archery range where the competition was about to begin. The royal banners of France and England hung limply from their poles. No breeze stirred the dust of the parched earth, unlike the two previous days when a veritable whirlwind had made the shooting impossible. The sun climbed slowly in the hazy sky. A large crowd of spectators clustered in the wooden galleries under the striped awnings. The ladies, like a bevy of bright birds, chatted and laughed in high brittle voices while fanning themselves energetically. The gallants lounged behind their damsels and bantered amusing comments in boisterous voices. Neither of the kings nor their courts sat in the royal boxes.

Gareth mounted the gallery steps two at a time, then pushed his way along the back wall until he was directly behind the Countess of Thornbury. Fitzhugh and Walter followed. The press of the bejeweled audience in their heavy velvets and brocades made the rear of the gallery a hot and smelly place. Walter cursed his damnable luck when he saw Guy Cavendish seat himself next to his mother. Ormond flattened himself against the rough-hewn wooden wall. A protruding splinter scratched his neck.

Narrowing his eyes, Gareth clenched his fists at his side. "Yonder is the brazen jade!"

"The countess appears very friendly with the chit," Fitzhugh observed.

Hogsworthy replied with a mirthless laugh. "I wonder if Lady Alicia knows she is consorting with a common bawd. God rot it! She is even holding the strumpet's hand like a daughter's!"

Fitzhugh shook Gareth by the shoulder. "Lower your voice or you will give our game away."

The angry lord growled in the back of his throat. "Look now! See how Ford struts like an orange rooster. At any moment, I expect him to throw back his head and crow like one."

Walter mopped more perspiration out of his eyes with his sleeve, then stood on his tiptoes to see over the feathered hats of the crowd in front of him. A trumpet fanfare announced the commencement of the first round. Sir Andrew tossed his garish doublet to his squire, then fastened on his leather wrist guard. While the other contestants took their places at the firing line, Andrew drew near to the railing where the countess and her companions sat. With a toothy smile and many crowd-pleasing flourishes, he bowed to the women, kissed their fingers and received a ribbon token.

Gareth sneered. "What a farcical dumb show! Look

you, he is tying the harlot's ribbon around his arm next to the countess' favor.''

Fitzhugh chuckled. ''Andrew is going soft in the head like an aging melon.''

Before Gareth could respond, the crowd applauded the first bull's-eye of the match. The quivering arrow belonged to Sir Andrew Ford.

Rosie could not control her gasp of surprise. Andrew had hardly aimed before he loosened his arrow. She expected it to fly over the painted stag's head. Instead it embedded itself between the two white eyes.

The shorter Frenchman who shot beside Andrew gave the Englishman a scowl that would curdle milk. Then he pulled his bowstring. Meanwhile, Andrew turned and bowed low to the countess.

Lady Alicia waved her fan in return. ''Nod your head to him, Rosie, and smile. Andrew adores attention.''

''I had noticed that already,'' she replied, as she waved at him.

The Frenchman's arrow landed just below the stag's chest. He glared at his opponent as if his miss were Andrew's fault.

Without losing a jot of his brilliant smile, Andrew pulled an arrow from his quiver, notched it in his bowstring, turned and fired all in a single fluid motion. Rosie didn't see where the arrow went. *How awful! He must have completely missed the entire target.* The crowd cheered and stomped their feet.

She tapped Lady Alicia. ''How now? What happened?''

The countess paused her clapping. ''Mark the place of Andrew's first arrow. Now there are two, cheek to jowl.''

Rosie leaned forward and squinted at the target over a hundred feet away. Andrew's two arrows appeared joined at their tips. The exuberant lord spun around and took another bow which only encouraged the partisan crowd to cheer him louder.

Lady Alicia nudged Rosie. "Clap, or else Andrew will think you are displeased with his performance."

Rosie held up her hands above her head so that he could see she applauded him. When he smiled at her, Rosie's heart skipped a beat.

Three more times, both men shot their arrows. Three more times all of Andrew's hit the same mark while the Frenchman's shots grew wilder. The crowd did not need the judge to announce that Andrew had won the round. The Frenchman gripped his bow, then broke it over his knee. He tossed the pieces at Andrew's feet then stalked away amid the booing and hissing of the English. Andrew came to the railing again while the lackeys set up fresh targets. Guy offered him his wineskin.

Andrew tilted it and drank deeply. "My thanks, Guy, you were always a thoughtful squire." Then he turned to Rosie and beamed. "How now, my lady Rosalind! Have I caught your eye?"

Her heart turned a somersault in response. How dashing he looked in his slightly rumpled state! His loose shirt was open at the neck and a sheen of perspiration emphasized the corded muscles of his chest. His exertions had mussed his wavy hair and she thought he looked particularly raffish with a lock of it falling casually over his forehead. Leaning on his bow, he reminded her of childhood tales of brave Robin Hood. Andrew's virility captivated her, despite her attempts to quell the excitement that rose within her. *You have caught my eye, my heart and nearly all my wits, you rogue.*

Aloud she replied, "Aye, my lord. I am much amazed by your skill with the bow," which was the truth.

Lady Alicia chuckled. "Our Andrew has always been a man of surprises," she remarked with a knowing look.

He flushed and took another drink.

Guy leaned around his mother and winked at Rosie. "Don't let Andrew's gray hairs mislead you, sweetheart. He may be approaching his dotage, but he is still the finest shot in England."

Andrew returned the wineskin to its owner. "I salute your good father, Guy. He made me practice until my fingers bled."

The trumpets announced the second round. With a deep bow to the ladies, Andrew returned to his mark. Many of the women in the gallery called to him by name and waved in a manner that Rosie did not think was very ladylike. He returned their attentions with many smiles and blowing of kisses. His behavior irked Rosie and she fanned herself to disguise her annoyance. Some of those noble ladies acted as if they owned him. Rosie told herself that she did not care a whit. After all, she was merely in his employ for a brief time.

That reminder gave her cold comfort.

If she had thought his first five bull's-eyes had been pure luck, the next two rounds convinced her that Guy's remark was true. Andrew's final opponent, the Chevalier de Fauconbourg, had shot well, but even the French audience applauded Andrew when he was presented the prize of a purse of coins.

He rejoined his ladies in high good humor. "Didn't I tell you, my dears? Didn't I say they should have awarded me the prize two hours ago? Ah, but it gave me good cheer to tweak the noses of those Frenchmen just a little. They have such remarkably long noses to tweak.''

Lady Alicia patted his hand like an indulgent mother, then she tapped Guy. ''Rosie said she would love to see your new warhorse.''

Rosie gasped. ''Haint, I mean, I never said—''

Guy made a face. ''But, mother—''

The countess interrupted both of them with a silvery laugh. ''Nonsense! Of course Rosie must visit Moonglow. Guy, take the child and, mind you, no meddling with her.'' She gave her son a very stern look. ''Need I make myself any clearer?''

Guy looked faintly insulted. ''Nay, mother, I grasp your meaning to the hilt.'' He took Rosie's arm and pulled her from her seat. ''Come, Lady Rosalind, allow me to introduce you to my horse.'' In a lower tone, he muttered in her ear, ''Did you know that a whore and a horse make good company for a man can ride both equally well?''

Rosie pinched the back of his hand and was pleased to see his grimace. ''Mind your good mother, my lord. You are to treat me like a blessed lady.''

He arched his eyebrow mischievously. ''Blessed ladies do not pinch.'' He helped her down the steps.

Lady Alicia turned to the victor of the archery match. ''Now, good Andrew, attend me for I have serious news to pour into your ear.''

Chapter Thirteen

The viewing of the horse was not a success. Rosie had rarely been close to one before, and Moonglow was an enormous beast. She stayed well back while Guy spoke to it in loving tones and fed it a carrot.

"He's skittish because he's young and did not like to travel across the Channel," he explained. "But you need not fear him, Rosie. He's only a big baby at heart."

She did not budge. "Haint afeard, my lord. Not of anything." She tossed her head to give her lie an appearance of truth.

A faint light twinkled in the depths of his cobalt eyes. Guy whispered to his horse. "Methinks the lady protests too much."

Rosie was relieved when he finally returned her to the archery range. The gallery was practically empty except for Andrew who sat on the narrow bench close to Lady Alicia. The subject of their discussion must have been dire indeed, for Rosie had never seen Andrew look so serious. The two men-at-arms lolled at the base of the steps while Jeremy practiced his own marksmanship at the firing line.

Guy stopped at the bottom of the stairs. "Have we

been gone long enough, mother, or should I take Rosie to look at kennels as well?''

The two glanced up from their conversation and both smiled, not at Guy, but at Rosie. She experienced a ticklish prickling on the back of her neck. *They have been a-talking about me.* She lifted her head with a confidence she did not feel. *Mayhap Lady Alicia has put a large flea in Andrew's ear for buying a whore.*

The countess rose and shook out her skirts. ''Nay, Guy, no need to go larking off to the hounds on such a hot noontime. We are finished and I am parched with thirst.'' She gave her hand to Andrew who kissed it with great tenderness. ''Adieu, my friend, and remember all that I have said, or twill grow heavy on your conscience by and by.''

''Never fear, my lady. Your words are engraved upon my soul.''

Guy helped his mother down the steep stairway. ''Shall I accompany you back to the tent?''

She smiled at him. ''Nay, my boy. Off with you, but do not forget you are to joust with the king this afternoon. I shall applaud you anon.''

He kissed her on the cheek. ''And I shall wear your favor.'' He waved to Andrew and gave Rosie an exaggerated wink. ''Come see Moonglow take the course this afternoon, sweetheart. I know how much you liked him.'' Without waiting for her retort, he strode off toward the center of the English encampment.

Lady Alicia took Rosie's hand in hers. ''And just how did you find Guy's precious horse, my dear?''

Rosie swallowed back what she really thought of the charcoal-gray brute. ''He's mickle big, my lady.''

She laughed lightly. ''In case it has missed your no-

tice, I do have large sons.'' Then she bent down and
kissed Rosie on the forehead.

Her kindness took Rosie completely by surprise. Her
cheeks heated with shame. ''Ye...you should not have
done that, my lady,'' she murmured, not looking at her.
''I hain...*am not* worth an oyster to you.''

Lady Alicia cupped Rosie's chin in her soft hand and
smiled down at her with a wrenching tenderness in her
eyes. ''Oh, my dear child, you are worth far more than
you can possibly imagine.'' Then she gave herself a little
shake and released the confused girl from her thrall. ''La
and a day, Andrew! I am gone. Take good care of this
sweetling until we meet again. Reece!'' she called to her
bodyguard. ''I expect you are wanting your dinner by
now. Come!''

With another laugh and a girlish wave, the Countess
of Thornbury departed. Andrew came down the steps
one at a time, as if he carried an enormous burden on
his shoulders.

''Are you tired, my lord?'' Rosie asked him.

His serious expression melted into a brilliant smile.
''Nay, lass, I am newborn this very moment. Great Jove,
Rosie! You *are* a gladsome feast for my eyes.''

She wondered if he had drunk too much of Guy's
wine. Andrew gazed upon her with warm approval, the
lines around his mouth curling with a new tenderness.
She felt a curious swooping pull in her breast. *Tis only
hunger for me, and sunstroke for him.*

Alicia's revelation had opened Andrew's eyes. Now
that he knew who Rosie's mother probably was, he saw
the resemblance immediately. He had been an ass not to
have caught it earlier, but he had never expected to
chance upon a jewel in a dunghill. Rosie was the femi-

nine image of her older brother. Andrew sighed. Lady Alicia had given him the task of telling that rascal. Andrew feared that the surprised brother would not take the news with good grace. In the meantime, Andrew resolved to redouble Rosie's schooling. Since she was born to a gentle estate, the sooner she learned how to act like a lady, the more likely her brother would accept her.

Rosie put her hands on her hips and cocked her head. "Methinks your success has given you a headache. Do you want to lie down?"

Andrew swallowed hard at the suggestion. In all honesty, he wanted to lie next to her and teach her a number of unladylike things. Instead, he turned his smile up a notch. "I am as right as rain—if any ever falls on this wretched valley." He hefted his purse of coins. "And I have something that begs to be spent, lest it burns a hole in my pouch. Jeremy!" He signaled his squire to join them.

Jeremy retrieved his spent arrows, then trotted over to his master. With a wink and a chuckle at the perspiring boy, Andrew drew a silver farthing from his prize money. The squire's eyes widened when his master dropped the coin into his palm.

"You have done well this morning, my boy." Andrew clapped the surprised youth on his back. "I decree that the rest of this most glorious day will be spent by all of us in the hearty pursuit of pleasure. Therefore, Jeremy, return my equipage to our domicile on winged feet, then spend this trifle on whatever pleases your fancy."

Jeremy glanced at Rosie who shrugged her pretty shoulders. "Have you been too long in the sun, my lord?" the squire asked.

The boy's stunned reaction only amused Andrew.

Sweet mercy, twas good to be alive! "Nay, my little waterfly! I am invigorated by its torrid rays—and by the shining beauty who stands by my side." He bowed to the bewildered Rosie. "Mark me now, Jeremy. We will attend to our own dinner, but, I pray you, do not return so pickled in drink that you cannot serve us a sumptuous supper. Now, be off with you, scamp!"

Jeremy grinned, bowed and took to his heels in a dead run.

With a chuckle, Andrew remarked to Rosie, "Methinks my good squire fears that I will come to my senses in short order, so he had best spend my largesse as quick as he can."

Bafflement tinged her beautiful eyes. "Methinks this new fancy of yours is madder than the last, my lord. You gave him enough money to feed a poor family for a month."

Andrew ignored the truth of her observation. He was in too good spirits to be pricked by his conscience. "Aye, but there are no poor families here, only we who have no cares in the world."

Her lovely brow knitted into a frown. Andrew placed a finger across her delectable lips before she could utter another protest.

"Peace, sweet lady. If it is your desire to benefit the poor, than we shall do just that." He gathered her hand in his. "Come, we shall lighten my purse and enrich a score of hardworking venders."

He led her to the outer ring of the encampment where merchants from many countries had set up a bustling trade fair. Their first stop was the food stalls. In short order, they had tempered their noontime hunger with a delicious repast of pigeon pie, piping hot apple tartlets, a crock of snails in a light garlic sauce, a generous handful of cherries and a wedge of pale French cheese. They washed everything down with brimming mugs of ale. Dark slabs of spicy gingerbread studded with almonds rendered Rosie mute with delight. It pleased Andrew to watch her consume the simple fare with such gusto and enjoyment. The child must have been starved half her life. He vowed she would never again feel the sharp pangs of hunger. Her pleasure made his own food taste better.

Andrew wiped his hands and lips with his handkerchief, then passed it to Rosie and gestured that she follow suit. He did not point out the cherry stains on her bodice. Why spoil her day with needless anxiety?

He clapped his hands and rubbed his palms together. "Finished, my dear? Good, for my purse is still quite full and you have ordered me to empty it into the coffers of these poor purveyors and craftsmen."

Rosie returned his handkerchief. "Nay, my lord, you mistook my meaning, but—"

He flourished the scrap of linen like a banner. "Say no more, my lady!" he bellowed so that several dozen people turned to stare at them. "I will take you this instant to the perfumers, and the glovers and the drapers!"

She gasped in the most delightful manner. "Haint ever—"

He held up his hand for silence. "Of course, I quite forgot! Our first visit must be to the jewelers! *How* could such an important destination have slipped my mind?"

Rosie tugged on his sleeve. "My lord!" she whispered. "You are attracting attention."

Andrew looked around him and pretended to be surprised. He jumped up on the bench that had been their makeshift picnic table.

''What ho! Good people, I crave your indulgence and your most excellent judgment. Regard my lady.'' He pointed to his blushing companion. ''Such fine skin, such a bright eye, such rosy cheeks. But soft! Look you, my good friends! No bauble graces this fair swan's neck! Not a pearl. Not an emerald. Not even a lowly garnet.'' He slapped his forehead with the palm of his hand. ''Alack and a day! What a churlish cad am I!''

''Sir Andrew!'' Rosie pleaded in a whisper.

He cheerfully ignored her. ''I admit it. I am a heartless brute.''

Rosie raised her voice. ''Andrew, sit down, I pray ye.''

He chuckled at her slip, then he continued his address to the growing crowd. ''A knavish, paper-faced pantaloon is what I am to have been so remiss. But, my lords and fair ladies, do you think I can amend this glaring fault? Will my sweet lady then forgive me?''

His audience cheered and several of the men shouted, ''To it, my lord! Deck her proper!''

Rosie blushed a darker shade of pink. She bent her head and studied her hands in confusion. Andrew acknowledged the command of his audience, then he jumped down beside her.

''There, sweetheart. You have heard the *vox populi*— the voice of the people. I must take you forthwith to the nearest jeweler or I shall never again dare to show my face among this good company.'' He took her hand. ''Come along like a good girl, and pray, do not make a scene.''

Utter astonishment etched her pretty face, then she replied in a fierce whisper, ''That was the grandest piece of tomfoolery that ever I clapped eyes on.''

He squeezed her hand. ''Exactly!''

Andrew hummed a little tune as he all but pulled Rosie through the holiday crowds. "Now, if I were an enterprising seller of baubles and beads, where would I set up my booth?" he bantered. How utterly charming Rosie looked when she was completely mystified. He must mystify her more often.

He spied his neighbors. "Good day, Sir Jeffrey and Lady Karina! Gloriously hot, isn't it? Lady Rosalind, here is Sir Jeffrey, a good friend and most excellent jouster." Andrew whispered "Curtsy" under his breath.

Rosie executed a perfect reverence. He had to admit that she had learned that maneuver right well.

"My lord, my lady," she murmured in a soft, dovelike tone.

After an exchange of a few more idle pleasantries, the Brownlows moved on. Rosie opened her mouth to say something, but Andrew forestalled her by spying the elder Cavendish brother.

"A pox on him," Rosie muttered as Andrew dragged her over to Brandon. "These Cavendishes sprout out of the ground like weeds."

"Smile, my dear! Brandon is your dearest friend and, by my beard—if I had one—it looks as if he has bought some fortunate young lady a pretty frippery. What ho, Brandon!"

The blond giant gave him a sick smile and attempted to hide the length of lace he had just purchased. Andrew swooped down on him, plucked the creamy bit of froth out of Brandon's hand and made a great show of examining it.

"How now, my boy, what have we here? Do you plan to wear this in the tournament this afternoon?"

Brandon puffed out his cheeks with resignation. "'Tis for a cheerful wench who has given me great pleas... "

He coughed and looked at Rosie, "Your pardon, *Lady* Rosalind. A gentlemen does not speak of such tales when a *lady* is present, does he, Andrew?" He snatched the lace out of Andrew's hands and stuffed the item into his pouch. "If you must know all, tis to trim her petticoat."

"Ah!" Andrew nodded as if Brandon had just revealed the secret of the ages. "But does this generous wench *possess* a petticoat to trim? That is the burning question."

Brandon chuckled. "I will investigate that when next I see her. Good day, Andrew, Rosie." Then he leaned down and whispered in her ear. "You are doing very well, sweetheart."

Rosie did a poor job of hiding her grin at his compliment. "So are you, it seems, my lord," she replied pertly.

With a wink to Andrew, Brandon disappeared into the crowd. Andrew led Rosie down the row of bright-colored stalls. Suddenly, she gripped his arm.

"The devil take him! Tis Quince, and he is coming straight for us." She halted and half turned away from Andrew. "Quick, my lord, afore he spies me."

Andrew shot a quick glance at the bawdmaster. Though the odious man drew closer, he made no sign that he had recognized Rosie. Andrew stepped between her and the oncoming Quince. Dipping his head slightly, he said in an undertone, "Take courage, my sweet. Ladies do not walk with their heads down unless they are in church during Lent."

Her lower lip trembled and her complexion had turned pale. "If Quince sees me, he will take me back. I know it."

Andrew looked briefly over his shoulder. Quince was

almost within earshot. "Hold up your head, Rosie," he instructed her in a firm voice. "Do not look at him, look *through* him. Tis an old ploy we of the upper crust use to avoid pesky creditors. To it with verve!"

Taking a deep breath, Rosie lifted her chin, and assumed all the dignity she could muster. Squeezing her cold hand for reassurance, Andrew led her past the greasy seller of flesh. As they swept by him, Quince doffed his stained cap.

"Good day, my lord and lady," he greeted them in a smarmy voice.

Andrew pretended that he did not hear the man, though he watched his every move out of the corner of his half-lidded eye. Quince did not slacken his pace but kept on going, bowing and scraping to every gentleman in the throng. After a few tense minutes, Quince completely disappeared.

"Be light of heart, Rosie. He is gone."

She shivered and still clung to his sleeve. "He will beat me within an inch of my life if he realizes he just bowed to me. God's teeth! If I were a man, I would cut out his heart in this marketplace!"

One corner of Andrew's mouth twisted upward in a sneer. "Trust in me. I will render that piece of crow's meat into thin strips of parboiled fat if he ever again lays but a finger upon you."

She snorted in an unladylike fashion. "Trust, my lord? You speak very bravely—for now—but what will become of me in July, I wonder?" She did not look at him, but stared straight ahead. Her green eyes hardened into chips of ice.

Andrew did not know how to answer her. He was not sure what would happen to her once her brother knew of her existence. As he wrestled with this dilemma, he noticed a hanging sign that proclaimed the wares of a goldsmith from Flanders.

He welcomed the reprieve. "July is far away, but look what is here before us now!" He pulled her into the three-sided tent.

Rosie's solemn expression melted when she saw the glorious golden array spread out on a board covered with black velvet. "By my troth, my lord! Tis like someone caught the sun and conjured its beams into the metal. Haint eve… I have never seen the like," she breathed.

"Nor I," Andrew replied, basking in her happy glow. Rosie should smile more often. Her lips were made for laughter—and for kisses. He cleared his throat. "*Ladies* are always decked with the finest of the jeweler's art, and so shall you be. Which one do you like?" He pointed to a row of delicate gold chains.

She shook her head gently. "Ye…you cannot be serious. Twill cost all your prize, my lord. These are too fine for me."

Andrew smiled at the stall keeper. "My lady is overcome with the beauty of your art, good master. Allow us a moment to catch our breath." Then he bowed his head over her and murmured, "Banish your past, sweet Rosie, and enjoy what this day brings."

She leaned back and gazed into his eyes. "Teach me how I should forget to remember, my lord."

Her soft-spoken plea impaled his heart. He smoothed her brow with his thumb. "If I could, I would wipe away all your sorrows until your memory was newborn. Allow me to begin by draping you with sunshine."

Turning back to the display, he lifted a gold chain of exquisitely fashioned roses. "Here is a fitting necklace— roses for my Rose." He placed it around her neck and closed the clasp.

With a look of awe, she touched one petal, then another as if they might disappear at any moment. "Tis cool against my skin."

Cocking his head, Andrew admired the effect. "You will warm it soon enough." *I am already on fire.*

"Haint ever touched real gold afore," she whispered.

He cheerfully excused her lapse in vocabulary. "Tis your beauty that enriches the work." He turned to the goldsmith and spent a few challenging minutes while they haggled over the price. The necklace took most of his purse, but no matter. At this moment, Andrew felt far richer than his marriage to a wealthy wife had made him.

Rosie closed her hand over his. "My lord," she whispered as if they were in a church. "This necklace has cost ye far more than your wager. Are ye sure that—"

He stopped her mouth with a kiss.

Chapter Fourteen

Andrew had planned only to brush lightly against Rosie's lips, but once he touched their petal-softness and tasted the heady wine of her sweetness, he could not stop. Like a thirsty man in a parched desert, he gathered her closer to him and drank deeply from her wellspring.

At first Rosie stiffened with surprise, though she did not push him away. Then, as his tongue traced the soft fullness of her lips, she relaxed into his embrace. As he moved his mouth over hers, she returned his kiss with a passion that belied her outward calm.

Raising his head, Andrew gazed into her liquid eyes. "Ah, Rosie," he breathed. "You have bewitched me."

She ran the tip of her pink tongue around her lips, still moist and swollen from his kiss. "Is that what it is, my lord, or something else?"

He swallowed. *She thinks I expect payment for my gift. God help me, she is right.* "If I have offended you, my sweet Rosie, allow me to take back my sin." With a teasing smile, he bent down to kiss her again.

Rosie closed her eyes and rose on tiptoe to meet his embrace.

A harsh guffaw stopped them. "Casting pearls before swine, Ford?"

Andrew looked over his shoulder and clenched his jaw. Sir Gareth Hogsworthy, flanked by his minions, stood just outside the entrance to the goldsmith's tent.

The knave curled his lip. "I asked if you were decking a pig."

Rosie reacted angrily at the sneer of contempt in the man's voice. "Go to, ye waggish, evil-eyed moldwarp!"

Andrew put his arm around her shoulders. She shook with her fury. He gave her a little squeeze. "Tush, my dear. Pay him no mind. He crawled out from under a rock and is of no consequence."

Gareth swaggered nearer. He eyed Rosie's gold necklace. "Tis a sad waste of the jeweler's art to hang such a pretty piece on a whore."

She struggled against Andrew's grasp. "Bladder of lard!"

Several of the bystanders laughed at her apt remark.

Andrew tightened his hold on her. He feared she might attempt to do bodily harm on the reeky cad. "Remember you are a lady now, Rosie," he cautioned her in a low tone. "And ladies do not answer remarks tossed by the riffraff."

Gareth planted his feet wide apart and put his hands on his hips. "If that creature is a lady, I will eat my hat!"

Andrew chuckled to himself. *Rejoice in your ignorance, Hogsworthy. I would not give you twenty-four hours to live if the truth were known.*

Aloud, he said, "That savory dish can be arranged in good time." To the onlookers he added, "Pray you, good people, forgive my lord's vile temper. Tis an unfortunate affliction that he has borne since childhood. He would strike up an argument with his own shadow if there were no other victims in sight. My lord, we bid you good day.''

He led Rosie past the glowering knave. Gareth grabbed him by the shoulder and wheeled him around to face him. The man stank of poor wine. ''Hold, Ford! I will take what I have paid for—now.''

Rosie backed away.

Andrew chuckled nastily. ''Not today—or ever, my lord. A fool and his money are often parted.'' He shook himself free of Gareth's grip, then took Rosie by the arm. ''Speak to Master Quince, not to me,'' he called over his shoulder in parting.

Looking back at the irksome man, Rosie gasped. ''My lord! He has a knife!''

Andrew whirled as Hogsworthy lunged at him with a wicked-looking dagger clasped in his fist. He side-stepped the blow's full impact. The blade tore into his padded sleeve. A searing, burning pain coursed down his left arm. Still in motion, Andrew tripped his opponent. The heavier man fell facedown into a stinking puddle of mud and manure.

Just then Brandon and Jack stepped out of the crowd. With a boyish grin, Brandon placed his boot on Hogsworthy's rump. ''The footing is tricky hereabout, eh, my lord?''

The crowd laughed with appreciation.

Encouraged, Brandon drew his sword from his scabbard. ''If you desire a bit of play before supper, I am your man.'' He tickled Gareth behind the ear with the point.

Andrew groaned. He had no desire for his headstrong former pupil to tangle with the maddened Hogsworthy. Alicia would kill Andrew if Brandon were injured.

"Give way, my boy." He smiled despite the pain in his arm. "Do not blunt your blade on that thick gentleman."

Brandon bared his teeth with a sardonic smile. "Take our old teacher back to his tent, Jack. I will linger here awhile and amuse myself."

Andrew wished he had the strength to cudgel the hot-head. "Brandon—" he began, but Jack stepped between them and took hold of Andrew. He wrapped Andrew's good arm around his shoulder.

"Peace, old man," Stafford murmured as he half dragged, half carried his mentor out of the goldsmith's tent. "They say that when age is high, the wit burns low. Come along!" He glared at Rosie. "And you, too, wench. There may be some use for you yet."

"Jack!" Andrew retorted more sharply than he had intended. "Curb your tongue. Rosie is a lady and you would be wise to remember that."

Stafford snorted. "This jest of yours grows stale. When you sink to a public brawl over a common whore—"

Andrew summoned his strength in his good arm, and cuffed Jack. The blow staggered the youth and both men almost fell. "I'll thank you to keep a chivalrous tongue in your head!"

Jack tightened his hold on him. "Zounds, graybeard! You still have a mighty clout—and a blind eye." He shot another scowl at Rosie who followed behind them.

Andrew prayed his young lady would curb her quick tongue. Her temper matched Jack's and he did not have the energy to keep them from tearing into each other. Thankfully, Rosie said nothing.

How had the bright day turned so black? she wondered. She clutched Andrew's feathered hat as Jack led the way through the encampment. Every so often, Andrew turned his head and give her one of his endearing smiles. She tried to smile back, but the bright crimson stream of blood that soaked his sleeve and dripped from his fingers terrified her. His complexion had lost its healthy glow and assumed a grayish pallor. He now looked as old as his years.

Misery hung like a millstone around her neck. *Tis my fault, damn my cursed tongue!* She shouldn't have insulted Sir Gareth. After all, she was his inferior. She could wind up in the stocks for her offense, or worse, handed over to that vile lord for his own cruel punishment. Judging the black look on Jack's face, Rosie knew she would receive no sympathy from him. Stafford would probably drag her back to Quince.

A low groan escaped Andrew. Rosie hurried to his side.

"Don't touch him!" Stafford's voice lashed her as painfully as a whip.

"Peace, Jackanapes," Andrew slurred. "Tis only a scratch, but the churl has ruined one of my favorite doublets. Imported from Italy." He smiled to Rosie. "Bloodstains are the very devil to remove, you know."

She placed her finger on his lips. "Hush, my lord. You strain yourself."

Andrew kissed her fingertips. "Sweet Rosie."

"A canker rose," Jack muttered.

Her breath burned in her throat, though she answered nothing. A terrible bitterness mingled with frustration engulfed her. She swallowed the sob that rose in her throat. *No tears now!* She gritted her teeth.

Jeremy had not yet returned from his afternoon of pleasure seeking when Jack dragged Andrew inside his pavilion.

"Not on the bed, I pray you. I have only three sets of linens with me." Andrew pointed to his chair. "Put me there."

Once seated, he assumed more control of the situation, though the effort cost him. "Jack, pour me some redeeming wine. The jug is hereabout. Rosie, open that." He pointed to a brass-bound trunk. "In it, you will find a leather chest. Aye, good girl."

"Ha!" sneered Jack, handing Andrew a brimming goblet. "Good for nothing but trouble."

Andrew's eyes darkened. "One more word against my lady, and I will kick your carcass out of here. You test my patience to the limit."

Jack said nothing in return, but drank down a large mouthful of the wine. Rosie ignored him. She poured water from the bedside ewer into a wooden bowl, then soaked a piece of linen in it.

Andrew watched her preparations with nodding approval. "Untie my sleeve, sweetheart. As for my shirt, I fear tis a complete loss. Pity. I shall miss it."

"God's death, Andrew!" Jack exploded. "Cease this puling over your deuced wardrobe!"

Andrew raised his brows, then gave Rosie a wink. "Methinks our Jackanapes does have a heart after all. Can it be he is actually worried over my personal well-being?"

"The devil take you," Stafford muttered, pouring another drink.

Rosie said nothing. Using the gentlest touch, she cut away the gory sleeve. She sucked in her breath when she saw the extent of the damage. Hogsworthy's dagger had sliced a thin path from the elbow to the wrist. Blood continued to gush from the wound.

"Do not faint on me now, my dear," Andrew murmured.

She wrinkled her nose and fought a wave of dizziness. "Haint ever fainted." She wrung out the cloth and blotted the mess.

Andrew clicked his tongue against his teeth. "Ah, sweet Rosie, I shall have to deduct a penny for that lapse. You know better."

She didn't look up at him. "With all due respect, my lord, shut up."

Jack choked with rage.

Andrew merely chuckled, then held up his good hand. "No offense, Jack. I deserved that rebuke. Besides, Rosie gets her temper from her...an ancestor, no doubt." He watched her efforts to staunch the blood. "Hmm. Open the chest and find a small blue glass bottle."

Such a rarity was hard to miss. Rose held up the rounded vial. Andrew nodded. "Excellent! Uncork it and pour some of that powder into the wound—just a pinch. Tis made from the horn of a unicorn."

Awed by the mere name of that magical animal, Rosie carefully opened the bottle then sprinkled a glistening path of white powder down the length of the wound. She corked the bottle with reverence.

"There is a needle in that wooden cylinder and you will find a skein of black thread. Aye. Thread the needle and sew me back together again."

Rosie thought she would gag. "Stick a needle in ye?"

Andrew's smile broadened. "Aye. Do not worry twill hurt me, my dove. I hurt enough as it is. A little more pain is nothing."

Jack hunkered down beside Andrew's chair. "He used to sew us up after a few misdirected cuts with a broadsword, wench. I'll hold his arm steady. You mind that you make a neat job of it.''

Andrew sighed and rested his head against the high back of the chair. ''Jackanapes, you and I must confer about your insufferable lack of good manners. However, now is not the time. Two boons I beg of you. First, before sweet Rosie gives us a demonstration of her needlework, I desire another draft of that good wine. Second, I bid you swear upon…upon your dear mother's soul that you will not utter one more word against this much maligned maiden.''

Jack poured the wine, then held the goblet to Andrew's lips while he drank. A shadow of annoyance crossed his face. ''I do swear that I will say nothing ill to…Rosie,'' he repeated in a chill tone.

Andrew waved away the drink. ''Excellent! Thus fortified, I am ready. Commence your handiwork, my dear.''

The first stitch was the hardest. Rosie wavered when Andrew sucked in his breath at her first stab. Then he began to whistle through his teeth while she made several more stitches down his arm. True to his word, Jack held Andrew's arm steady. He sighed with relief when Rosie knotted the final stitch and cut the thread.

Andrew stretched out his legs. ''Now, more wine— not for my mouth, but pour it over my arm. Hold!'' He pointed to the bowl full of bloody water. ''I prefer my wine in a goblet or in me—but not on my rug. Jack, hold the basin and catch the runoff. Rosie, begin!''

He moaned when she did so, and gritted his teeth. When she had liberally washed his arm with the wine, she patted the injury dry. Andrew closed his eyes.

''You will find rolled bandages in the bottom section

of the chest. Two should suffice,'' he instructed. ''Bind me snug.'' His voice drifted.

Rosie located the clean linens. Deftly, she wound them around his forearm, taking care to keep the material free of wrinkles.

''You have the light touch of an angel,'' Andrew murmured.

''My foster brothers and sisters often cut themselves, my lord. There were seven children and it seemed one of them was always in bandages.''

Andrew nodded his head, though he kept his eyes closed. ''Seven is a mystic number. Now, Rosie, this is one more thing I need. Look for a small wooden box marked Poppy.''

She bit her thumbnail. ''I cannot read, my lord.'' There were at least a half-dozen boxes in the medicine chest.

Jack pointed to a small, fantastically carved one. ''That.''

She gave him a quick look out of the corner of her eye. ''My thanks, Lord Stafford,'' she muttered.

Andrew droned on. ''You will find a small spoon made of horn.''

He shifted in his seat and winced with pain. ''Now, find a clean cup, measure out one small spoonful of the poppy—not too much—and add water. Mix well.'' His voice sank into a whisper.

Rosie followed his directions, though her hands shook. Meanwhile, Jack eased Andrew's boots off his feet, then his doublet and paned breeches. Andrew winced and grunted with each movement. Jack held out his hand for the poppy mixture. His gaze bore into Rosie. Without a murmur of protest, she gave him the medicine. He supported Andrew's head while he drank it down.

Then Jack stood, and hoisted Andrew to a standing position. "Turn down the bedding," he told Rosie.

She all but flew to the inner chamber. As soon as she had smoothed the sheets and plumped the pillows as she had seen Jeremy do, she stood back while Jack lowered Andrew into the bed. Jack's tenderness surprised her.

"Will he be all right?" she asked in a tiny voice.

Jack placed his palm against Andrew's forehead. "He sleeps, thanks to the poppy. Watch for fever during the night and keep his forehead cool with damp cloth." He gave her a steady look. "'Tis strange for me to see him like this. I was usually the one in bed with something sewed up and drunk on poppy, while Andrew was the one who kept watch all night."

He strode out to the large chamber and poured himself a third cup of wine. Rosie licked her lips, but did not dare to ask him if she might have some as well. As he drank, he looked at her. When he finished, he wiped his lips with the back of his hand.

"You sew a fine seam." He poured another cup. "If truth be told, I would have puked my guts had I sewn him up. Here." He held out the cup.

She all but snatched it from his hand, in case he changed his mind. "Thank you, my lord." She savored the rich, red liquid.

He gave her a wintry smile. "We are not square yet, Mistress Rosie, but I will honor my vow. Take good care of him, or you will answer to me. Do you mark my meaning?" He seemed to grow in size, filling the chamber with his brooding presence.

Rosie stiffened. "Aye, my lord."

He nodded once, then turned on his heel and stormed through the tent flaps. She drew in her first deep breath since Andrew had been injured. Though she had never before thought prayer was worth much, she now sent a swift one heavenward.

The fingers of twilight had already crept through the encampment by the time Jeremy returned to his master's pavilion. The squire's smooth face contorted with anger when he saw Sir Andrew and heard Rosie's tale.

"This comes from playing with a polecat," he growled, his tongue loosened by wine. "You are to blame for this misadventure."

Rosie refused to be cowed by the boy, even if he was the son of a gentleman. The tongue-lashing she had endured from Jack had been more than enough. "I did not start the fray. Twas Gareth who drew his knife."

Jeremy stepped closer until he practically touched her. "Tis no never mind. *You* were the point of their dispute. Twas an ill-favored sea that cast you on this shore." Icy contempt flashed in his eyes. "Sir Andrew has never before stooped so low for his entertainment. I pray to God that he never will do so again."

Andrew stirred in his sleep. Rosie brushed past Jeremy. Though she held her head high, his words had pierced her straight to the heart.

Jeremy grabbed her arm. "Stay away from my lord. You have done enough for a lifetime!"

She wrenched free. "He may be fevered. I must keep his forehead cool."

The squire blocked her. "Nay, guttersnipe. You will not lay a finger on him again. Tis my office to attend my master in his need." He pointed to his rolled pallet that was stowed between two of the coffers. "*You* sleep there this night. As for the morrow..." He paused, his anger hardening his pretty features. "Let the devil take the hindmost—and you with him!"

Without waiting for her reply, Jeremy entered the bedchamber and dropped the silk curtain behind him. Rosie stared after him, her emotions in a mad whirl. She wanted to box the boy's ears yet beg for his forgiveness. His anger was no less than her own for herself. She wandered over to one of the stools, sat upon it and stared out through the parted tent flaps until the sky turned black and the lackeys lit the camp fires.

The only light within Andrew's tent came from a single lantern in the bedchamber. In the semidarkness, Rosie kicked off her slippers, then struggled out of her wrinkled, stained gown. She gave the garment a cursory inspection. Ruined beyond repair, she thought with a dull ache in her head. She balled it up and tossed it into a far corner. Then she pulled out the pallet, unrolled it as far away from the bedchamber as possible and lay down upon it.

Far into the night, she watched Jeremy's shadow move back and forth as the squire ministered to his master. Andrew neither moved nor spoke. Only his drugged breathing told Rosie that he lived. She drew her knees up to her chin and allowed a solitary tear to roll down her cheek.

Every accusation that Jack and the squire had spoken hammered in her ears. They were right. Andrew would be well and whole this very minute if he had never met her. Instead, come the morning, he would be the laughingstock of the entire English court. She could hear their jeers now. The most fastidious of knights had debased himself for the sake of a barefoot harlot. No doubt, Sir Gareth supped tonight and would dine tomorrow on Sir Andrew's notable lapse of good taste.

Rosie whispered a curse or two on Hogsworthy. Sir Andrew was the best of the breed. She had almost trusted his glowing promises. Now for his sake, she must end his insane fantasy, since he seemed unwilling or incapable of doing it himself. She would slip away in the darkness, and hide herself among the ragtag throng of camp followers. He would never find her there, even if he had the inclination to search for her. On the other hand, he might awaken tomorrow and be relieved that she had disappeared from his life.

Rosie stared at the drape and tried to imagine Andrew on the other side of it. Now that she had decided to go, she found no comfort in her decision. Her heart twisted with bitter sorrow that she must leave him when he was so ill. She knew he would think she was only a fair-weather mistress who ran at the first sign of distress. Good! It would be better if he despised her for her cowardice.

With a sigh drawn from the depths of her despair, Rosie got up and peeled off several of her petticoats, leaving only the plainest to act as a skirt. A pretty gown of taffeta did not belong on a common goose girl's back. She fingered the gold chain that she still wore around her neck.

She knew she could sell it back to the goldsmith. The money would be enough to buy her passage home to England. And once there she could pursue her dream of a life on her own.

Rosie undid the clasp and held up the chain in the weak light. The golden roses winked at her. Who would believe that a beggar girl in a petticoat rightfully owned such a beautiful and costly thing as this? her common sense asked. She would be arrested for theft and hanged before midday. No one would trouble himself over her fate. Rosie knew she had many faults but stealing was not one of them.

She crossed the rug on noiseless feet, and found Sir

Andrew's book of songs. Next to it lay one of his fine handkerchiefs. She wrapped the necklace in it, then opened the book and laid the jewelry between the thick pages. *If Andrew chances to think of me at all, he will find his gift here.* She closed the book softly. Then she touched the curtain.

Holding her breath, she lifted a corner and peeked inside. Jeremy sat by the bed, nodding toward sleep. Andrew looked peaceful in his repose, as if he dreamed of angels. She wanted to tiptoe inside and kiss his lips, just once, but Jeremy would pounce on her like a cat on a mouse. Instead, she kissed her fingertips and fluttered them toward her knight.

"Thank you for the lovely dream, my lord," she whispered. "I shall always remember you."

She allowed the curtain to slide through her fingers until it hung in place again. Then she turned and crept toward the entrance. After one last, lingering look around the pavilion, Rosie slipped through the flaps. The sleeping guardsman and the two lackeys who drowsed by the fire did not see her melt into the night.

Chapter Fifteen

Thursday, June 14

Andrew floated to the surface of his dreams. As he awakened, he drew in a deep breath. "Rosie?" he murmured.

"My lord!" Jeremy replied with relief in his voice. "You have slept half the day away."

Andrew opened his eyes, then grinned at the sight of his hollow-eyed squire. "And I perceive that you have not slept at all. Where is Rosie? Is she also wan and pale with the night watch? By my bones, I feel new made. Where is the lass?"

Jeremy turned away from his master and poured some fresh water into the basin. "She is not here, my lord," he mumbled.

Andrew detected the boy's evasiveness at once. He pulled himself into a sitting position. "How now, Jeremy? Where is my young lady?"

The squire flinched. "Gone, my lord," he finally replied.

Andrew knotted the bedclothes in his good hand.

"You let her wander out alone? You are as dense as pease porridge, you clotpole!"

Jeremy straightened his shoulders and gave his master a hard look. "I did not see her go, my lord. Rugby, who was on guard, said he did not see her on his watch nor did either of the potboys. She stole away like a thief." The line of his mouth tightened. "No doubt she ran back to her whoremaster with all of your valuables tucked in her apron."

Andrew glared at his squire. "Methinks there is more to this tale than meets my eye. If you are so certain sure of her thievery, take an inventory." He spat out his words contemptuously. Inside, he prayed. *Please, Rosie. Do not let me have misplaced my trust.*

Jeremy drew nearer to the bedside. "Please calm yourself, my lord. You will break open your wound and excite a fever."

"I will break open your head if you do not do as I bid, maltworm!"

Clenching his jaw, Jeremy went out of the bedchamber. He swore under his breath as he threw open the chests and coffers. Andrew lay back against his pillows and awaited the verdict while his fears mounted for Rosie's safety.

"What ho, within!" Brandon shouted from outside the pavilion. Without waiting for a reply the two brothers entered, accompanied by Lady Alicia and Jack.

The countess proceeded directly into the bedchamber where she seated herself beside Andrew. She produced a covered bowl from her basket. "You've done yourself a fine turn this time, Andrew," she chided as she uncovered the dish and stirred its contents.

His stomach rumbled with hunger at the savory aroma of her soup. "A scratch, my lady, and of no consequence.'' He lowered his voice. ''But it appears that Rosie has fled.''

Alicia nearly spilled the soup on the bedcovers. She quickly put the bowl down on the side table. ''Where?''

He shook his head. ''I know not, my lady.''

Her eyes blazed with blue fury. ''Boys,'' she called to the three young knights. They tumbled into the bed-chamber with jests and quips at Andrew's plight. ''Hold your rattling tongues,'' she ordered. ''Rosie has gone.''

Brandon shrugged dismissively. ''What of that? Good riddance, I say.'' He chuckled. ''At least, now I am excused from my wager.''

''Dolt!'' Andrew was so furious, he could barely speak.

Jeremy reappeared. ''All is in order, my lord. She has taken nothing.''

Jack cocked an eyebrow. ''Did you find a golden chain of roses?''

The boy shook his head.

''Twas hers to keep,'' Andrew mumbled. A pain of emptiness burrowed into his soul and fed both his anger and his fears. ''Well, don't just stand there like great oak trees, you rascals. Find her!''

Jack hunkered down beside the bed. ''Peace, old friend. Let her go. Count yourself lucky to be rid of her. Now Gareth will leave you alone.''

Andrew ground his teeth. ''I do not fear that puffed-up clack! But I do fear what would happen to my sweet Rosie should she fall into his clutches.'' He swung his legs over the side of the bed and tried to stand, but a wave of dizziness gripped him. '''Sdeath! I am as weak as a kitten.''

''And as addled as one, too.'' Alicia eased him back against the pillows.

His angry gaze swept the faces of the four young men around him. "Find her. Get my men-at-arms and my grooms to help you. Turn this wretched camp upside down and inside out, if you must, but I want my Rosie back here! Now!"

Guy shook his head. "You cannot be serious, Andrew."

"'Tis his fever talking," Jeremy added.

Andrew grabbed the brass candlestick from the table and hurled it at his squire. The surprised boy ducked. Guy caught the missile before it hit the canvas wall.

Jack's eyes widened. "God's nightshirt, Andrew! You have gone mad. You have never lost your temper before—not like this. The chit has bewitched you. You are well rid of her."

Andrew would have struck the prattling fool if he had the strength, but Alicia took up the argument for him.

"Jack Stafford! You do not know what you are saying. You will swallow your own words one day, I promise it!"

Andrew attempted to control his emotions. "You burn precious daylight. Be gone! Do not come back without her."

"But she is only a strumpet—" Brandon began.

With a roar, Andrew heaved one of the pillows at him. It struck the knave in the face. "Harken to me, you scantlings. Rosie is no whore. She is a lone, frightened doe lost amongst an army of wolves who would tear her apart if they could. She is more of a lady than many who call themselves by that title, and she deserves your respect and honor." His head ached as well as his arm. He swore at his weakness.

Alicia rose. Her stately presence commanded silence from all of them. "Fie upon you! You dare to call yourselves knights? Where did your oath of chivalry fly to? Knighted only two months and you have already lost it? Rosie is a *woman* who needs your protection. Is she not worthy of that?'' Alicia looked at each youth in turn.

"I will fight any man who swears she is not," Andrew added.

Tension thickened until Jack broke it. "I will search for her, old man. I treated her ill yesterday and I am to blame for this mishap." He looked at Guy and Brandon. They nodded.

Andrew released his pent-up breath. "We are *all* to blame, most especially myself. I took her for a plaything and lost a real lady. Find her for me, boys."

Alicia's lips trembled with her fear. "And pray she is safe."

Without another word, the three young knights left the tent. After sending Jeremy to the vintner's for a strop of wine, Alicia turned to the patient. "You must tell him soon," she said. She held out a spoonful of her savory soup.

He nodded. "Aye, as soon as they find Rosie."

"Pray God they do, or he will hate himself for a lifetime."

He dredged up a sigh. "I have done nothing but pray since I awoke, my lady. Do you think God will answer such a rake as me?"

Alicia gave him a comforting smile. "You are not as evil as you like to believe, Andrew Ford. Now, open wide."

The wind off the Channel whipped the dry dust of the Val D'Or into a whirlwind. Guy pulled his hat lower over his eyes and drew his cloak high across his nose and mouth to protect himself from the stinging flecks.

Twas a day to stay inside and amuse oneself with games of chance or love. Few persons ventured forth in this foul French weather. Even the rabble of camp dogs curled themselves into tight furry balls and waited for the windstorm to abate. Guy peered through the swirling dust. Where in God's name had Rosie found shelter in this?

An hour later, he met Brandon near the eastside stables. "Not in here, nor in any of the hayricks." The elder Cavendish wiped his tearing eyes with a corner of his cape. "I scouted Gareth's lair as well. He has a wench, all right, but not our Rosie."

Guy passed his wineskin to his brother. "Have you seen Jack?"

Brandon took a long swallow, then nodded. "Aye, he questioned the girls at the Golden Cockerel. They swear no one has seen Rosie since the night Andrew bought her."

Guy chewed on the inside of his cheek and considered their options. "Do you think it likely that she's fled to the coast?"

Brandon shook his head. "How would she know which way to go? Who can see a hundred feet ahead in this hell's broth? And she does not speak any French. Nay, the girl is hiding here somewhere. I feel it in my bones." He handed the wineskin back to his brother. "Go to, Archangel. Mayhap you are truly a blessed guardian after all."

Guy knotted his fist. "I owe you a drubbing for that, poltroon."

A half smile crossed Brandon's face. "At your convenience—later."

They parted on that note. Seeking temporary shelter inside the stable, Guy wiped the dust out of his face while he considered where next to look. Then he remembered his father's hunting lessons. A frightened animal will head for its burrow or to a place where it can become invisible. A slow smiled creased his face. Winding his cloak tighter around him, he plunged back into the lashing wind and headed toward the outer fringe of the camp where the vendors and entertainers huddled.

He spent the next few hours moving from booth to tented shop. Thanks to the ill wind, few patrons strolled among the stalls that day. He met some willing wenches with blond hair and green eyes, but none were Rosie. When he had almost given up, he found her.

A faded-blue kerchief covered her golden curls. With the sleeves of Andrew's night shirt rolled to her elbows, Rosie labored in the rear of a cook tent. A huge mound of glistening oysters were piled on the wooden trestle table in front of her. Guy pulled his cloak closer to his face so that she wouldn't recognize him. He lounged in the shadows on an upright keg and drank a mug of ale while he watched her shuck the oysters. The mottle-faced cook shouted at his row of sweating scullions and banged on his kettle of simmering stew for effect. Guy waited until Rosie picked up an empty basket and ducked outside behind the tent. He rose and followed her.

He found her pulling handfuls of oysters out of a large barrel of brine. "Good evening, my lady," he murmured in her ear.

Rosie shrieked, dropped her basket and tried to run. Guy caught her around the waist and swung her over his shoulder.

"Let me down! Haint done nothing!" She pounded him with her fists.

Guy chuckled as he turned toward Andrew's bright

pink tent. "Nay? What happened to the necklace you had yesterday?"

She grew very still.

"Spent it already?" he asked.

"Never ye mind," she retorted.

Guy thought he heard her sniffle a bit. *Serves her right for causing Andrew such distress.*

With her head hanging down like a neck-wrung goose, Rosie bumped against Guy's shoulder. She knew exactly where he was taking her and she tried to quell her rising panic. The constable would never believe her story and she knew that Sir Andrew would not be inclined to testify on her behalf. No doubt he was very angry with her. She closed her eyes. How long would they keep her in the stocks? she wondered. She clenched her teeth to stifle the fears that rose in her throat. She could stand whatever they did to her. The years with old man Barstow had taught her to be strong.

Since she had not seen where Guy was going, she blinked with surprise when he parted the tent flaps and unceremoniously dumped her in the middle of the familiar Turkish rug. There was a general round of "Bravo!" and "Well done!" from the assembled gentlemen.

Sir Andrew, dressed in a fine suit of dove grey taffeta with silver slashings on his sleeves and teardrop pearls decorating the front of his doublet, sat in his high-backed chair. His left arm was held in place by a sling made of scarlet taffeta. Joy at seeing his return to health bubbled in Rosie's throat, but she scotched her cry of delight when she saw the thundercloud in his expression. *He doesn't want me. Tis his gold he seeks.*

"Haint got your bleeding necklace," she snarled in her worst accent.

"Found her in an oyster barrel," Guy announced.

Sir Andrew did not twitch a brow. "Jeremy! Fetch the tub and send the boys for plenty of hot water."

A plague on it! He's a-going to drown me!

The squire leapt to the task with a smirk on his face. Rosie hid her trembling hands under her borrowed apron.

Sir Andrew studied her with his enigmatic gaze for several moments while Jeremy sloshed buckets of water into the tub. Then a wry but indulgent glint appeared in the depths of his hazel eyes.

"I perceive that you have spent your day consorting with the lowest sort of the piscine species." His mouth quirked with faint amusement. "Furthermore, your vocabulary has taken a shocking dip. I fear you have just forfeited two pennies." He leaned toward her and spoke in a lower, tone. "And I am sure that you did not sell your necklace. You have too much good sense to do that." His eyes flashed a pleading look.

A flicker of hope warmed her. She wet her dry lips. "Methought ye, that is, *you* would read a good book while I was gone, my lord," she replied, staring directly at him. "The one I balance on my head."

With a slow, secret smile, he nodded. "Ah, exactly! Brandon, fetch me my lute book." He pointed to it.

With a puzzled frown, Brandon handed him the heavy tome. Opening the book on his knee, Andrew found the page where his handkerchief lay. His smile deepened when he lifted the necklace from its folds.

"Behold, my dear! I have found something that has caused great distress among our friends." He shot them a stern glare. "My lords and squire, I thank you for all your pains upon my account. As you can see for yourselves, all's well that ends well. Therefore, I bid you a good evening. That includes you, Jeremy. Keep watch outside and discourage any visitors. I have seen a multitude today.''

The Cavendishes and Jack exchanged startled glances with one another, then they picked up their capes and hats.

Guy gave Rosie a stiff bow. ''I crave your pardon, mistress. Henceforth I will be your most humble servant.''

Brandon grinned and shrugged at the same time. ''You hoodwinked us all, Rosie. I am the better for your lesson in honesty. Adieu, sweetheart.''

Jack swept her an exaggerated reverence. ''And I, not to be outdone by my companions, do judge myself a dolt and ass, and I beg your pardon.''

Speechless with shock at this new turn in her fortune, Rosie could only nod in reply. Jesting and punching one another, the three young knights stumbled out into the howling wind.

Jeremy did not look at her, but he turned very red in the face. ''Wh-who would have thought it?'' he stammered. ''I am gone,'' he added as he grabbed his cape and followed after the others.

Rosie turned to Andrew. ''And now what?''

Andrew gave her an irresistible grin. ''Strip, my dear.''

Understanding washed over her. ''But I had a bath the other day.''

He nodded. ''Aye, but since then you have managed to perfume yourself like the Billingsgate fish market.'' He pointed to the tub.

Not sure if Andrew was still angry at her defection,

Rosie decided not to argue with him. She quickly untied her apron, petticoat and nightshirt and let them slide off her body. Without daring to look at him, she stepped into the steaming water and sank down. The warmth felt wonderful after a long day bent over a table slitting open oyster shells.

"Wet your hair, my sweet, then lean back so that I may have the pleasure of washing your tresses," he murmured near her ear.

She turned and saw that he now knelt behind her with his assortment of soaps and oils within reach. "But your arm," she protested as she watched him deftly remove his doublet and roll up his right sleeve.

He flashed her a smile that sent her pulses racing. "Tis much better now that you have returned safe and sound."

She ducked under the water for a moment, then leaned back and enjoyed his gentle touch as he worked the soap into her hair.

"Are you a-going to beat me?" she finally asked, not looking at him.

He paused. "Do you want me to?"

"Nay, but are you very angry with me?"

He poured a jug of rinse water over her. When she stopped sputtering, he asked, "Why did you run away? Have you been ill-treated?"

She wiped the last droplets out of her eyes, then turned to him. "Nay, my lord. You have been kindness itself."

He sat back on his heels with a perplexed look on his face. "Have I ever threatened you with bodily harm?"

She shook her head. "Nay, you have been very patient with me." She regretted her foolish action.

He narrowed his eyes. "Did someone speak unkindly in your ear?"

Rosie didn't answer. She refused to place any blame on the men who had spent the entire day looking for her.

"Ah," Andrew said. "I see that I have hit the mark. They blamed my little scratch on you?"

Instead of answering him, Rosie took a deep breath, held her nose and sank under the water. She stayed there as long as she could, then splashed to the surface. Andrew waited with several towels.

He wrapped her hair in one and squeezed out the water. "Youth is full of passion and fire," he observed in a husky voice. "My young friends are like squirrels, especially my imp of a squire. They chatter a great deal, but have no thought behind their swaggering speeches. Wisdom comes with age and wrinkles such as mine. Over time, I have learned to think before acting. Tis a lesson you would do well to learn."

Rosie looked at him through the veil of her wet hair. "You have no wrinkles that I can see, my lord."

Her compliment ignited a warm glow of pleasure in Andrew's chest. His advancing years often pricked his vanity and it pleased him that Rosie did not think him an old man. With a broad smile, he offered her his good hand and helped her out of the tub. He allowed himself the sinful pleasure of gazing fully upon her seductive young body and her innocent beauty. After all, he *did* own her, in a manner of speaking.

The bathwater ran down her flat stomach and over her rounded hips. The candlelight complemented the peach-tinted cream of her skin. He desired to caress the moist satin of her breasts and to suckle the pink tips of her nipples. Liquid fire surged through his loins. He wrapped

her in a soft blanket. For a long moment he held her
dewy body in the crook of his good arm.

"Ah, Rosie," he murmured in her ear, "you could
provoke all the deadly sins."

She giggled. "Haint ever." Then, like an eel, she wiggled out of his loose embrace and went over to the mirror where he had put the comb and brushes. Sitting on
a stool, she worked on the tangles in her hair.

Andrew drew in a ragged breath to steady himself,
then shouted, "Jeremy! Bring us our supper and remove
the tub. My lady and I have a great hunger." *For thee,
dearest Rosie, if I only dare.*

As if he were a mummer awaiting his cue, the squire
whisked through the entrance carrying a cloth-covered
tray. The youth did not look at either his master or Rosie.
Andrew would have boxed the boy's ears if he had
gawked at the nearly naked girl. Zounds! The blanket
clung to her body, outlining every delightful curve.

After setting the table and serving the food, Jeremy
turned his attention to the tub. Andrew dismissed the
squire from his mind. His thoughts centered on the fair
nymph who had set him afire.

"Will you join me, Rosie?" he asked in a strangled
voice. *In bed for a lifetime?* He cleared his throat. "For
a bite of supper?"

Her beautiful eyes gleamed with delight. She put
down her brush and took her place opposite his chair.
"I've had nothing but oysters."

He groaned inwardly. *She is stuffed full to the brim
with the food of passion.* He cleared his throat again. "I
am quite partial to oysters."

She wrinkled her nose in the most adorable way.
"Aye, but they lose their appeal if ye have nothing else
to eat."

Andrew didn't trust his voice to answer. Instead, he cut her a large slice from the fresh-baked loaf of bread. With a cry of pleasure, she slathered it with butter and soft cheese, then consumed it greedily. He quaffed a large gulp of wine in an attempt to cool down his ardor. A mistake of the first order! His senses spun.

They ate their meal in silence, accompanied only by Jeremy's rhythmic dipping of the bath water from the tub into buckets. Andrew had no idea what he put into his mouth. He could taste nothing but his growing desire for his supper companion. He chewed and swallowed but took no satisfaction from the food.

From the moment Guy had dumped Rosie on the rug like a sack of grain, Andrew had wanted to clasp her to his heart. The realization that he had almost lost her further inflamed his desire. He ached to bursting and he prayed that the leather lacings of his codpiece would hold. The twinkle in her eyes as she demolished a half-dozen boiled plover's eggs, the dimple at the corner of her mouth when she bit a dark, ripe cherry, her pink tongue that darted to catch the fruit's red juice—all enticed and beguiled him. He gripped the arm of the chair with his good hand and wished Jeremy would finish his deuced bailing.

At last the squire stood and pointed to the empty tub. Andrew fished a silver shilling out of his poke and tossed it to Jeremy. "Take the tub and yourself away, my boy, and amuse yourself in an educational manner." The squire's eyes widened with surprise. Andrew had been very liberal with his money. "If not educational, try profitable. In either case, do not return until after the midwatch."

For the first time that day, Jeremy smiled. He bowed to his master, then to Rosie. Hefting the water-logged wooden tub with a low grunt, he removed himself with appreciable speed. Andrew crossed his legs.

Rosie mopped the cherry juice from her chin, then cocked her head. "What are you looking at, my lord?" she asked with a charming half smile.

"You."

She fidgeted with her napkin. "Don't know why. I look like a drowned mouse."

He shifted in his chair and leaned over his nearly untouched supper. "Nay, my sweet, my eyes are glad to see you."

She flushed, then bowed her head in confusion. "And I to see you, my lord," she whispered.

He cleared his throat, then reached across the table for her hand. "Rosie, would you share my bed with me this night?"

Chapter Sixteen

Rosie sucked in her breath. His request and the gentle caress of his fingers sent waves of excitement mixed with fear coursing through her. She had dreaded the arrival of this moment. She would give the earth to lie with Andrew and to be his lover, but she knew he didn't mean it that way. He was claiming his bought-and-paid-for virgin. Ha! How was she to accomplish that trick so late in the game? Her precious vial of pig's blood was long gone. She shuddered to think what he might do to her when he discovered that she had duped him.

She took a deep breath, but didn't dare look into his handsome face. "You paid for that pleasure, my lord. Tis yours to take."

He kissed her fingertips and licked the traces of honey from them. The warmth of his tongue sent shivers up her arms.

"Nay, Rosie, that is not what I asked you. What I paid for were your services in my great counterfeit before the king. I did not buy a maiden's favors. I never have." He kissed her hand again. "Rosie, look at me. Will you lie with me for the sheer pleasure of my company?"

She longed for the fulfillment he asked, but she realized that her intense feelings for him had nothing to do with their business arrangement. He had never said that he loved her. He only wanted to take his pleasure, just like all the other noblemen whom she had met over the past few days. Women were merely the means of attaining that goal.

She withdrew her hand from his. "If you wish it, my lord," she replied in a calm voice. She must not betray how much he meant to her.

He got up and came around the table. To her shock, he dropped to one knee before her. "And what do *you* wish, sweet Rosie?" His mellow voice simmered with barely checked passion.

To be loved forever. She whispered, "Take me gently."

"Of course," he replied, with a significant lifting of his dark brows. "Because you are a virgin. I had forgotten."

Rosie wet her lips and girded herself with resolve. She owed him the truth, no matter what it cost her. "Am not."

He cupped her chin in his hand and swirled the pad of his thumb across her lips. "Not what?"

She drew a deep breath. "I am not a virgin." She closed her eyes and waited for him to explode.

Instead, he tapped her on the nose. When she opened her eyes, she saw that his were bright with merriment. "How now, my dear?"

She gave him a stiff little smile. "Well, mayhap I am practically one."

"Curiouser and curiouser," he murmured in a light-hearted manner. "Prithee, how can you be almost, but not quite a virgin?"

An unwelcome heat crept into her cheeks. "Twas this past May Day. Simon Gadswell—he was the son of our squire—bought me ribbons and sweetmeats and told me how pretty I was."

"He spoke the truth in that, sweetheart."

"And he kissed me—several times, methinks."

Andrew clasped her damp, clammy hands in his warm, dry ones. "I agree. I am sure twas more than once. No man in his sound wits would stop at only one kiss from your sweet lips. Go on."

She shuddered with humiliation, then was angry with herself for being embarrassed. "Then he…um…touched me and I…that is…" She buried her burning face in the hollow of his neck. "I let him take me in our hayloft. Simon made a quick job of it."

Andrew's good arm encircled her and pulled her onto his knee. Gently, he rocked her back and forth. "I expect it hurt you," he murmured.

Rosie gritted her teeth at the painful memory. "Aye, but he said he loved me for it. And I believed him, like a ninny."

"Naturally." Andrew's voice rumbled from deep inside him. "He got what he wanted. And I presume he abandoned you soon after that?"

Her mind burned with the remembrance of what followed. "Aye," she answered with a snap. "Tis why Barstow sold me to Quince. Ha! Quince thought he had gotten a virgin. He never knew the truth. Before the auction, one of the girls gave me a little vial of pig's blood to prove my claim…but…but I lost it." A knot of regret rose in her throat. "Forgive me, Sir Andrew, but I cannot bloody your bed. Are you very angry with me?"

He threw back his head and let out a great peal of

laughter. "Indeed not, my pretty deceiver! My sheets are made of the finest cotton from Cyprus. Quite costly—far more than I paid for a certain virgin. Do you think that I would wish to have them stained with the blood of a swine?"

Rosie couldn't help but join in his mirth, and her tense muscles relaxed. He stood up, bringing her with him, and smiled with satisfaction. Her heart turned over in response.

"Then to the question at hand, Mistress Rosie. I humbly beg the honor to show you exactly how a real gentleman cherishes his lady. I have a wealth of experience in these matters. Trust me, sweetling."

His affectionate teasing cheered her. For the first time she relaxed in the company of a man. They exchanged glances and a slender fragile thread of trust grew between them.

Rosie cocked her head. "Pray tell me, my lord, do your other lovers recommend your lessons?"

"I have never had a complaint in over twenty years."

She gasped at the length of time. "By the book, you must have started in your cradle."

His eyes shone with amusement. "Not quite *that* early."

He slipped his good arm around her tiny waist and drew her closer to him. He whispered her name, sending shivers of delight through her. She stood on tiptoe and wound her arms around his neck. Only the pressure between their bodies kept her blanket in its place.

Andrew lowered his mouth. She felt the heady sensation of his lips against her neck. She clung to him. His lips feather-caressed her with a tantalizing promise. Her skin burned where he had touched it. Then he moved his mouth over hers, and devoured its softness. Parting her lips, she rose to meet him and welcomed the velvet warmth of his kiss. She drank in his sweetness. When the need for air became pressing, he lifted his head.

"Will you lie with me and be my love, Rosie? I will prove to you all earthly pleasures."

Her blood pounded in her brain, her heart soared and her knees trembled at his words. Pretending to consider his offer, she glanced at him then said playfully, "Aye, haint got nothing else better to do this night."

Rosie's damp blanket dropped to the rug somewhere between the supper table and his bed. Though the evening shadows had fallen, the silken chamber took on a glow with Andrew at its center. His compelling presence entranced her. She looked into his eyes and saw the heart-rending tenderness there. Excitement rippled through her and her bare skin prickled pleasurably as his gaze caressed her.

"Ah, Rosie," he breathed her name like a prayer. He held her snugly against him.

She inhaled sharply at the contact. Desire rose in her breast.

"Do not be afraid," he whispered. "I will not hurt you."

She cleared her throat, pretending not to be affected by his vitality that hummed under her fingertips. "Haint... I mean, *I am not* afraid." She banished all the shadows of the past that clutched her heart.

His intoxicating scent of wood smoke and exotic oil from the East enveloped her. Dizzying currents ran through her.

His fingers skimmed down the hollow of her back. His touch was almost unbearable in its tenderness. The mere brush of his hand sent a warm tantalizing shiver through her. His uneven breathing fanned her cheek as he held her close to his chest.

"Give me your lips, my love."

Her soul sang in response. She lifted her face to his and rose on tiptoe to meet him. His lips touched hers like a whisper.

His first kiss was as light and honey-sweet as a summer zephyr. She quivered under its agonizing tenderness. He worshipped her lips slowly until she could stand it no longer. She laced her fingers through his thick hair and gave herself freely to his passion.

His tongue coursed over her lips as if searching for the entrance and she opened for him. When he withdrew, her mouth burned with his fire.

With infinite tenderness, Andrew eased her down to lie among his pillows. As he stood beside the bed, his gaze wandered slowly over every quivering inch of her. Rosie colored under the searing heat of his scrutiny. The prolonged anticipation of what would happen next was almost unbearable.

She reached up to him. "Do I please you, my lord?"

He chuckled deep in his throat. "Aye, Rosie, so well that all my fine speeches have flown from my mind."

He pulled his shirt over his head and tossed it aside. The candlelight etched the musculature of his chest and shoulders, giving her a new awareness of his strength. Her heartbeat hammered in her ears. She found it difficult to breath.

With a seductive smile, Andrew untied the three laces that held his golden codpiece in place. His appeal was devastating. A delicious shudder heated her body.

"Do I look too old for you, my dear?" Andrew teased.

She ached for his touch. "Nay, my lord. I perceive

no wrinkles at all.'' Her heart skipped with her longing for him.

He untied his hose and peeled them over his narrow hips, then down his hard legs that were corded with muscles. When he stood before her in all his manly glory, Rosie sensed the barely controlled power that was coiled within his magnificent body. She thought she would die for the pain of wanting him.

''Will you come to bed now, my lord?''

''Aye, my love,'' he replied in a low husky voice.

Rosie swallowed with difficulty as he dropped down next to her. He leaned over and kissed the pulsing hollow at the base of her throat. She purred and wriggled closer to him. He moved higher and nibbled her earlobe. Then his lips fluttered across her cheek toward her mouth in a series of slow, slivery kisses. His caresses were light, yet painfully teasing. She took his face in her hands and drew him to her.

Andrew smothered her lips with a demanding mastery. She wound her arms around his neck and held on tight. It was a kiss for her bruised soul to melt into.

When they finally parted, he cupped one of her breasts in his hand. She moaned with pleasure as he outlined the circle of its creamy mound with one slow-moving fingertip. His sensuous massage opened a floodgate of desire within her, quickening all her untried senses. The rosy peaks of her nipples grew to pebble hardness. He laughed at her delight when his lips brushed their tips.

''Do I tickle your fancy, Rosie?''

''Oh, Andrew!'' was all she could gasp. Instinctively, she arched toward him.

His sleek hard body caressed hers, hip to hip, thigh to thigh. His heartbeat thudded against her own. She molded her curves to his contours. Andrew took her hand and guided it down to the most private part of himself. He groaned when she fondled its silky smoothness.

"Hold, sweet executioner! I am not as strong as I thought I was."

He slid his hand between her thighs and inched upward to her core. When he touched her there, waves of fire throbbed through her. She writhed under his gentle torture and gripped the pillow behind her head. Never in her most wanton dreams had she imagined this ecstasy. She peaked and exploded in a starburst of fiery sensations. As she descended, she breathed in deep soul-drenching drafts of satisfaction.

Before she had time to relish the moment, Andrew touched her again, drawing her into another whirlwind of passion. She gasped as he lowered himself over her. With a whispered "aye," she surrendered herself completely to his love.

Together they soared into golden, fire-flashed heights, then burst into bright comets and floated back to the present on feathered clouds of bliss. Andrew's love wrapped Rosie in a silken cocoon of euphoria. Uncontrollable joy bubbled through her. She savored the deep feeling of peace that settled over her.

Andrew rolled onto his back and gathered her to him with his good arm. He breathed a long sigh of contentment. Pillowing her head on his broad shoulder, she tucked her chin next to his chest with a murmur of pleasure and drank in the comfort of his nearness. In one joyful moment he had unlocked her heart and bared her soul.

They slept for a while, then Rosie slowly awoke to find him nuzzling her neck. Her willingness shone in her eyes and on her lips. Now they took the time to explore each other, then to arouse and finally to give to each other the full measure of their beings.

When dawn's light filtered through the sides of Andrew's pink palace of love, Rosie watched him waken. The glow of his smile melted her heart.

"Good morrow, Rosie. Pray, what are you looking at?"

"Your own sweet self." She smiled in reply. "Without a feather, or a satin doublet or an outrageous codpiece in sight."

Chapter Seventeen

Saturday, June 16

Andrew lounged in the early-morning shade cast by his pavilion and watched Lady Mary teach Rosie how to play shuttlecock and battledore. Every so often his sweetheart glanced up and smiled at him. The dimple in her cheek winked provocatively. He smiled back. God in heaven, twas good to be alive and loved by so wonderful a girl!

Jack sat cross-legged beside him. He snickered to the Cavendishes. "What, ho, cousins! Mark how our esteemed tutor and his latest protégé bill and coo like springtime doves."

Andrew ignored that remark. What right did the infamous Jack of Hearts have to jibe him?

Guy tossed his peach pit over his shoulder and wiped his sticky fingers down the front of his doublet. "Aye, Jackanapes. Methinks old Andrew looks ten years younger than he did a few days ago. Could it be that he has fallen a victim of Cupid's arrows?"

Andrew paid no attention to the boy. Why should he,

when Rosie looked so delightfully delicious in her mint-green gown? He applauded when her racket connected with the feathered shuttlecock and sent it flying over Mary's head. He barely felt any pain in his arm at all—only a little stiffness in his fingers.

Jack cleared his throat for attention. "Since oysters have proved such an inducement to love, let me bathe in a barrel full of the creatures."

Brandon gave his cousin a telling lift of his eyebrow. "You need no help, Jack," he remarked. "Rather, a cold blast from the north to cool your hot blood. That, or a hot wench," he added with a sly grin.

Andrew frowned at the trio. "You are in the presence of a lady—of two ladies, in fact. Behave yourselves accordingly."

Jack chortled. "Oh? Like Guy behaves with Lady Bardolph?" he asked with a mischievous grin.

Brandon choked on his peach and stared at his younger brother. Guy flushed darkly and returned him a guilty grin.

Andrew shook his head. Guy was not yet twenty and too young to fall pray to Olivia's wanton wiles. "Rosie and Olivia are as alike as oil and water," he observed. He sent Guy a particularly pointed look. "I might add that Lady Bardolph is well-used laundry water. Take note, fledgling."

Jack laughed at Guy's discomfiture. "I second our good mentor's opinion—from personal experience. Ah, but Rosie! When she tires you, old man, give her to me for an hour or two of sport. I long to tussle with her."

The other two laughed.

Andrew's bile welled up in his throat. He resisted the urge to wring the young rooster's neck. Instead, he clapped his hands and called Jeremy to leave off polishing his armor and fetch the lute.

"You and you." He pointed to the Cavendish brothers. "Relieve the ladies of their rackets and partner them in a pavan. Rosie must practice her dance steps and I fear she has grown too used to mine. Jeremy, play for them and mind your chord changes."

With a bit of good-natured grumbling, the young giants pulled themselves to their feet and ambled over to the ladies. Jeremy dragged his stool out of the tent, and tuned the lute strings.

"Again?" Rosie called to Andrew when Guy offered her his arm. "'Sdeath, Andrew. You will have my feet bleed yet!"

Andrew merely waved the slate that he kept near at hand. "A lady does not swear, my dear."

She made a face at him, then laughed. Jack snorted.

"And what of me? I can dance a better turn than Guy any day of the week. Let me partner that delicious dainty morsel."

Andrew gripped the young knight's shoulder and shook him hard. "Rein in your voice and come inside the tent with me."

"Now? Tis as hot as sin in there!" Jack protested.

Andrew stood and glared at him. "This is not a request, but a command. Though I know you are now past my authority, I exercise it."

Jack opened his mouth to utter some vulgar oath, but snapped it shut when he saw that Andrew's merry face was serious. He scrambled to his feet, brushed off the dust from his tights, then meekly followed the older man. Andrew dropped the flap down behind them to insure their privacy. He pointed to the wine jug.

"Pour us both a cup, Jack. Fill to the brim for I have

thirsty work ahead of me, and methinks you will need yours before I am done.''

Jack turned a shade pale. "Have I gotten some wench with child?''

Andrew decided to let him sweat a little. Twas time the lad took some thought of his reckless frolicking among maidens high and low. "Wine," he ordered. He sat down heavily in his armchair and wished he had not promised Alicia that he would do this delicate task.

In silence, Jack splashed the ruby liquid into the silver goblets. His hand shook a little.

"Which one is it?" he asked as he handed Andrew his wine.

Andrew pointed to the low stool at his feet. "Sit!" he barked. For once, the prattling Jackanapes did so in trembling meekness.

"Rosie—" Andrew began, but Jack interrupted.

"By my life, Andrew! I have not touched her, I swear it!''

Andrew held up his hand. "Peace, you twittering fool. Allow me to finish for tis a hard tale to tell and one that will take away your breath.''

The young man muttered into his wine.

Andrew gave him a stern look. "Speak gently of Rosie. Would you say the same things about your sister as you do about her?''

Jack looked up at him with a mixture of confusion and surprise in his blue eyes. Then he grinned. "God's nightshirt! You caught me square with that one! So I have not got a little bastard on the way. Whew!''

Andrew did not flinch. "Bastardy is no laughing matter.''

The other frowned. "You talk in riddles, old man, but I will play your game. Nay, I would not speak about a

sister the same way as I do about a toothsome wench.
But you forget one important fact—I have no sister. Nor
a brother. Alas, I am an only child.'' He pretended to
sob.

Andrew kicked his kneecap.

Jack swore and rubbed it. ''I grow weary of your discourse, Andrew. Speak your mind and be done with it.''

Andrew wanted to toss his wine into the brat's face,
but it would be a waste of a good vintage and would
not help the situation. ''Very well, Jack. The long and
the short of it is this— Rosie is your younger sister.''

For the first time in memory, Jack did not utter a
sound. Instead a multitude of emotions played across his
face. Then he smiled. ''How long have you sat up at
night thinking of this quip? My sister is a whore from a
goose farm? Then I am the son of the Ottoman Em-
peror.''

Andrew leaned closer to Jack. ''Nay, you are the son
of Sir Gilbert Stafford and the heir of Fenderwick.''

Jack swallowed a large mouthful of wine. ''Sing me
a new song. I know this old tune already.''

''Our sweet Rosie is the natural daughter of your
mother, Lady Margaret Stafford, by a secret lover who
died shortly after her conception.''

Jack furrowed his brows. ''You *are* serious. Nay, tis
some perfidious claim that the chit has made for her own
profit. You are more besotted than I first thought.''

''And you have sheep's wool for brains,'' Andrew
replied in an even tone. He had known this conference
would not be easy. Jack had the stubbornness of a mule,
and on occasion the intelligence of one. ''How much do
you remember of your lady mother?''

Jack ran his finger around the rim of his goblet. ''She
died after I had been fostered to Sir Thomas. I must have

been thirteen. She was cold in the ground before I got the news.'' His mouth tightened into a hard line.

"And before you left your home?'' Andrew prodded with gentle care. Jack rarely exhibited his deeper emotions.

The youth shrugged his shoulders but did not look at him. "My father kept her in her apartments most of the time. Said she was sick and could not be disturbed by a noisy boy.'' A muscle ticked in his jaw.

Andrew chose his next words carefully. "Your father is a hard man—and a vengeful one.'' He paused and waited for Jack to erupt. When the lad remained silent, he continued. "As I understand the tale, he married your mother for her estates when she was little more than a child.''

Jack sneered at him. "Tis not unusual. *You* married for wealth.''

Andrew sent a silent prayer for forgiveness to Gwendolyn's innocent soul. "Aye, but I loved my little wife as best I could, though she never outgrew her childish mind. Ours may not have been a true marriage, but I made her happy with games, toys and songs. On the other hand, your mother matured into a desirable woman, yet your father sired you as a matter of cold duty. Then he returned to the arms of his mistress, leaving Lady Margaret unloved and unwanted. Can you blame her when another man offered her his love?''

Jack continued to toy with his goblet. "I know nothing of this.''

"You were only a babe in leading strings when your mother conceived her daughter. To save the child from your father's jealous wrath, she placed her on the altar steps of Saint Giles.''

Jack snapped his head up. "At Stoke Poges?''

"The very same."

The boy whistled through his teeth. "Tis a mere co-incidence."

"Lady Alicia thinks not. She knew your mother well and loved her."

Jack drained his wine. "Then I will speak with her. I must have more proof than your tale."

Andrew nodded. "She will convince you as she did me. But before you go, stand before my looking glass and search your face carefully, Jack. You look like your mother. Mark the shape of your mouth and the tilt of your nose. Remember your smile and laugh. Then observe Rosie—her face, not her body. If you are not blind, you will see the resemblance."

Jack crossed the rug and stared at his visage for a long while. Andrew watched him. The youth in the glass seemed to change and grow more mature. Then Jack gave himself a shake and turned to leave.

"One more thing, Jack."

Pausing midstride, he cocked his head. "Aye?"

"No matter if you believe my story or not, say nothing to your father. He will believe it, and Rosie's young life will not be worth a groat. Her mere existence is a thorn in his vanity."

Jack considered this for a moment, then nodded. "I would not have Rosie's life endangered, no matter who she is. I am not my father."

"Thank the good Lord for that!"

He gave Andrew a piercing look. "What will become of her?"

"I will take care of her."

His lip curled. "As your mistress?" He did not wait for the answer, but pushed his way through the tent flaps.

Andrew stretched in his chair then mulled the boy's question. Jack had hit the mark dead center, and the rebuke in his voice pricked Andrew's conscience. He buried the uncomfortable feeling, finished his wine, then strolled outside.

The stately pavan had changed into a merry country dance. No doubt, Lady Mary had called the tune. Andrew grinned as he watched Rosie twirl and laugh. Her face glowed with a happiness that had not been there a week ago. Out of the corner of his eye, he saw that Jack also watched the merry romp. When Jeremy brought the frolic to its conclusion, young Stafford slipped away and headed in the direction of the countess' tent.

Godspeed, Jack—and good luck, Alicia.

Hidden by Lord Brownlow's tent, Fitzhugh and Gareth watched the dancers applaud themselves.

"The lass learns quickly," Fitzhugh remarked. "She dances almost as well as you do, Gareth."

Hogsworthy replied with a muttered oath. "I will fiddle her fine joints to dance to a different tune—under me," he snapped.

Fitzhugh chuckled. "So you have said—repeatedly."

Gareth glared at him. "Do not mock me, Ned. I *will* win in the end."

Fitzhugh had the good sense not to answer. Gareth gnashed his teeth when he saw Rosie skip up to Ford and kiss the man on his cheek. The jade had grown far too bold, thanks to Ford's foolish pampering. She needed to be reminded of her place, and Gareth knew just how to teach her. A sour smile ruffled his lips as he contemplated the lessons he would give the wench.

Monday, June 18

A few days later, one of the king's young pages arrived at Andrew's tent with a large bundle wrapped in unbleached muslin and a message from His Grace. Rosie welcomed the respite from her dinnertime etiquette lesson. She fanned herself with one of the napkins and wished they were back in England where it was cooler. It had not rained once since she had arrived in France. No wonder the French were natural devils, she thought. They lived in hell.

Andrew's fine brows flickered a little when he read the king's message. "I fear I must disappoint you, Rosie. I cannot take you to the joust this afternoon."

She hid her disappointment behind a false smile. She had never before seen a tournament and had looked forward to this one.

Andrew patted the page on the head. "Tell the Master of Revels that I will come anon." He gave the child a silver penny. "Run along, poppet, and do not make yourself sick on sweetmeats with my largesse."

The child grinned with gap-toothed pleasure and trotted out, polishing his new riches on his green-and-white tabard.

Rosie shook her head at him. "You know he will do it, my lord."

He chuckled. "Aye. Tis why I gave him the coin. Every little boy should have the opportunity to get as sick as a dog on marchpane. Now, let us see what fripperies the Master of Revels has sent me. By the book!"

He held up a short cloak and shook out its folds of scarlet satin. He ran his finger over the crossed keys that were embroidered in gold thread on the shoulders. "Hoy day, Rosie! I shall look like a boiled prawn in this!" He twirled a crimson satin hat with golden scallops stitched on its upturned brim.

She had never beheld such finery, not even in all of Andrew's overflowing coffers. "Pray tell, what is this for?"

He adjusted the cape on his shoulders and admired the effect in the mirror. "A masque, my sweet. A piece of mummery to amuse a court that has grown bored with itself. Something to tweak the long nose of the French king, I presume. In any event, I am to appear at the king's banqueting pavilion within this hour for rehearsal of my part."

He grew more serious. "I fear you cannot come with me this time, Rosie. I must keep you from sight of the court until the feast. Jeremy! Run to the Countess of Thornbury and ask if Rosie may idle away a few hours in her company."

The long-suffering squire nodded and dashed away. Rosie kicked off her slippers and wiggled her stocking toes with relief. The shoes still pinched no matter how long she wore them.

"Mayhap, Lady Alicia would like to play a hand or two of primero." Rosie had just mastered this card game and had discovered that she could beat both Andrew and Jeremy with regularity.

Andrew pretended to be horrified. "Nay! Tis not in the least ladylike to win all of the countess' silver coin. Sir Thomas would have my head in a basket."

Rosie shrugged. "Tush! We will play for comfits or cherries."

He gave her an amused look. "And you will grow too fat for the fine gown I have commissioned for you. Then what would you wear to the king's feast?"

She curled her lips in an impish grin. "I could go in my petticoats. You said I looked fetching in them."

He leaned over and kissed her on the forehead. "Aye,

you minx, fetching to my eye, but I fear you would shock the great Cardinal Wolsey.''

She tilted her head back for another one of his heart-tugging kisses. "And King Henry? Would I shock him as well?''

Andrew caressed her lips with his mouth.

"You would incite unholy thoughts in our young monarch. Nay, you must stay properly clothed—except for me.''

She twined her fingers amid his brown and silver hair and pulled him closer for a deeper kiss. "Must you go just now, Andrew?'' she whispered. She yearned for more of his passionate attentions. Her heart overflowed with love for him that she knew she could never reveal.

A sigh of regret escaped from his lips into hers. "Aye, when the king commands, we all must obey.''

A discreet cough interrupted further dallying. Jeremy looked very red in the face, either from running in the hot sun or from catching his master at play. Rosie adjusted her bodice and straightened her golden necklace. Jeremy could be such a killjoy at times.

"The earl and his lady have gone to visit the French encampment for the day,'' announced the boy. "The Cavendish brothers and my Lord Stafford are already at the tiltyard in preparation for the joust.''

Andrew pursed his lips. "Perdition take it! Try Lady Mary.''

Jeremy shifted his feet. "I did, my lord. She and Sir Martin accompanied the Thornburys, and Lady Marianne is skylarking about.'' He shrugged.

"Humph! Lady Marianne, sweet soul that she is, couldn't defend a flea from a cat.'' Andrew's face betrayed his anxiety.

Rosie took his strong hand in hers. "Do not fret upon

my account, Andrew. I will be safe enough here by myself. I give you my solemn promise that I will not run away again.''

He knelt down beside her chair. ''I know you would not, sweetling, but the camp crawls with evildoers.''

She placed her finger across his lips. ''Thanks to my upbringing, I am quite handy with a knife. I can butcher a goose in the twink of an eye.''

He kissed her finger. ''Tis not a goose that worries me.''

She tucked his hair over his ear. ''Tis not a goose I would prick with my knife. Have no fears for me. I can take care of myself.''

He savored her lips again—a hard, lingering kiss as if he wished to burn his passion into her memory. ''Pray God that you do, my sweet. I will station one of my men to guard you.'' Then he cleared his throat. ''Jeremy, gather up my scarlet finery and let us away. Rosie, take pen and ink and practice writing your name on a piece of foolscap as I showed you.''

She groaned. Penmanship was her least favorite occupation.

He gave her a stern look, though he marred the effect with a sudden smile. ''Ladies should know how to sign their names. I will inspect your efforts upon my return. If not…'' He pointed to the slate, now scored with marks and chalky smudges.

Rosie wrinkled her nose. ''As you desire, my lord.''

He rolled his eyes in mock agony. ''Do not ask me what I desire, sweet Rosie. You know it already. I will leave Nym outside on guard,'' he added, naming one of his men-at-arms. Then he turned on his squire. ''Jeremy! Quit standing there like a hobbledehoy! Let us be gone!''

Blowing her a kiss, he strode out. He shut the flap, leaving her alone in the hot airless tent.

Rosie bathed her face in a basin of cool water, then spent the next frustrating hour alternately writing her letters and making enormous blots. Her perspiration mingled with the ink on the paper and further marred her work. The sun beat down on the canvas roof.

After a while, she tossed aside the quill and bathed her face again. She poured herself some wine and liberally watered it. Then she opened the tent flap and prayed for a stray cooling breeze. She heard cheers and a fanfare of trumpets coming from the distant tiltyard. She wondered if Jack Stafford had fallen on his face yet. She put no credence in his boast that he was the finest jouster of the lot. She yawned and didn't bother to cover her mouth as Andrew had often chided her to do. There was no one in sight except her guard. Even the camp dogs had disappeared. Everyone was out enjoying themselves except her.

Nym stirred from his spot in the scant shade. "Sir Andrew said you're supposed to stay inside, mistress," he muttered.

She sighed. "Tis hot and stuffy."

"Aye, mistress, tis that."

Rosie lowered the flap and paced restlessly around the ornate border of the Turkish rug. After finishing her wine, she got out the deck of cards from Andrew's portmanteau. She returned to the table, pushed aside her writing materials and shuffled the cards. Andrew had told her that all ladies were expected to know how to play several diverting games of chance. She laid out a hand of patience and attempted to beat the deck. She poured herself more wine, but did not add as much water to it this time. The long, lazy afternoon dragged on.

After losing a third round, Rosie tossed down her hand with disgust. She yawned again and decided that a nap would be the best way to make the time pass. She went into the inner chamber, clambered on top of Andrew's large bed and soon drifted into a light sleep.

A sudden movement roused her. When she opened her eyes, a heavy woolen blanket was thrown on top of her. Then she was scooped up and tossed over someone's shoulder.

"Put me down, Guy! Tis too hot for such tricks."

The churl only laughed.

She tried to kick him, but her toes flailed in the air. "Jack! Brandon! Stop! Andrew will be furious! This is no way to treat a lady!"

Her abductor slapped her soundly on the backside. Even through several layers of skirts and petticoats, the blow stung. "True enough, but you are no lady, are you, Rosie?"

A stab of panic coursed through her as she recognized Sir Gareth's voice. She quelled her icy fear through sheer willpower. She would need her wits to escape this man. She had already seen what violence he was capable of.

He chortled in a nasty fashion. "You are a guttersnipe in borrowed feathers," he continued. "But I will amend that mistake shortly. I intend to pluck you bare."

Rosie shuddered. "Help!" she shouted. "Nym! Help me!"

With a terrible oath, Gareth cuffed her. "If you are screeching for that oaf Ford left outside, he is... indisposed."

Rosie's ears rang and she felt sick to her stomach. *I must leave a sign so they will know I have not run away again.* She fumbled with the clasp of her precious necklace. It slipped from her neck and fell on the edge of the rug. Fortunately, neither Gareth nor his silent accomplice noticed it. Rosie prayed that Andrew would find it soon.

"Help me!" she shouted when they ducked through the entrance.

Gareth struck her again, much harder this time.

"Sweet Jesu!" she murmured, just before she fainted.

Chapter Eighteen

The supper hour had already arrived by the time Andrew and Jeremy returned from the masque rehearsal. Andrew was in excellent spirits. He had been given an especially large part to memorize and he knew he would be the center of attention when they presented their piece before Henry and his queen. Jeremy ran ahead to set the table. Andrew whistled the tune of the new galliard he had just spent the past hour learning. He prided himself on the height of his leaps.

The squire met him at the entrance. "Rosie's gone!"

Andrew ground his teeth. "I expressly told her to stay inside, but she flouts me at every—"

The youth interrupted, "Nay, my lord. She was taken and Nym has a large bump on the side of his head."

Andrew tensed. Jeremy tied open one of the tent flaps. Inside, Nym lay on the rug nursing a gash behind his ear. "He dragged himself in here but passed out before he could help her," Jeremy explained in a low voice.

"Fetch water and clean his wound," Andrew instructed. He knelt down beside the guardsman. "Who did this foul deed?"

Nym grimaced as he pulled himself into a half-sitting

position. "The devil, my lord! I was struck from behind.
From a distance, methinks I heard Mistress Rosie a-
calling help, but…" He grew silent.

Rage engulfed Andrew. He wanted to tear through the
entire encampment, slashing open every tent until he
found his beloved. Then cold reason took the upper
hand. He realized that he needed help. "Touch nothing
but Nym's head," he told his squire as he strapped on
his sword and scabbard. "I will return anon."

He dashed through the village of pavilions toward the
Cavendish family campsite. He prayed that the Thornburys had returned from their visit to the French. The
soft glow of candlelight shining through the canvas
cheered him.

"What ho, Sir Thomas! I am in dire necessity!" Andrew shouted outside their tent.

He almost wept with relief when the earl himself lifted
the flap.

Sir Thomas Cavendish furrowed his graying brows
when he saw his former squire. "How now? What is all
the fuss about?"

Andrew barely paused for breath. "My Rosie has
been snatched from under my nose. My guard lies sore
injured and my own blood boils. I have come to beg
your help and Buttercup. I fear the worst."

The earl stepped outside in the gathering twilight. A
fierce spark leapt into his Nordic blue eyes. "Softly, old
friend. You know better than to begin a hunt while hot
under the collar. Jan!" he bellowed for his current
squire. A tall young man appeared around the side of
the tent. "Fetch my sword and dagger. Put Buttercup on
her leash. Tell my wife—"

"Tell me what, Thomas?" Lady Alicia appeared in
their entranceway.

Andrew groaned inwardly. She would kill him for his neglect. "Rosie has been abducted by some enemy of mine, my lady. God help me, I wish it were not true."

Her eyes flashed. "Thomas! You must find the poor child!"

Thomas swore under his breath as he guided her back inside. "Aye, my love, but until I do, I request that you remain here in safety. Nay, Alicia, I will brook no arguments now. Haven't the time. When the boys return from their bathing, send them after us. Tell them to come armed. Nay, not a word!" He kissed her hard on the mouth, then backed out of their tent and dropped the flap.

Jan reappeared with Thomas' heavy sword in one hand and the leash of a large, yellow hound in the other. The earl grunted his approval as he girded himself. He gathered Buttercup's leash in his hands, then turned to Andrew. "Show me where she was. Step lively!"

Ford needed no urging. He ran to keep apace with the earl's long strides. Buttercup strained at her leash and wagged her whiplike tail with anticipation. When they reached Andrew's tent, Thomas released the dog and allowed her to explore the interior. He called for more light, then he dropped to all fours and investigated the rug.

"Someone with dirt on his boots came in here. Observe." He outlined the faint mark. "Tis not yours nor the boy's for you make a religion of wiping your feet. Tis your villain, I warrant."

He crawled forward, following the tracks. Buttercup joined him, sniffing deeply. Andrew watched them, his heart hammering in his throat.

"Aye, girl. Scent him out." When they reached the inner chamber, Thomas stood and leaned over the rumpled bed. He plucked one of Rosie's long blond hairs from the pillow.

"The lass lay down—asleep, no doubt. See here?" He pointed to the prints of two boots beside the bed. "The knave grabbed her here."

Andrew gritted his teeth. "I will flay him alive."

Sir Thomas grunted. "Must catch him first, my boy. Buttercup, mark!" He pointed to the place where Rosie had lain. "And here, mark!" He pointed to the boot prints.

Buttercup circled the spot on the rug. Then she jumped on the bed and circled the pillows. Andrew made no complaint when her paws added more dirt to his bedding. He cared for nothing but Rosie's safe return.

Thomas watched his dog with grim satisfaction. "Most sensitive nose in Christendom. Can smell out a single man in a mob. Like her great-grandsire Deuce. Pup looked fit to die, but he turned out to be the best tracker I ever had."

Buttercup quivered. The hair on the scruff of her neck bristled.

Thomas licked his lips. "Find him! Seek, Buttercup. Find him!"

With her nose inches above the rug, the dog circled the main chamber again. Andrew opened his mouth to complain that she wasted time, but Thomas held up his hand for silence. Buttercup hovered over a spot near the edge of the rug. Jeremy crept closer to the huge animal, and pounced on a small object that Andrew had missed.

"'Tis her necklace." He held up the slim gold chain with its roses.

Thomas patted the dog. "Good girl! Seek! Find her!"

Like an arrow shot from a bow, Buttercup jumped through the open entrance. She circled the ground outside, then trotted to the left around the rear of Lord Emerickes' tent.

The earl, Andrew and the two squires followed close behind her.

In the purple gloaming, Thomas' eyes gleamed with the thrill of a chase. When Andrew had served as his squire, he had often seen that look and it boded ill for the pursued.

"The game is afoot!" the earl rumbled under his breath. "Do you know whom we seek?"

Andrew gripped his sword hilt. "Methinks tis Sir Gareth Hogsworthy. He has coveted Rosie and plagued me for keeping her."

"Aye," Thomas replied. "But where has he hidden the lass? The man is no lackwit. He would not drag her back to his own lair."

Andrew nodded grimly. He did not want to contemplate what Gareth would do to her once he felt he was safe from discovery. *Rosie, my love, hold on! I will save you, or die. I am dying now.*

Buttercup led them away from the nobles' area. Then she veered to the right, and cut around the tents of the royal servants. People glanced up with wide-eyed surprise as the dog and her followers raced past them, but neither Andrew nor the others spared a breath to enlighten them.

They crossed one of the wide avenues that radiated out from the center of the English encampment. Buttercup swept into the plainer, smaller tents of the hundreds of clergymen who had accompanied the great Cardinal Wolsey to France.

Andrew mopped the sweat from his streaming face with his sleeve. "My lord, methinks Buttercup has taken a wrong turn."

The earl shook his head. The dog picked up the pace. She headed for the last ragged row in that holy section. Thomas stopped so suddenly, Andrew nearly fell over him. Ten feet ahead, Buttercup circled outside a brightly-lit tent. The flaps were closed and were securely tied from within. Muffled laughter seeped through the thin canvas.

"Methinks we have found our quarry," he whispered.

Andrew started forward, but the earl held him in a vise grip. "Never charge a maddened boar, my boy. You get more by stealth." He gave a low whistle and Buttercup bounded back to his side. Thomas rubbed her ears and held her by her collar. Then he turned to the panting squires.

"Creep close and cast an eye through the flaps if you can. Be nimble on your feet, boys. If they spy you, race away from us. Now, foot it!"

The squires slipped past them. Andrew chaffed at the wait.

"Why send those striplings to do a man's job?" he whispered.

"Because they can run faster than either of us, Andrew. We are not in the springtime of our youth, no matter how sprightly your Rosie makes you feel." He squeezed Andrew's arm. "Hold fast! We'll get her back."

The squires flitted among the deep night shadows. When they reached their objective, they slithered along the side until they passed slowly by the slit entrance. Andrew held his breath. The boys doubled back and made a second pass.

"A pox on their hides," he whispered to Thomas. "They will give the game away." His nerves screamed under his skin.

The squires disappeared behind a neighboring tent. The sounds of merrymaking continued unabated. Jeremy materialized out of the darkness. His face looked white in the faint light of the quarter moon. His lower lip quivered.

"Aye, she's there, but…" He gulped.

Andrew dug his fingers into the boy's shoulder. "Is she hurt?"

Jeremy swallowed. "They have tied her down across a trestle table, my lord," he whispered. His voice shook with his anger.

Andrew's wrath boiled up in his throat. He unsheathed his sword. He would kill them all. Thomas tightened his grip on his arm. "Nurse your fury in silence a moment longer. Jan, how many within?"

"Five," the older squire said. "Two lords, their squires and a cleric."

Andrew ground his teeth. "There is no man of God in there, but one who worships Satan. I'll send him to his infernal master."

Thomas drew his great sword and his dagger. "Jan, find my sons and lead them here. Jeremy, return to your tent and prepare for your master's return. He and the lass will require food and warmth. See to it!"

Both boys dashed away in the darkness. Then Thomas turned to Andrew and grinned wickedly. The earl's teeth gleamed in the moonlight, giving him an unearthly look. "Shall we join the feast, my boy?"

Andrew didn't trust himself to speak, but merely nodded. He gripped his sword tighter. The two men and the dog crept up to the tent. Thomas motioned to Andrew to stay by the entrance with Buttercup while he circled to the rear. The minutes dragged on leaden feet. Andrew felt as if he would jump out of his skin.

Then the peace of the night was shattered by the earl's battle cry. "A Cavendish, to me!" he roared in blood-curdling tones. Andrew sliced open the tapes that held the flaps and charged inside. "Attack!" he shouted to Buttercup.

Many things happened at once. Buttercup sprang at Hogsworthy whose back had been to the entrance. Thomas, still bellowing his war cry, slashed a large rent in the rear. The other four men tumbled over each other in their frantic haste to get away from the dog's fangs.

Andrew noted little of this. Instead, his gaze was riveted to Rosie. Her beautiful eyes dark with fear, she lay dressed only in her shift on the table. A cloth had been jammed into her mouth to silence her cries. When interrupted, Gareth had been in the act of unlacing his codpiece.

The earl touched the villain's private parts with the tip of his sword. "Move a whisker, I beg you. Twill be my pleasure to relieve you of this."

Gareth blanched and stood very still. Meanwhile, the dog had backed the other four into a whimpering, cowering huddle. With a strangled cry, Andrew severed Rosie's bounds then gently pulled the cloth from her mouth. Recognizing him, she burst into tears and turned away, hanging her head in shame.

Andrew covered her with his masquing cape and held her close to his chest. "Rosie, tis all right. You are safe now with me."

She shivered inside the scarlet satin and gave herself over to convulsive sobs. The pitiful sound tore at his heart. While he held her tight, he stared over her head at the putrid knave who had degraded her so abominably.

"You are not fit to walk in the company of men,

Hogsworthy. Your name should be stricken from the list of honorable knights for the distress you have caused this fair maid.''

Despite the proximity of the earl's sword point, Gareth had the gall to retort, ''I see no damsels in distress here, but only a whore being well-used—bought and paid for by me. You had her for over a week. Tis my rightful turn now.''

The earl nicked Gareth's sensitive skin. The man shrieked several curses. ''Is this how you fight your battles, peacock?'' he jibed Andrew. ''You call on your old master? Afraid to dirty your pretty clothes?''

The fire of Andrew's rage had already spent itself, leaving an ice-cold hate in its place. He narrowed his eyes and regarded the other man as if he were a mangy rat in a trap. ''Nay, I do my own fighting. I challenge you to a joust of war, Hogsworthy. The tiltyard at two o'clock tomorrow afternoon. Look to it, you loathsome canker, for I swear to you that my sword and my lance will not be blunted. They thirst for your foul blood.''

He lifted Rosie off the table and carried her out of the reeking place. There, he encountered the Cavendish brothers and Jack. ''Your good father and Buttercup have brought a crew of patches to heel and they would be much glad of your assistance in some hearty sport. Do not prick Hogsworthy too badly for I have vowed he is mine alone.''

Brandon and Guy exchanged grins and drew their swords. Jack came alongside Andrew and touched Rosie's cheek. She flinched.

''Is she hurt?'' he asked in a hoarse voice.

Andrew kissed the quaking girl on her forehead. ''Aye, Jack, in body and in spirit.''

Jack's handsome face hardened. "Then I will ride with you against her foe."

Andrew looked deep into the young man's eyes and saw a brother's revenge burning there. "Tomorrow at two in the tiltyard."

Jack nodded and then followed after his cousins. Andrew shifted Rosie into a more comfortable position and started back toward his tent.

Her sobs subsided into hiccups and whimpers. "I…I am so as…ashamed," she said through her tears.

He brushed another kiss on her forehead. "Not your fault, my love," he soothed.

"I tr…tried to fight them off." Her teeth chattered with shock.

"Shush, my sweet," he crooned. "You upheld your honor as a lady."

His words brought a fresh round of tears. "Haint a lady. Never was except in your imagination. Any half-wit can see that now."

People stared as Andrew stalked past them. He ignored their questions. Only the angel in his arms mattered to him. "I see no one but my much maligned darling."

Rosie closed her eyes. "Haint nobody's darling. I am nothing."

"Hush," he whispered and kissed her tangled hair.

Jeremy and the potboys had already filled the tub with rose-scented hot water by the time Andrew returned. The squire averted his eyes and went about his duties silently while his master unwrapped Rosie from the garish cape, removed her shift and eased her into the bath. She did not protest, but continued to weep while he gently washed away Gareth's brutality.

Jeremy placed the medicine chest within easy reach.

Andrew shot a look of gratitude to the boy. He colored, then held out a large towel by the hot brazier to warm it. Andrew helped Rosie out of the water, then wrapped her in the heated towel and carried her to his bed. Jeremy had already turned back the coverlet and plumped the pillows into an inviting mound. Whispering words of endearment and sweet nothings, Andrew patted her dry as if she were a baby. Then he dabbed her wrists and ankles with his soothing balms.

"Mull some wine," he told the squire in a low tone.

Rosie brushed her hair away from her face and looked at Andrew for the first time since he had rescued her. "You cannot fight that man," she said in a quivering voice. "He is much bigger and methinks he is good with his sword."

Andrew stroked her cheek with his knuckle. "And I am not?"

She chewed on her lower lip before answering. "You are the world's champion with a bow and arrow, my lord, but jousting with lances and swords? That needs more than a keen eye and a handsome doublet." She took his hand in hers and lifted it to her lips. "You could be killed. Do not do this rash thing, Sir Andrew. I have no honor worth fighting for. Do not spill your noble blood for my sake."

Jeremy held out the cup of warm spiced wine. Andrew mouthed the words *poppy powder* and pointed to the small box in his chest. The squire portioned measure and mixed it in the wine.

Andrew offered Rosie the cup. "You prattle like a magpie, my sweet. Drink this." He watched as she swallowed it down to the last drop.

"Pray tell, what makes you think that Hogsworthy will gore me?"

She settled back against the pillows. "He is so big and—"

Andrew pulled the coverlet up to her chin. "And I have been trained in arms by the greatest knight in England, the Earl of Thornbury. Also Jack has offered to ride at my side and defend me should I fall."

Her eyelids fluttered as she fought against the effects of the sleeping potion. "You are both mad. Throw me back into the gutter where I belong. Live… another…day." With a sigh as soft as a butterfly's kiss, she fell asleep.

Andrew smiled down at her, then he leaned close to her ear and whispered, "I cannot live without you."

He stood, stretched and then blew out the bedside candle. Afterward he took a long soak in the tub, followed by a rubdown under Jeremy's capable hands. He had to prepare himself for the morrow. He had not jousted in over a month and he knew he was woefully out of practice. He prayed that his years of experience would stand him in good stead. Then he sighed. Too many years. He was nearly forty and had been slowing down in recent months.

"Burn that." Andrew pointed to the red-and-gold cape that still lay on the rug where Rosie had dropped it. "And the cap that goes with it."

Jeremy's eyes widened. "But tis your masquing attire. I can clean it like new again, my lord."

Andrew shook his head. "The very sight of them will remind Rosie of this black day and I will not have her suffer more on account of my vanity. I have lost the desire to prattle, prance and preen before a jaded court with pasteboard smiles. Their applause dulls my ears. These fancies of mine have turned to ashes in my mouth. Burn them!"

After a light supper, he tiptoed back into the bed chamber. He doffed his dressing robe in the darkness, then climbed into the bed beside the sleeping Rosie. He gathered her in his arms and held her close throughout the hours remaining of the brief night.

Dawn came too soon.

Chapter Nineteen

Tuesday, June 19

Rosie opened her eyes and winced at the brightness that shone through the pink walls of Andrew's tent. For a moment, she wondered if she had merely dreamed that horrendous nightmare, but the dull pain of the rope burns around her wrists and ankles confirmed the harrowing experience. She groaned and buried her head in the pillows.

"Good morrow!"

Rosie rolled over and gaped when she saw the stately Countess of Thornbury sitting and sewing by her bedside. The older woman smiled at her with love in her eyes.

"Did you sleep well?"

Rosie started to sit up, and suddenly realized that she had nothing on. "Aye, my lady. No dreams." Her mouth felt as if she had eaten stale bread.

Lady Alicia smiled. "Good! Sleep is the best medicine for all ills."

Rosie rubbed her eyes and cast a glance toward the

larger section of the tent. "Where are Sir Andrew and Jeremy?" she asked with a sinking feeling in the pit of her stomach.

"Gone to the tiltyard. You have slept till almost midday." The countess trimmed her embroidery floss, then folded her work and placed it in the basket at her feet. "Tis time you were up and abroad."

The events of last night spilled from the black recesses of Rosie's mind. Andrew was going to fight Sir Gareth today. "Nay," she whispered.

The countess stood up and gave the bedclothes a sudden yank. "Arise, my chick. You will feel more yourself when you have washed, dressed and eaten something. Quickly, my pet. The sun will not linger for a slugabed. We must be at the arena before the combat begins."

"I cannot, my lady," Rosie replied in a tormented voice. *I cannot watch Andrew die for me.* "I...I will only shame him with my presence."

Lady Alicia lifted a fine, arched eyebrow. "Mark me, Rosie. All the encampment knows that Lord Hogsworthy has dishonored Sir Andrew Ford's lady and they know that Andrew has challenged that blackguard."

"Everyone?" Her throat felt as if it were closing up.

The countess nodded. "The rumor of it ran like wildfire. Even the dogs have chewed on it with their breakfast." She pulled the trembling girl out of the haven of the bed and pushed her toward the washbasin.

"Since *you* are the lady in question, you must be present when your honor is avenged," Lady Alicia continued.

Rosie gripped the sides of the washstand. A heavy despair settled on her. "But I *am not* a lady," she snapped. "Surely rumor's tongues have wagged that truth as well."

The countess rummaged through the pile of clothing on the trundle bed. "Nay, it did not." She held up a simple peach gown made of silk and linen. "'Tis a hot day yet again and this should keep you as comfortable as possible."

Rosie stumbled through her washing and dressing as if still in a dream. Her fears for Andrew's safety coiled around her heart and clasped it in an icy grip. She could barely choke down the few pieces of cold chicken and honey bread that Lady Alicia forced on her.

The countess took up the large hairbrush and worked it through Rosie's tangles with patient, gentle strokes. "Do not be so downhearted. Our Andrew may look like a sugarplum, but there is more to that man than meets the common eye." She paused and hugged Rosie. "Just as there is much more to you than you think. Besides, young Jack stands ready to take up the fray should Andrew fall."

Rosie's dampened spirits sank even lower. "But why? My Lord Stafford knows who I really am."

A strange smile fluttered across the countess' face. "Aye, my dear, Jack does indeed. Nothing could keep him out of the arena today."

Anger flared in Rosie's breast. "Then he is a fool to waste his life, for all he wants to do is bed me. He has said so often enough."

Lady Alicia stopped her brushing and smiled with exasperation at Rosie. "Jack has changed of late, and in so doing, has become more of a man. You will see anon. Pull on your stockings, and hurry."

Rosie swallowed further protests. "Will the king be there?"

The countess shook her head. "Nay, thank the Lord. Henry is the guest of the French king for dinner this forenoon while our queen hosts Queen Claude on our side. Our sovereign has no time today to sort out the petty disagreements between two of his minor knights. By the time His Grace returns, the matter should be concluded.''

Rosie gazed sadly at her. ''I feel so helpless,'' she whispered her anguish. ''What can I do?''

In answer, Lady Alicia tied a beribboned lace handkerchief around Rosie's sleeve. ''Before the combat begins Andrew will tip his lance to you. Tie this around it as a sign of your favor—and give him your best smile.''

Rosie fingered the frivolous scrap. ''I will try.''

The countess tied a second one around Rosie's other sleeve. ''This one is for Jack. Above all else, Rosie, pray.''

She bit her lip until it throbbed with pain. Praying had never come easy to her. ''They say that Jesus was kind to Mary Magdalene and she was a harlot. Mayhap He will listen to me—just this once.''

Lady Alicia adjusted the veil on Rosie's coif. ''Amen to that.'' She handed her a white-feathered fan, then led her out into the glaring sunshine.

The Cavendish brothers stepped out of the nearby shaded area. With their faces washed and hair combed, both young men looked especially handsome wearing their short doublets in the Cavendish colors of red and black. After bowing to his mother, Brandon fell in step with her.

Rosie was too embarrassed to look at either youth. Guy startled her when he touched her shoulder and offered her his arm.

''Good day, my lord,'' she mumbled, looping her arm around his.

''How are you feeling?'' he inquired in a low tone.

She cast a sidelong glance at him and saw only honest concern on his beautiful face. "Do you want a courtesy answer or the truth?"

Tilting up her chin, Guy forced her to look directly at him. "I spy the truth in your eyes, Rosie. Take heart. Old Andrew can fight like the very devil when his back is up."

She shook her head. "His arm has not yet healed."

Guy's lips thinned into a hard line. "I know."

Brandon looked over his shoulder and winked at her. "The wagers are running two to one in Andrew's favor, Rosie. I will be a rich man."

"Or a grieving one," she whispered to the ground.

Guy squeezed her hand. "'Tis bad luck to speak of it. I saw Jack and Andrew an hour ago. They are in the best of spirits."

She said nothing. The walk to the jousting arena seemed to take forever. As they drew closer she heard the hum of the large crowd like a horde of angry bees in summer. "By my larkin!" She gripped Guy's sleeve.

The tiltyard was enormous. As they crossed the wooden bridge over a man-made ditch that surrounded the high-banked rampart, Brandon shouted, "Make way for the Countess of Thornbury. Make way!"

Lords and ladies, varlets, scullions and potboys all turned curious eyes on Lady Alicia and her party. The crowd's noise increased in pitch and excitement. People pointed at Rosie and whispered behind their hands. She felt as if every man mentally undressed her as she walked past them.

"Hold up your head and look proud," Guy whispered.

"I wish I could die," she replied.

"Not today. Remember you are a lady," her escort murmured.

Rosie gritted her teeth. "Am not!"

Guy gripped her hand. "Andrew will prove you are one within this next hour. He is truly your champion knight. Do your part, Rosie. Make a bold show of your support. Smile, damn you!"

Startled out of her self-pity by Guy's vehemence, she lifted her chin and pulled back her shoulders. She smiled left and right with a great show of teeth but no joy in her heart.

"Look, Rosie!" Brandon pointed to a huge artificial tree that soared over a hundred feet above the plain. Hundreds of colorful shields hung from the branches amid the withering leaves of hawthorn and raspberry.

She stared at the artifice and wondered if the many ropes that anchored it in place would hold.

"Tis the Tree of Honor," Brandon continued. "Look midway up on the right. You can just spy Andrew's silver swan peeping down at us."

"Which one is that...that man's?" Rosie could not bear to utter his name.

"Hogsworthy?" Guy asked. He scanned the laden branches. "There just below Andrew's. A little to the left. Three jagged red lines on a field of silver." He pointed higher. "Mine is practically at the top. You have to step back to see it well. Tis a grinning wolf on a red background with crescent in the upper left corner." He looked very pleased with himself.

Brandon snickered. "Guy's shield is nearer to heaven for he has such a heavenly face, eh, Archangel?"

The countess rapped her son with the handle of her fan and gave him a cross look. Guy swore a number of violent things under his breath.

One of the marshals led them to the south gallery. As the aggrieved lady, Rosie was seated in the center of the front row with the countess beside her. Brandon and Guy sat on the bench behind them. A gentle breeze fanned Rosie's flushed face. Dozens of banners, some the Tudor colors of green and white, others the French blue and gold, ruffled overhead around the huge arena.

Trembling from head to foot, Rosie smiled until she thought her face would crack. Brandon passed his mother a goblet of watered wine. She drank from it, then urged Rosie to take some.

"Twill help you relax."

Rosie wished she could down the whole thing and pass out.

"Where is the earl, my lady?" she asked, scanning the rows of people around them. "Methought he would be here."

Lady Alicia laughed and pointed toward a high box opposite them. "He sits with the judges. Henry appointed him the king of arms for today. He will make sure the fight is fair."

Rosie took another sip of her wine. She almost spilled the remainder on her skirts when a fanfare of trumpets blasted their strident call.

The high wooden gates at the right end of the field opened and three riders cantered into the arena. The leader wore Hogsworthy's red and silver, as did his squire who carried Gareth's banner on a long pike. The middle rider's colors were blue and gold.

Guy leaned forward and whispered in Rosie's ear. "Fitzhugh is acting as Gareth's supporter. He was there last night."

Rosie shuddered. She didn't need to ask where

"there" was. She would never be able to erase that vile scene from her memory.

With their visors up, the trio swept around the near side of the arena. When they passed Rosie, Hogsworthy spat deliberately at the ground directly in front of her. Fitzhugh merely sneered. The squire, whom Rosie also recognized as a member of that hellish feast, did not raise his eyes to hers.

"Alackaday, I am undone!" she murmured behind her fan. "They were there too—they *know*."

The noblemen in the gallery behind her booed and shouted vindictives at Hogsworthy.

The countess dismissed the villains on the field with a flick of her fan. "Pay them no mind. They are nothing but bedbugs. Listen to the spectators. You have already won their hearts."

Tis Andrew's heart I want to win, instead of only his wager.

The trumpets sounded again, calling the challenger to the field. The gates on the left swung wide. Rosie gasped with awe and wonder as Andrew, Jack and Jeremy charged in at a full gallop. She had never pictured Andrew astride a horse. Now she couldn't take her eyes off him. Though his white steed was caparisoned in sky-blue and silver colors and had many silver bells and tassels flying from the bridle, Andrew never looked more warlike. His armor flashed back the sun's rays and long, colored ribbons streamed from his helm like a trailing wind.

The crowded stands around the arena swelled with cheers as Andrew flew past them. Jack looked positively dowdy as he followed his mentor. Rosie's heart lifted at the sight and nearly burst with pride when her champion reined to a stop before her. No matter what happened to her later, she would never forget this moment.

Andrew flashed her a smile as brilliant as his armor. Then he tipped his lance to her. Its sharpened point reminded her of the serious business ahead. Lady Alicia nudged her.

"Your handkerchief," she whispered.

With shaking fingers, Rosie loosened the lacy cloth and tied it around the end of the lance. She didn't want to touch the wood that was fashioned to kill. Andrew grinned and winked at her.

Next Jack extended his lance. Rosie was afraid to look at him. She tied the second handkerchief to his equally sharpened tip.

"Smile at him," the countess hissed.

Her lips trembling with the effort, she lifted her face to look at Jack. His piercing blue eyes were hooded like those of a hawk. Then he gave her a low bow from the saddle. She covered her mouth with her hand to hide her cry of surprise. Jeremy, his face a pale mask, dipped his banner to her as he rode by. Behind the countess, Brandon shifted in his seat and hunched forward. His former merriment vanished from his face as he watched his mentor and his best friend ride to the far end of the field. He knotted his fist until his knuckles stood out white against his skin.

Rosie swallowed and looked away. *If anything happens to Andrew or Jack, Brandon will surely kill me.*

In a high-pitched voice that grated on her already taut nerves, the ermine-caped pursuivant announced the names and titles of the challenger and the defendant, as well as the reason for this joust of war. It took Rosie a moment to realize that she had been named as Lady Rosalind—Stafford? She glanced at Lady Alicia.

"Head up! Smile," the countess prompted her.

"But how can they call me a Stafford?"

The countess patted her hand. "You needed a last name, and it could not be Andrew's, now could it?"

Rosie clutched her fan. "I am shaking too hard to smile."

Brandon reached over and put his hand on her shoulder. Caught off guard by his gentle approval, she jumped.

"Wave to Andrew," he whispered. "He will appreciate it."

High in the judges' box, Sir Thomas Cavendish pointed his white stave and bellowed, "*Laissez aller!* Let the combat begin for the honor of the Lady Rosalind Stafford."

"Lord have mercy!" Rosie moaned.

The next fifteen minutes were utterly terrifying for her. Silently, she prayed for Andrew's success as she watched the two men thunder down the course with their deadly lances aimed at each other's heart. On the third pass, Gareth's point caught Andrew's shield and tumbled him off his horse. A jarring crash echoed around the arena, and the crowd went still.

With a small cry, Rosie leapt to her feet. Only Guy's hands on her shoulders restrained her from climbing over the railing and running to Andrew's aid. At the far end of the arena, Jack lowered his visor and signaled for his lance. When Andrew rolled over and clambered to his feet, Rosie sagged with relief. Guy eased her down onto her seat. His mother offered her the half-empty cup of wine. Rosie drank without tasting the fruity vintage.

Gareth dismounted slowly at the near end of the arena. Both squires rushed to their masters with their broadswords. Unsheathed, the naked steel gleamed wickedly. Rosie shivered.

Though Andrew was a few inches shorter and a few years older than his opponent, he moved with more agility. Despite the heavy armor he wore, he danced around Gareth, wielding the sword at every turning. Rosie followed each move with her heart in her mouth.

"He fights well," she exclaimed to the countess.

Behind her, Guy chuckled. "Andrew is one of the best swordsmen in England. He schooled Brandon and me. We still cannot best him."

The combatants continued to trade ear-ringing blows. Rosie felt she had aged a decade since the fray had begun. By now both men staggered with fatigue. Andrew appeared to have trouble holding up his shield. Finally, he backed away from Hogsworthy, and tossed the heavy protection aside. Then he gripped his long sword with both hands and advanced.

"Tis his injured arm," Brandon muttered in an undertone. "He must end this quickly now."

Rosie trembled as fearful images of what might happen gathered in her mind. She twisted the handle of her fan until it snapped in two. Hogsworthy swung in a wide arc. Andrew ducked. From his crouching position, he lunged and delivered a stunning blow to the other man's breastplate. Like a mighty oak felled by the woodsman's ax, Gareth wavered a moment, then toppled backward in the deep sand.

Andrew followed through with a second slash to the man's sword arm. The weapon rolled from his opponent's limp hand.

Guy sucked in his breath. "God's blood! Methinks Andrew broke Gareth's arm with that blow. I could feel it in my own bones."

Andrew pointed the tip of his sword at Gareth's neck. The crowd cheered, while Rosie shuddered.

"Andrew will not kill him, will he?" she asked Lady Alicia.

"The cur deserves it," Brandon answered, "but old Andrew has always been a tenderhearted fool. Rest easy, Rosie. Watch." He gestured to the judge's box. The Earl of Thornbury, majestic in the ermine-trimmed red robe of his office, rose from his seat and held out his white stave.

"Hola!" he shouted. His deep voice filled the arena and silenced the audience. "Cease and desist all further combat. We declare for the challenger, Sir Andrew Ford. Honor has been satisfied."

Andrew turned away from his defeated opponent, then saluted the judges with his sword. The earl pointed his stave at Gareth.

"Sir Gareth Hogsworthy, the charge against you has been proved by combat. You are guilty of dishonoring the Lady Rosalind Stafford in words and in deed. You have disgraced the order of chivalry. For your punishment, you will sit astride the palisade in full armor until the sun sets this day. You will have no water, no food nor succor. I command the marshals to see that this punishment is completed to the full measure. In the hearing of this company and on behalf of the lady whom you so wrongfully mistreated, I abjure you, Sir Gareth. In the name of King Henry, I banish you from this place and from the future company of knights. By this time tomorrow, you will be gone from the soil of France or face the penalty of death."

The earl paused, and pointed to each end of the list where Fitzhugh and Jack waited with lances poised. He shook his stave and ended the joust with the traditional cry, *"Chevauchez les bannières!"* The squires dipped their banners in acquiescence. Fitzhugh and Jack saluted the king of arms, then rode out of the arena.

With an exhausted sigh, Rosie slumped against Lady Alicia. "Pray, is it over?"

Brandon chuckled. "Aye, for Andrew. But tis only started for Hogsworthy. In this heat, he will cook merrily inside his armor. The sun will not set for many hours."

Rosie shook her head. "Though I hate the churl, I feel sorry for him."

Guy turned down his lips. "Spare your feelings. Think on Andrew instead. Lo, he comes. Now give a happy greeting to your champion."

Rosie looked up to see him approach their seats. The nobles around her cheered and applauded. Their joyous noise filled her with a bursting pride and she added her applause to the general tumult. At the base of the dais, Andrew pulled off his helm and cowl. Sweat streamed down his face and slicked his hair against his head. Rosie and Alicia stood as he saluted them.

Andrew smiled up to his proven lady. "Prepare a bath for me, sweetheart," he said between gasps for breath. "The wretched dust of France plagues every part of me. God's teeth, gentleman! I have not had such good sport in a month of Sundays."

Before Rosie could make a reply to her lord, Brandon leaned over and whispered, "Mark you, his appetite will be high tonight. Make sure that you satisfy *all* of his needs. Andrew deserves no less from you."

Her temper flared. "My thanks for your advice, Sir Brandon, but I have learned what is expected of me. You men think all women were put on earth solely for your pleasures. Sir Andrew proved nothing by his victory. I see it still makes no difference whether I am a lady—or a strumpet."

Chapter Twenty

Despite her angry retort to Brandon, Rosie greeted Andrew with a steaming bath and a warmer smile on her face. The display of his courage had revealed another facet of this most complex man. While he relaxed in the tub, Rosie attended to his cuts and bruises. His arm wound had reopened a little, and she tenderly cleansed and rebandaged it. Meanwhile, Jeremy procured the choicest foods from the cook tent. After he had set their table, he bowed to both his master and Rosie. Then he left them to enjoy their supper and privacy with each other.

Wiping his mouth with his napkin, Andrew sat back in his chair and beamed at her. "Tomorrow, we will continue your dancing lessons. Your pavan needs much work and the time speeds apace."

Rosie crumbled a sugar wafer in her hand. "My lord?"

His eyes crinkled with merriment. "The king's banquet, sweetling. Surely such an important event has not slipped your mind."

Studying him for a moment, she tried to discern if he was jesting with her. "Methought the joust confirmed my counterfeit ladyship. You have already won your wager, though you have paid a high price to do it.''

His grin broadened. ''Not so. The king was not present this afternoon. Nay, my wager was to set you before Great Harry and all his court at the final feast. If you can hoodwink His Grace there, I have won.''

She rolled her eyes. ''You fell too hard on your head this afternoon and some of your fine brains spilled into the sand. This doggish stubbornness of yours will be your undoing. It gives me cold comfort.''

Andrew kissed her hand with many gentle caresses of his lips. ''Then let me warm you,'' he whispered. ''Come to bed, Rosie.''

Her passion for this impossible man rose in her like a leaping fire. His tender persuasions clouded all her common sense. Willingly, she gave herself to him and reveled in his exquisite lovemaking.

Afterward, she lay in his arms and listened to his even breathing as he slept. Though she savored the feeling of satisfaction that seeped through her, the leering faces of Gareth and his evil cohorts intruded into her imagination. She stared up at the tent's peaked roof and tried to shake away her disquiet.

With a sigh, Rosie pressed a soft kiss on Andrew's shoulder. Exactly what did Andrew want from her that she had not already given to him? His obsession with his wager had already cost him a great deal of money, bodily injury and the enmity of Sir Gareth. Now Andrew teetered on the brink of complete folly. What if the king discovered that he had brought a common harlot into his presence? She shivered at the thought and snuggled closer to his warm, strong body.

In his sleep, he tightened his arms around her. Despite her apprehensions, she smiled in the darkness. Her lips tingled in remembrance of his wealth of kisses. She knew she would do everything in her power to win the wager for Andrew. She would even dance that wretched pavan into hell itself—or at King Henry's banquet. She loved this clever madman past all reckoning, no matter the ultimate price she must pay.

And then what? The question nagged her. What will happen to her when the kings departed and the servants packed up the lavish tents and the colorful banners? Andrew had promised to pay her the money she had worked so hard to earn. Was that to be her final reward—a few pennies and a cheerful kiss goodbye?

Her memory fluttered back to that improbable night she had first met him. How grateful she had been then for just a good supper, a clean bed and his comforting promise not to touch her! How stupid she was! Hadn't the Cavendish brothers and even Jeremy warned her that she was merely the latest of Andrew's temporary fixations? She was God's own fool to have fallen in love with such a heart-breaking rogue. Rosie pressed the heels of her palms against her eyes as if she could blot out that sobering thought. Long after the midwatch, she finally fell asleep.

Andrew spent the next few days schooling Rosie in her manners, speech, dancing and general deportment. Every morning a flock of French seamstresses fluttered around her, fitting her for the sumptuous gown she would wear. Brandon and Guy occasionally visited to monitor her progress but Jack Stafford noticeably stayed away. While Rosie wondered at his absence, she had no time to give the matter much thought. Every evening she fell into Andrew's bed exhausted by the humidity and the day's lessons. Every night her lord taught her how to love him all over again. With chains of patience and tenderness, he bound her closer to himself.

Saturday, June 23

By the night of the king's banquet, Rosie was a tangle of nerves. Lady Mary and her maid had arrived an hour earlier to help Rosie dress. Closeting Rosie in the bedchamber behind the closed drapery, Lady Mary worked her magic not only on Rosie's toilette but on her spirits.

"Hoy day, my dear! You will take the court by storm." Mary laughed with girlish glee.

Rosie twitched her shoulders. "It itches."

Mary smoothed her chemise. "Cloth of gold is a beautiful material but tis true, it itches. But how splendid you look. You shimmer when you move. I cannot wait to see all those lords and ladies bowing to you!"

Rosie stared into the mirror while Mary wove strings of pearls in her hair. "How can I look them in the eye?" she whispered.

Mary giggled. "Imagine everyone standing there without a stitch of clothing on. You will carry the moment very well."

Rosie grinned. Just thinking of Andrew naked and in bed was very pleasurable indeed. Then she saw the pearls that Mary draped around her neck. "Hold, my lady. Tis too marvelously rich for me. I fear I will lose it."

Mary ignored Rosie's protests with a laugh. "I trust you." She pinned a filmy golden veil to the wreath she had made of Rosie's hair and pearls. "There now. You are fit for a king."

Rosie strove to look as calm as Mary. Stepping back from the mirror, she adjusted the fall of her skirts. The

French seamstresses had created the most beautiful gown she had ever seen. Panels of vibrant red satin fell from the waist to the hem of the gleaming cloth of gold underskirt. Every move that Rosie made caused the satin to sway in an enticing, seductive manner. She practiced walking up and down the cramped chamber. She wore more petticoats than ever before and they rustled like leaves in a breeze. Rosie plucked at the enormous puffed sleeves of red satin that were slashed to show off the golden undersleeves that spilled from under the tight satin wristbands. Pearls, and tiny diamond-shape mirrors trimmed the square neckline and weighted down the satin panels of the overskirt.

After tugging one last time on the gold cord that laced her split bodice together, she lifted her chin. "I am ready, Lady Mary. Lead me into the lion's den."

Andrew scrambled to his feet when the maid drew back the drapes. Astonishment arched his brows and his mouth fell open. Brandon and Guy, who had been lounging on the coffers, fell over their own feet in their haste to stand. Jeremy, with a small salver of wine cups in his hands, froze in place. Jack Stafford stood transfixed in the entranceway.

Rosie fidgeted under the silent male scrutiny. "Has my hair turned green? Should I charge you each a halfpenny to stare at me like I was a two-headed dog?"

Andrew recovered his wits first. He swept her a gallant bow. "Beloved lady, you outdazzle the dawn! It appears that our little bud has blossomed into a most beauteous red rose. What say you, gentlemen?"

"Oh, ho, Rosie!" Brandon's laughter rumbled up from his great chest. "Had I not witnessed this transformation, I would not have believed it!"

"Aye," Guy agreed, clapping Brandon between the

shoulders. "You have conjured a miracle, Andrew! Rosie, you are a marvel."

Jack crossed the rug, lifted her hand to his lips and kissed it with surprising reverence. "You are indeed every inch a lady," he said in a low undertone. "Bards will sing of your beauty after this night."

Rosie stared into his clear blue eyes. "My Lord Stafford—" she began.

He shook his head. "Nay, I am only Jack to you, sweet Rosie."

She cocked her head and wondered what he had been drinking. He gave her the *oddest* smile, not at all like the lecherous ones she was used to seeing on his lips. "Jack, I apologize for the joust. I did not tell them that my last name was Stafford. Pray do not—"

"I told the pursuivant," he said.

Rosie flashed him a stern look. "If you mean to make a jest of me—"

He interrupted her for a third time. "Never, Rosie!" He laughed.

"Nay, Rosie," Brandon added with a wicked glint in his eye. "Methinks Jackanapes means to make a jade of you and—"

He had no opportunity to finish. Jack turned on him and threw his best friend to the ground. "Speak with a civil tongue when you talk of Rosie in my hearing or you will rue it, Brandon. This I swear."

Andrew stepped between the two ruffled roosters. "Gentlemen, I pray that you settle this dispute at another time and place. We cannot pause now for a bout of wrestling, nor will your wardrobes abide it. In the meantime, Brandon, you will do well to heed Jack."

Rosie knotted her brows into a perplexed frown. "My Lord Staf...that is, Jack, I do not understand."

He gave her another kiss, this time on her cheek. "I know. I cannot tell you the whys and wherefores of my mind now, sweetheart, but I beg you to trust me. One day I will explain, but until then, know that I stand at your right hand, ready to defend you against all manner of evil."

She leaned closer to him and whispered, "Methinks your wits have been parboiled inside your helm, but I am happy to humor your delusion."

Andrew drew her hand in his. "Enough of this prattling, my children. Brandon, escort your lady aunt, and let us away. I hope you have been lucky in your gaming skills this past week, or else you have your letters of credit signed and sealed. My wager is as good as won."

He led his party out of his tent. They traveled up one of the five broad avenues to the center of the English encampment where the royal pavilions stood. Rosie shielded her eyes against the late afternoon sun. At every step some nobleman or gentlewoman called greetings to Andrew and to his Lady Rosalind Stafford. She smiled and nodded first left, then right.

I must not become too enamored of this beautiful name. Tis borrowed finery like the gown and pearls I wear.

Andrew chuckled. "You are a triumph already, my dear, and we have not even arrived at the banqueting hall." He called over his shoulder to Brandon. "Count out your sovereigns now, my boy!"

Rosie prayed that the evening would go as well as its beginning. She tightened her grip on Andrew's arm.

A vast sea of people wearing the most splendid garments joined their procession. The brightly decked courtiers laughed and tossed compliments to each other like showers of sweetmeats. Ladies' veils and long, hanging sleeves fluttered in the freshening breeze from the Channel.

Andrew adjusted the tilt of his black velvet cap across his broad forehead and winked at Rosie. "You outshine me, sweetling. I am a drab crow next to your fine feathers."

She shook her head. How could he say that when he knew he was the most handsome man in sight? Once again, his apparel excelled all others. The full coat he wore was an extravagance itself. Made of a black velvet brocade and studded with sparkling topaz gemstones, it fell to his midthigh and drew attention to his muscular legs clad in black silken hose. The padded sleeves made his impossibly wide shoulders look even more so. Under the coat, he sported a jerkin made of the same cloth of gold as her gown. His jeweled dagger hung from his equally bejeweled belt. He was the living personification of the star god Orion.

His codpiece was his most flamboyant to date. The satin triangle flashed with a myriad of topazes against the black background of his black satin breeches. People could not help but stare at its sheer audacity of so many bright jewels clustered on one prominent area. Andrew caught her staring at him.

"How now?" He grinned at her. "Is something amiss?"

"I pray that we do not meet with a real crow, my lord, for he would covet your...ah...your jewels."

Andrew chuckled low in his throat. "Hmmm, is that so? Only a crow, my sweet? Pity. I had hoped to attract a certain red Rose."

Rosie swallowed hard, choking back the wave of tingling awareness that coursed through her. The task ahead of her was great enough without her desire muddling her brains. She needed to keep all her wits about her and she had best remember that.

When they reached the encampment's hub, Jack dashed ahead toward a curious fountain. He ran up its two wide steps, grasped one of the many silver goblets that hung from chains around the base, and dipped it into a waist-high basin. "A toast to my Lady Rosalind!" he cried to the milling crowd. "Who will join me?"

"Jack has lost his last shred of dignity," Rosie whispered. "He is making a spectacle of me. Please, Andrew, do something."

Instead of shouting at the youth, Andrew dragged her up the steps to join him. On close inspection, she saw that two kinds of wine flowed without ceasing from twin spouts. A gilded statue of Cupid cavorted over the stream of malmsey while a cheerful golden Bacchus presided over the rivulet of claret.

Andrew took a goblet and glanced to her. "Which is it to be tonight, my dear? The god of Love or the god of Wine?" His beautiful hazel eyes flashed a wicked challenge.

"I could use the god of Courage," she replied with as much cheer as she could muster, "but I will choose Love in its stead."

He could not have looked more pleased. "You choose wisely. May this wine give you that which you most crave." He dipped the cup into the malmsey, kissed its rim and held it out to her.

I crave only you, Andrew Ford, but no wine on earth will grant me that wish. She smiled, took the cup, and quaffed a large draft. Kissing its rim, she returned the goblet to him.

He grinned and drank over her kiss. The Cavendishes and their merry aunt joined the toast. Then they proceeded toward the most lavish pavilion Rosie had ever seen. She tugged on Andrew's sleeve.

"There? Tis the king's palace?" She gaped at the series of connecting tents that stretched before them. The sun's waning rays glanced off the sides of the golden canvas. Painted leaves, trellises and pillars decorated the outside. Banners of green and white snapped from every tent pole.

Guy crowed at her awe. "Nay, tis only Great Harry's banqueting hall. His palace lies yonder." He pointed to a larger building of canvas that was painted to look like brick and plaster. Real glass covered the large arched windows.

"Tis a wonderment," Rosie conceded. A monument to vanity, she added to herself. Why couldn't the king have been contented with his banqueting pavilion? It was gaudy enough by itself.

Lady Mary's husband, Sir Martin Washburne, waited together with his daughter and the Thornburys at the torchlit entranceway. Rosie swept the handsome earl and his beautiful countess a deep curtsy.

Sir Thomas' eyes gleamed with approval. "You have done well, Andrew. Very well indeed."

Lady Alicia kissed Rosie on the cheek. She smiled then brushed away a tear. "If only your dear mother could see you now."

My mother would have probably sold everything on my back for a pretty penny. Aloud, Rosie thanked the countess for her compliment. She wondered why more tears dewed the lady's thick lashes.

Leading Buttercup on a red leather leash, the imposing Earl of Thornbury, now flanked by his equally imposing sons, created a wide path through the crowd for Andrew and Rosie to follow. The countess, Lord and Lady Washburne together with Jack and Marianne brought up the rear. Rosie had the momentary sensation that she was being led to the gallows.

The dusty ground was paved with bricks, and over this sturdy floor lay several layers of Turkish rugs that were even more lavish than Andrew's prized possession. "Ohhs" and "ahhs" escaped Rosie's lips as her lord led her deeper inside this true-life vision from a poor girl's dream. The harried lord chamberlain pointed to empty places at a long banqueting table in the main section of the hall. Andrew lifted Rosie over the bench, then sat down on her right. Jack quickly took the place on her left while the Cavendish clan sat opposite them. Buttercup settled herself under the table at Sir Thomas' feet.

The clamorous din swelled when a fanfare of golden-throated trumpets announced the entrance of the king and queen. Andrew helped Rosie to her feet and gave her a reassuring wink before they made their reverence. The royal couple ascended to the head table and took their places under a wide canopy made of cloth of gold.

"Tis the most costly thing I have ever beheld," Andrew whispered. "And I have seen a great many lavish accouterments in my time." He kissed her earlobe.

Rosie barely heard his remark, though she shivered with delight at the momentary touch of his lips. King Henry in all his magnificence had captured most of her attention. The twenty-nine-year-old monarch was so splendidly arrayed and so bejeweled that he sparkled with his every movement. His sleeveless coat of purple velvet strained at his massive shoulders. When the king turned, the cloth of gold lining caught the torchlight. A jaunty purple bonnet trimmed with ermine perched atop his reddish-gold curls.

Rosie stared at the king's ring-studded fingers, at his

diamond-and-sapphire buttons that marched down his gold brocade doublet and at his massive collar of huge golden links. Smiling at his subjects, Henry twirled an eye-popping diamond the size of a walnut that hung on a chain from his collar. Almost engulfed by his presence, sweet Queen Catherine looked like a plump woodland duck.

Rosie squeaked with alarm when some of the fur around Henry's neck moved. A long, ringed tail waved in the air. Two bright black eyes set in a puckish furry face blinked at the scene. She clutched Andrew.

"Fear not, tis only the king's current pet. Tis called a marmoset and comes from the New World. Henry dotes on the creature." he explained.

She made a quick sign against the evil eye. The animal reminded her of a gargoyle on a church rain spout. Another riff of trumpets announced a ponderous fat man dressed entirely in scarlet. He mounted the dais with difficulty then turned a piggish eye on the assembly.

Jack leaned over her shoulder. "Tis the great Cardinal Wolsey himself," he whispered. "He is the real power behind the throne, though he looks like a hog dressed in red satin."

Rosie suppressed a giggle. The cardinal made a huge sign of the cross and the crowded hall fell completely silent while he intoned a mercifully short prayer of praise and thanksgiving. At the "Amen" the hall erupted with joyful clamor as the fifteen hundred courtiers sat down to dine.

Thankful that she was hidden from the king's view by Andrew's enormous puffed sleeves, Rosie began the most lavish meal she had ever eaten. Lifting her lavender-perfumed napkin, she discovered that her trencher was a plate made of real gold. So was her goblet that the steward filled with claret. So were the great candlesticks that dotted the center of the table. So were the ewer's basins and the massive salt cellars. Her vision swam with gold.

The first course of baked turbot, cold smoked salmon and asparagus in a light lemon sauce was followed by a spun-sugar subtlety made to represent the season of spring. The second course of roasted peacocks, quails and fresh cucumbers in a vinaigrette followed. Under the table, Buttercup growled to claim her territory when several small greyhounds attempted to steal her scraps. One of the grooms of the hounds who moved along the banquet tables snapped his small whip and shook his bells at the quarreling dogs.

After drinking a few goblets of the choice wine, Rosie felt much more at ease. Both Jack and Andrew watched over her in a delightfully protective fashion and the entire Cavendish family treated her as if she were one of them, instead of an interloping commoner.

Waves of servers continued the progression of rich food while the noise increased under the gilded canvas roof. Noblemen shouted to each other across the heads of the multitude. Ladies spoke in strident voices and shrieked when the king's little monkey scampered among the goblets and platters. People called for more wine, more venison, more quince in comfits. The dogs snarled and bickered under the tables. Great Harry's boisterous laughter rose above the general hubbub while he pelted his friends with sugared almonds and marchpane fruits. The king's favorite harpist, Blind Dick, sang before the high table but Rosie could barely make out a word or two of his song.

A dull headache formed behind her eyes. She hid the discomfort and smiled, made polite conversation and tried to remember all of Andrew's etiquette lessons. She hoped she would be able to stand up after this long meal was over, for Andrew had told her there would be dancing to follow. The heat from hundreds of bodies melted the decorative sugar creations and softened the candles in their holders. Great globs of hot beeswax plopped on the damask tablecloth and mixed with the stains and spills of the endless food and wine.

She took another sip of her claret and wished she could put her head in Andrew's comfortable lap and go to sleep. She nodded over her serving of pears in cinnamon and cream when a crashing sound startled her out of her daze. Standing on top of his table on the other side of the hall, Sir Edward Fitzhugh banged two platters together.

"I crave the king's ear!" he shouted.

Andrew narrowed his eyes. "What the devil does that popinjay think he is doing?"

Sensing a novelty, the pavilion miraculously quieted. The silence was almost as deafening as the noise. A prickle of warning shivered down Rosie's spine.

Andrew slipped his hand in hers. "Keep your head up, and do not chew your lip, my sweet. Your lips were meant for kissing, not for dinner."

She tried to give him a smile but her mouth felt as if it had frozen in place despite the stifling heat.

Great Harry rose, planted his hands on his hips and bellowed, "How now, my lord? Why do you break our good cheer with your rude noise?"

Fitzhugh smiled like a reptile. "I crave your pardon, Your Grace, but your feast has been dishonored. One of these gentlemen has dared to bring a whore into the royal presence."

Rosie stiffened. The hot chamber shimmered before

her eyes. Andrew gripped her cold hand. Jack swore under his breath.

The king chuckled and scanned the hall. "Only one, Fitzhugh? Usually there are more."

The guests laughed and applauded the king's wit. A hot blush stained Rosie's cheeks.

Fitzhugh shook his head. "Nay, sire. I do not mean a woman who is gentle born but one who is straight out of the foul gutters of London."

The king appeared intrigued. "And who is this far-flung wanton?"

Andrew massaged her icy fingers. "Keep your head high."

Rosie gulped for air. "How do I keep from fainting?" she mumbled. She wondered if she should throw herself upon the king's mercy and thus spare Andrew from the threatened embarrassment and royal displeasure. She started to rise, but he tightened his grip and held her in place.

"Do nothing but smile!"

Her lower lip trembled. "But, Andrew—"

"Smile!"

With a broad sweep of his arm, Fitzhugh pointed to Rosie. "There, Your Grace. Sir Andrew Ford has tainted your hospitality with a common tavern wench—a slut who takes all comers for a groat."

Rosie sagged. "God shield me!" she whispered through numb lips.

Andrew wrapped his arm around her shaking shoulders. "Keep your head high. Please, do not cry now, my love."

The king stared down at the couple. "Sir Andrew! Bring forth your lady!"

Chapter Twenty-One

Jack half rose out of his seat, but Andrew clamped his hand around the rash youth's arm. "Sit down, hothead!"

"Let me tell him who—"

Andrew tightened his hold on the boy until beads of perspiration broke out on Jack's forehead. "'Tis not the time for such a rash action. 'Twill make you look a fool and could put Rosie in mortal peril. Your father has many friends here."

Jack glared at him but sank back down, mumbling oaths. Andrew stood and turned to Rosie. The poor girl looked like a deer ready to bolt. Though his own mouth had gone dry, he flashed her a brilliant smile of confidence. He had called this tune in jest. Now the piper demanded to be paid.

"Take my hand, Rosie. Royalty does not like to be kept waiting."

She raised her fear-widened eyes to his. All the blood had drained from her face, making her look even more beautiful in the candlelight.

"I cannot," she whispered.

Andrew steeled himself to speak harshly. She must not lose her nerve now. "Cannot?" he retorted. "I thought I had bought a spitfire who stood barefoot on a barrel and challenged the world with her eyes. If you do not stand up now, I will wash my hands of you this instant.''

A steely glint replaced the fear in her expression. Her temper visibly rose. "Very well, my lord. Damn your bloody wager! Lead me to rack and ruin.'' She gave him her hand and glared daggers at him.

Forgive me, sweet Rosie, I promise I will make amends for this.

Andrew escorted her to the base of the dais. There he made a deep reverence before the king and queen. Rosie sank to the rug in a graceful curtsy and remained there with her golden head bowed.

Andrew cleared his voice so that every soul in the hall could hear him. "Your Grace, I have the honor to present to you my Lady Rosalind, the most beautiful of all England's fair flowers save for our blessed Queen.''

Henry's eyes gleamed with hungry appreciation as his gaze roved slowly over Rosie. He descended the steps and leaned down to cup her chin between his fingers.

"Rise, my child," he told her in a voice as seductive as silk.

Andrew chewed on the inside of his cheek as Rosie gracefully stood. Without a hint of the terror he knew she felt, she looked straight into the king's eyes and smiled.

Great Harry chuckled. "Aye, Ford, methinks you do not exaggerate this time. You are welcome to my court, Lady Rosalind.''

Rosie inclined her head. "My humble thanks, Your Grace,'' she replied in a voice as sweet as silver bells. "I am honored almost beyond speaking to be here this evening and to see you at long last.''

The king's smile grew wider. "Very pretty, Ford. And very prettily said, my dear." He looked over their heads to her accuser.

"Tell me, my Lord Fitzhugh, is this the same lady whom your good friend Sir Gareth so dishonored that he was punished and exiled?"

Fitzhugh, who should have recognized the danger in the king's mild tone, grew redder in the face and replied, "The very same, sire. Now that jester Ford seeks to make a mockery of you under your own roof."

Andrew prayed that his nerve would hold for the next five minutes.

The king lifted one sandy brow. "Does he now?" He glanced at Rosie.

She tossed back her head and turned up her smile a notch.

Good girl!

With his rage boiling unchecked, Fitzhugh plunged ahead. "That woman is no lady! She is a filthy whore!" he shouted.

Out of the corner of his eye, Andrew saw Jack grip the hilt of his dagger. *Keep your temper, Jackanapes, or twill be the Tower for us all.*

The king smiled. "She looks newly washed to me," he observed. "Be careful whom you call a harlot, my lord. Methinks there are a number of ladies here present who have not slept only with their husbands this past fortnight. You dishonor them as well. How many challengers do you wish to face in the tiltyard tomorrow, eh? Ten? Twenty? Fifty?"

Great Harry laughed and broke the tension. The hall filled with the answering laughter of the lords and ladies. They subsided when the king's expression changed to simmering anger.

"You have broken our good company this evening with your churlish accusations, Fitzhugh."

The idiot did not have the sense to know he was in serious trouble. "But, Your Grace—"

The king held up a hand glittering with rings. "Since you cannot be silent, you may leave—at once. Go, pack your baggage and be off to England. Skulk in your castle at Bodiam until we send for you again."

He snapped his fingers and two of his halberdiers stepped out of the corners of the chamber. They marched down the center between the tables until they stopped in front of Fitzhugh.

"These men will aid your leave-taking," King Henry remarked. "And, Fitzhugh, in case you or Sir Gareth harbor any further ill-feelings toward this wronged lady or her knight, be aware that they have my personal protection. Adieu!" He waved him away. Amid much laughter, the flushed lord and his escort left the hall.

Andrew released his breath.

"Fie upon you, Ford!" bellowed the king.

Andrew swallowed. Rosie shot him a quick glance.

"Your Grace?" he murmured in his throat. *God in heaven, protect Rosie and me from the king's protection.*

Great Harry chuckled. "You have been most niggardly in bedecking your dainty prize with jewels to accent her beauty."

Andrew was so relieved that he could not frame a clever reply.

"Permit me to amend this omission." Henry removed a small ruby ring from his finger, then took Rosie's hand and slid his gift onto her thumb. Her hand shook. Then he leaned over and kissed Rosie fully on the lips. She gasped and blushed.

"By the bones, my lords. Twas a kiss of an angel,"

the king announced to the assembly. "I perceive no wanton jade here, but only a sweet maid named Lady Rosalind."

The gladsome company applauded the king's judgment. Rosie's lips trembled. Andrew desperately wanted a large goblet of wine.

Then the king lowered his voice and spoke to the couple. "Guard your prize well, Ford. She is too beautiful by half."

Andrew swept him another bow. "Exactly, Your Grace."

Great Harry took Rosie's hand and turned it palm up. He touched each of her work-hardened calluses with his lips. Then he gave Andrew a conspiratorial wink. "Very well played, Sir Andrew. My compliments."

Andrew caught Rosie's hand as she sank into another deep curtsy. He bowed to the king, then led her back to their places while the hall shook with the sounds of cheers and stamping feet. Grinning like an imp, Jack helped Rosie to her seat. Brandon blew her a kiss while Guy lifted his goblet to her in a silent toast. Andrew collapsed beside her and mopped his face. Never in his life did he want to relive those past five minutes. He offered his wine cup to her. She grasped it with shaking fingers, but did not look at him. She took a long swallow.

Hoy day! I see I will have some fences to mend this night.

The rest of the banquet blurred in Rosie's mind. The dancing began after the last of the twenty-four courses had been served. Though she had expected Andrew to partner her, Jack claimed the first pavan. Andrew lounged on the bench grinning like a cream-fed cat while Guy and Brandon chortled and crowed over his success.

Rosie snorted. *His* success? Ha! If she hadn't kept her head, he would have lost his infernal wager—and his place at court, no doubt. She did not want to think about what might have happened to her.

Guy claimed her for the galliard, then Brandon partnered her during the basse dance. Then Jack led her through a breathless, twirling branle. Even the formidable Earl of Thornbury danced a pavan with her, and complimented her on her graceful moves. Meanwhile Andrew sat, and watched her with that look of self-satisfaction on his face. The more Rosie thought about his smug demeanor, the more she fumed.

When gallant Lord Washburne returned her after another basse dance, Andrew stood and took her by the arm.

At last! Tis about time he paid me some attention. "Let us leave this merrymaking while we still have our heads on our shoulders," he murmured as he guided her toward the entrance. "Our sovereign lord has had his eye on you for the past ten minutes, and I do not want to risk another encounter with him."

Rosie shot him a quick look of surprise, but then covered it with a mask of cool disdain. "Whatever you wish, my lord."

He chuckled. "'My lord' is it now? What happened to the name 'Andrew' on your lips?"

Rosie refused to allow her tender feelings for him to get in the way of her righteous anger. "Have you won your wager *now,* my lord?"

He expanded his chest. "Aye. A most enjoyable experiment."

I am nothing but an experiment? A plague upon you, my lord! She jutted out her chin. "So when will you pay me?"

He lifted his brow. "Ah, ever the businesswoman. I had forgotten."

He sounded mildly annoyed, but Rosie was past caring how he felt. Since he didn't need her anymore, she would take what he owed her and be done with the churl. In fact, the sooner she left him, the better it would be for them both. Why linger for another day or two? She knew that once he returned to his home in England he would toss her out with the rest of his rubbish. Besides, he had a wife, she reminded herself. He mumbled something that she didn't quite hear.

"My lord?"

"I said I will give you your fee as soon as we are home," he snapped.

Home! Ha! Yours, not mine. I have no home.

Rosie remained silent by his side until they reached his pavilion. Andrew opened the flap and ushered her inside with a flourish. Jeremy looked up from his card game with some of the potboys. A quizzical expression crossed his face. The lackeys scuttled out.

"How goes it, my lord?" He glanced from one solemn face to the other.

Andrew laughed without mirth. "The king was enchanted by my piece of work and rewarded her with a gold ring. The experience has fatigued us both." He sent Rosie a private message with his eyes.

She pretended not to notice it, but instead, began to remove the pearls from her hair. She knew she would be lost if she allowed him to lure her into his bed once more. She swept into the back chamber and pulled the drapes closed against him. Andrew whistled through his teeth.

Rosie tore out the plaits that had held her hair and the pearls in place. Then she removed Lady Mary's beautiful necklace and laid it on the bed. Cursing under her breath, she fumbled with the laces that tied up the bodice of her beautiful gown. She must escape before she lost her courage to leave him. Her rebellious heart broke within her breast.

Andrew rustled the drape. "I have reckoned your wages, Rosie. You have earned seven shillings and sixpence."

She fingered the king's ring. With that sum and the money she could get for the royal bauble, she would be well set up to buy her own bakery stall and to rent lodgings in a decent part of London. She stroked her golden necklace. She couldn't sell that as well. It was her one remembrance of him. Her eyes misted. She blinked away her regrets.

"I will take my money now, if you please, my lord."

He sighed. "Do you need help changing your gown?"

She pulled the gold cords apart and wriggled out of the golden garment. "Nay, I have dressed myself all my life. I had best not grow used to your help now." She bit her tongue and cursed the sting in her voice. Even though he had used her merely for his own purposes, he had always been kind to her.

He cleared his throat. "Very well, Rosie. I have put your coins in a small bag on the table. Your pardon but I find I am somewhat overcome with a headache and will walk about in the cool air for a while."

Without waiting for her reply, he left. She bit her knuckles to keep herself from breaking down in tears. So this is how it was to end. A cool parting without even a kiss to remember him by. She touched her lips. The king had kissed her well, but he couldn't hold a candle to Andrew. No one could kiss her into ecstasy as he did.

She gave herself a good shake then pulled on the

plainest gown in the pile. Since she couldn't tie up her laces without help, she covered her open back with a light wool cloak. She would be thankful for its comfort when the cold weather came—when she was back in London. She mounded Lady Mary's pearls in a lustrous heap and put them next to the candlestick where Andrew would be sure to find them.

Tonight Rosie would walk to Calais and board the first boat back to England on the morning tide. Thanks to her hard work, she had earned enough for her passage. After that, she would be free to do whatever she wanted. The thought left her with a heavy feeling. Drawing in a deep breath, she pulled back the drape.

Jeremy gave her a startled look. "Leaving?"

Rosie refused to be cowed by the youth, even if he was nobly born. "Aye," she replied. She lifted the leather purse from the table. "Mine?"

The squire curled his lip. "So my lord said."

Rosie swallowed hard. She did not want to depart with such anger in her wake. "Jeremy," she said in a softer tone. "Please tell your master goodbye for me. I fear I am not brave enough to do it."

He shrugged. "I knew you would bolt the minute he paid you."

"Tis for the best. You said he would lose interest in me after he had won his wager. You spoke the truth. He will forget all about me once he has returned to his wife."

Jeremy shook his head. "But his wife is—"

"Nay!" Rosie stopped him. "I cannot bear to hear of that lady. Fare thee well, my young lordling. You will make an excellent knight one day."

Before he could stop her, she dashed out of the tent. Her tears fell freely down her cheeks.

* * *

Andrew wandered around the tents near his own and pondered how he could smooth Rosie's feathers. If only he knew why she was angry!

"What ho, Andrew!" Guy called from the darkness.

Andrew gnashed his teeth. The last thing he needed now were the Cavendish brothers and their rapier wits. Brandon, Jack and Guy ambled toward him. They stank of malmsey wine.

Brandon threw himself to the ground at Andrew's feet. "Basking in your success, old man?" he asked.

Jack joined him. "By the saints, I was fit to burst when the king kissed sweet Rosie."

Guy chuckled. "Nay, you were jealous. You wanted the king to kiss *you!*"

Jack called him a foul name. Andrew rubbed his temples. He had lied when he told Rosie that he had a headache, but listening to much more of this sodden prattling would give him a pounding one.

"So, what is the reckoning? I have forgot the sum," Brandon asked.

"And do you want only coin or will you accept payment in plate and jewelry?" Guy added, elbowing his brother.

"Peace!" Andrew growled. "I will take it out in your hides if you do not hold your tongues."

Brandon rubbed the back of his neck. "How now? What has made you so somber? You should be celebrating! You are now a rich man."

"I became that when I married my little Gwendolyn all those years ago," Andrew murmured. He said a brief prayer for her innocent soul.

Jack hiccuped. "So—now you are richer."

Andrew dredged up a sigh of despair. "Nay—much

poorer tonight. I have lost the wager and I fear I may have lost it all.''

The young men gaped at him. Jack burst into laughter. "Aye, my mind mistook. Twas *you* the king banished from court, not Fitzhugh.''

"The king knew," Andrew said softly.

"What?" they chorused like schoolboys.

Andrew shook his head. "He knew that Rosie was not what she appeared to be. He marked her calluses and congratulated me.''

Guy whistled. "Tis well for you that His Grace has a sense of humor. You can keep Brandon's money, old man. And my three sovereigns as well. This piece of tomfoolery has been worth twice as much.'' He rolled in the dust and roared with laughter.

Andrew gave them a look of pure disgust. "Nay, I will not make a penny at sweet Rosie's expense. She has been bought and sold enough.''

Jack sat up. "Aye, what about Rosie? What do you propose to do with her when we leave France? I cannot bring her home to my father.''

Brandon snorted. "Why would you want to?''

Jack drew himself up. "Rosie is my half sister. My mother died because of my father's cruelty. I will not allow that to happen to Rosie.''

The Cavendish brothers grew still. Then Brandon spoke. "Are you jesting with us, Jackanapes?''

The boy shook his head. "Nay, ask your mother to tell you the tale, but swear to me that the secret remains with you.''

Guy exchanged looks with Brandon. "Done," he said.

"Does Rosie know?" Brandon asked.

Jack threw a dirt clod. "Not yet. I do not know how to tell her. The news is bound to come as a surprise."

Guy clapped him on the shoulder. "More like a shock, methinks."

Jack looked up at Andrew. "So, what do you mean to do with my sister? Make her your mistress?" He spat out the word.

"I would marry her tomorrow, if she will have me." Andrew gave a wry grin. "I suppose that means I must ask your permission first."

Jack scratched his head. "Now, here's a goodly jest! Very well, old man. As Rosie's only male relative, I must question your intentions."

The others laughed, but Andrew took the matter seriously. "I find I cannot go on without her, temper and all. She has a bastard's name, but I will give her mine for life. She is the lady of my heart."

"Amen to that!" Jack murmured.

"My lord!" Jeremy called in the darkness. "Where the devil is he?"

Andrew smiled at his squire's muttering. He lifted his voice. "Here, maltworm! Tush! Your noise will wake the Emerickes."

Jeremy nearly fell over a tent stake in his haste. "My lord, come quickly! Rosie has gone and methinks she means to sail for England."

Jack leapt to his feet. "'Sblood! Run away again? If you marry her, Andrew, you will need to chain her to your wrist!"

Andrew's heartbeat thudded against his chest. He grabbed his squire. "Which way did she go?"

The boy wet his lips. "Methinks toward Calais. I followed her a short distance and heard her ask one of Lord

Emerickes' men-at-arms which direction it lay. Then I came straight way to find you.''

Andrew let go of Jeremy. ''God's nightshirt! Rosie will fall into Quince's hands if I do not find her first.''

Guy got to his feet. ''We will help you. Tell us what to do.''

''Go to the devil, all of you!'' Andrew turned on his heel. ''I will do my own wooing myself.''

Brandon called after him, ''Methinks your wooing creaks and groans!''

Andrew raced through the drowsing camp. Dogs, startled out of their sleep, barked as he passed. He prayed that Rosie had not gone too far. He prayed that she had not stumbled into the wrong company. Most of all, he prayed that he could find her in the darkness. He leapt over tent pegs and skirted the embers of dying cook fires. Whenever he met a late-night wanderer, he paused and asked if they had seen her. At last, his persistence was rewarded.

''Aye,'' a perimeter guard replied. ''Not five minutes ago. She asked me to point out the Calais road.'' He gave Andrew a reproachful look. ''And she was a-crying.''

The man's words stabbed him to the heart and lifted it at the same time. Tossing the soldier a coin of some indeterminate value, Andrew redoubled his pace. The blood raced through his veins and his breath came in short gasps. *I am getting too old to go haring after a woman. From now on, I swear I will never let Rosie out of my sight.*

In the light of the waning moon, he saw her plodding down the rutted road. With a surge of joy, he circled around her.

"Rosie," he called to her softly. He didn't want to frighten her.

She halted and tossed back the hood of her cape. The faint moonbeams turned her hair to silver. She glanced over her shoulder. "My...my lord?" she whispered. For all her determination, fear tinged her voice.

He stepped into the road a few feet in front of her. She jumped, then backed up a pace or two. "Tis only Andrew," he said in the same tone he would use to gentle a skittish colt. "Why do you keep running away?"

Rosie hesitated, then replied, "I am looking for my place in this wide world, my lord."

He smiled, and opened his arms to her. "Then run to me, Rosie my love, and I will take you all the way home."

She tossed her glorious hair. "Where your wife lives?"

Her question caught him by surprise. "My wife has been dead for over a year, God rest her soul. My house is large and very empty. Come fill it with your laughter and your impossible ways."

Rosie cocked her head. "I will be no man's mistress, my lord."

Andrew stepped closer to her. "Good, for I am seeking a wife."

Her eyes grew round. "On a highway? Tis not your style."

He chuckled. "I *set* fashion, my love, not follow it. By this time next summer, all men of good taste will be searching for their brides on the high roads and byways." He reached for her. "What say you, Rosie? Will you take this old man as your husband? Will you trust me?"

For a heart-stopping minute she did not move, then she met his smile and took the hand that he offered. "You are not *that* old, methinks."

He drew her to him. "I have some gray in my hair."

She smoothed an errant lock over his ear. "Ha! I can count the silver strands on the fingers of one hand only."

He slipped his arm around her slim waist and discovered that she was trembling. "I eat too much at dinner. I am soft around the middle."

She rubbed his stomach. "There are some younger men I know who are much softer in their heads. My Lord Stafford for one."

How she had hit the mark! He threw back his head and laughed at the irony of it. "Tell me true, my lady, have I won or lost this night?"

"Do you mean me?"

He hugged her and reveled in her warmth. "Do I ever say anything I do not mean?"

She patted his cheek. "You say a great many words, Andrew. In truth, I only understand half of them."

He took her hand in his and kissed her fingers. "Then allow me the pleasure and the privilege of improving your vocabulary."

She laid her head against his shoulder. "Twill take a lifetime."

"Exactly!"

She looked up into his eyes. "You *did* say marriage?"

He kissed her hard. "Aye, and the sooner the better. At sunrise, I will rouse old Wolsey out of his great bed and demand a dispensation to be married at once. I am bound and determined to take you back to England as Lady Rosalind Ford. What say you to that?"

She slipped her arms around his neck. "Aye, Sir Andrew Ford, I accept your offer."

He pulled her hard against himself. "Then let us begin now. For your first lesson, repeat after me—"

She wrinkled her nose. "Now? Here? The morning is almost upon us and in faith I am very sleepy."

He grinned and kissed the tip of her nose. "Excellent! Repeat after me. I love you."

"I..." She kissed a corner of his mouth. "Love..." She brushed her lips across his. "You..." With a purr in her throat, she kissed him with reckless abandon.

Andrew and Rosie did not notice the golden dawn.

Epilogue

Sunday, June 24, 1520—Midsummer's Day

On the last day of the Field of Cloth of Gold, three momentous events took place, though later chroniclers wrote of only two.

In the midmorning, King Henry of England and King Francis of France laid the foundation stone for a chapel dedicated to Our Lady of Peace and Friendship, though both kings had no intention of keeping either peace or friendship with the other. The single dressed stone lay in the middle of the empty Val D'Or for a number of years until someone finally carted it away and used it in a wall.

At noon, under a blistering sun, His Eminence, Thomas Cardinal Wolsey, celebrated a solemn High Mass on a temporary altar set up in the tiltyard. It was attended by both kings and their courts. The Cardinal, in his worldly wisdom, granted the vast company a plenary indulgence—forgiveness for any sin that anyone might have committed during the past fortnight of feasting and frolic. During the final benediction, a large fireworks that was to have been used during the final pageant that night was accidentally set alight. The unexpected appearance of a fiery green dragon overhead caused a great deal of confusion among the attendees.

Much later that afternoon, Brandon's young page, Mark, reappeared in the Cavendish tent. The trembling child confessed to an insatiable curiosity about pyrotechnics. His hands were covered with gunpowder in mute testimony of his noontime activities. Once Brandon finally stopped laughing, he sternly admonished the boy never to play with fire again.

As the day drew to a close, the third important event took place. Sir Andrew Ford, resplendent in a golden doublet and a dignified codpiece, married his Lady Rosalind in a quiet ceremony conducted by Wolsey's confessor. Jack Stafford gave his sister away in marriage— but only after he and Lady Alicia had convinced Rosie of his brotherly relationship. The beautiful bride claimed to be speechless to gain both a brother and a husband on the same day, then she spent the rest of the evening talking about it.

On Monday, June 25, the skies over the Val D'Or finally opened and drenched the Field of Cloth of Gold in a heavy rain that lasted for several days. A week of traveling across choppy seas, on flooded roads and in chill winds failed to dampen the ardor of the newlyweds. Andrew and Rosie returned to his home in Warwickshire, where they settled down to a life of wedded bliss. Rosie stopped chewing her fingernails and spent Andrew's money on charitable causes. In the evenings, Andrew proved to be the most loving of husbands. During the day, he turned his formidable powers of concentration on his latest and most lasting obsession: the study and experimentation of the properties and diverse uses of gunpowder.

Lord and Lady Ford lived happily—and explosively—ever after.

* * * * *

Author Note

The Field of Cloth of Gold was the name of an historic occasion as well as the place where this event occurred. In the summer of 1520, England's master of statecraft, Thomas Cardinal Wolsey, hosted an unprecedented meeting between the young, handsome King Henry VIII of England and the equally young, handsome King Francois I of France. From June 7 through 24, a barren bowl-shaped valley on the northern coast of France located between the English-held town of Guisnes and the French town of Ardres became a stage where thousands of noblemen and their ladies from both courts tried to outglitter each other. The fortnight was a combination of a summit meeting between two leading world powers, an Olympic games, a World's Fair, an international fashion show and a culinary showcase. In short, it was the most sumptuous camp-out in history.

King Henry's retinue included over four thousand lords of his realm, their squires and retainers, hundreds of priests and lesser clerics, an army of potboys, grooms and lackeys as well as two thousand of the finest horses. His queen, Catherine of Aragon, was attended by one thousand members of her own household and a mere eight hundred horses. King Francois and Queen Claude were accompanied by an equal number of courtiers and retainers. A knight, such as Sir Andrew, was allowed to bring a chaplain, eleven servants and eight horses.

The fortnight was a nonstop round of feasting, gambling, jousting, wenching, archery, wrestling and shopping from the thousands of vendors who ringed the encampment. Cockfighting, masquing and exchanging polite insults with members of the opposite court were other popular pastimes. The French introduced the English to asparagus, prunes, turkey from the New World and, it has been rumored, lemonade. The English acquainted the French with salmon and Scotch whiskey. The hens of France were kept busy providing fresh eggs. Not only were they needed by the hundreds of cooks, but by the English courtiers who rode nightly through the French camp, pelting their counterparts with eggs.

Without a doubt, the Field of Cloth of Gold was *the* party of the second millennium.

I am deeply grateful to Deborah Staley of Maryville, Tennessee for her costume expertise in dressing Rosie and Andrew for the king's feast. Also many thanks to Anne Turner of the Folger Shakespeare Library, Washington, DC and to Betty MacKenzie, reference librarian at the Kings Park Library, Burke, VA for helping me research the Field of Cloth of Gold. I plead writer's license for reversing two historical events for the sake of the story: King Henry's feast actually took place on June 24th while the Mass in the tiltyard was on the 23rd. No, I didn't make up the dragon fireworks. It really happened, though no one knows who ignited it.

I love to hear from my readers. Please write to me at PO Box 10703, Burke, VA 22009-0703.

HARLEQUIN®
Makes any time special ™

WIN A DREAM

In celebration of Harlequin®'s golden anniversary

Enter to win a *dream!* You could win:

- A luxurious trip for two to **The Renaissance Cottonwoods Resort** in Scottsdale, Arizona, or

- A bouquet of flowers once a week for a year from **FTD**, or

- A $500 shopping spree, or

- A fabulous bath & body gift basket, including **K-tel**'s *Candlelight and Romance* 5-CD set.

Look for **WIN A DREAM** flash on specially marked Harlequin® titles by Penny Jordan, Dallas Schulze, Anne Stuart and Kristine Rolofson in October 1999*.

FTD · **RENAISSANCE. COTTONWOODS RESORT** SCOTTSDALE, ARIZONA · **K·TEL**

"Don't miss this, it's a keeper!"
—**Muriel Jensen**

"Entertaining, exciting and
utterly enticing!"
—**Susan Mallery**

"Engaging, sexy…a fun-filled romp."
—**Vicki Lewis Thompson**

See what all your favorite authors
are talking about.

Coming October 1999 to a retail store near you.

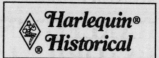

COMING NEXT MONTH FROM

HARLEQUIN HISTORICALS

- **STRATHMERE'S BRIDE**
  by **Jacqueline Navin**, author of A ROSE AT MIDNIGHT
  In this romantic tale set in Regency England, a world-weary
  duke is torn between his duty to his family and his love for a
  vivacious, free-spirited governess.
  HH #479 ISBN# 29079-9 $4.99 U.S./$5.99 CAN.

- **BRIANA**
  by **Ruth Langan**, author of CONOR
  In the third book of *The O'Neil Saga*, an embittered heir rescues
  a feisty Irish noblewoman from death and is revived by her love
  of life and her trust.
  HH #480 ISBN# 29080-2 $4.99 U.S./$5.99 CAN.

- **THE DOCTOR'S WIFE**
  by **Cheryl St.John**, author of THE MISTAKEN WIDOW
  A marriage of convenience between a nanny and a small-town
  doctor results in an emotional story involving self-discovery,
  healing and love.
  HH #481 ISBN# 29081-0 $4.99 U.S./$5.99 CAN.

- **BRANDED HEARTS**
  by **Diana Hall**
  While seeking revenge for a vicious attack on her family, a
  young woman fights her feelings for a cattle rancher whose
  warmth and caring tempt her to reveal the dark secret of her past.
  HH #482 ISBN# 29082-9 $4.99 U.S./$5.99 CAN.

DON'T MISS THESE FOUR GREAT TITLES AVAILABLE NOW!

HH #475 THE MIDWIFE
Carolyn Davidson

HH #476 LADY OF THE KNIGHT
Tori Phillips

HH #477 WINTER'S BRIDE
Catherine Archer

HH #478 THE SURROGATE WIFE
Barbara Leigh